BREAK

A BLOOD HUNTER NOVEL

BREAK OUT

A BLOOD HUNTER NOVEL

NINA CROFT

Entangled Publishing, LLC
2614 South Timberline Road
Suite 109
Fort Collins, CO 80525
Visit our website at www.entangledpublishing.com.

Edited by Liz Pelletier
Cover art by Heather Howland

Print ISBN   978-1-62061-227-9
Ebook ISBN   978-1-62061-237-8

Manufactured in the United States of America

To my mother, who always had a book close by.

CHAPTER ONE

Rico hurled himself behind the huge trunk of a tree and stood, back pressed against the rough bark, as the missiles whizzed past.

An arrow thwacked into the wood behind him, and every muscle in his body tensed. He reached gingerly around and snapped it off. In the dim light, he held the shaft to his face and cursed loudly—wooden arrows. It was almost as though they were expecting him.

"Goddamn heathen peasants." He might as well be back in the Dark Ages.

In the distance, a pack of hounds bayed for blood. His blood. But they weren't getting it.

He braced himself and peered around the trunk through the thick stand of trees, and spotted the crimson glow of a hundred torches not too far in the distance. Breathing in, he caught the oily scent of burning pitch.

A triumphant roar filled the air. The hounds must have

picked up his scent.

Rico cursed and darted off again, weaving through the dense forest with blurring speed. He could outrun the mob and the hounds, but it was a damn poor way to end an evening.

When the sound of voices faded behind him, he slowed down and finally came to a halt. Time to get the hell out of here. Leaning against a tree, he switched on his comm unit.

"What is it?" Tannis sounded irritated, and Rico frowned.

"I need picking up."

"It will have to be later—I'm busy."

He cocked his head to one side, listening for the sound of the mob, judging its distance. His pursuers would be on him soon. Tannis had better get unbusy and fast.

"Tannis, stop whatever it is you're doing, bring my goddamn spaceship, and pick me up."

She was silent for a moment. "I'll think about it."

The line went dead. He stared at the comm receiver on his wrist. She'd cut him off. Gritting his teeth, he imagined the pleasure of tossing her mutant body out of the ship's airlock. Only first, he had to get back to the ship. He pressed his finger down until he heard the line open.

"What?" she snapped.

"Tannis, are you aware that I've rigged *El Cazador* to blow if I don't input a unique numerical code every twenty-four hours? Come and get me or the whole ship goes up."

"Good try, but I don't believe you. You don't think that far ahead."

He took a deep breath. "Do you remember that time last year?"

"What time?"

"The time I saved your worthless life. At great personal risk to myself."

"Yeah. So?"

"So bloody well reciprocate."

A shaft of burning pain shot through his leg and he jumped, then stared down in disbelief at the arrow sticking out of his calf, an inch below the knee. "I've been shot," he said.

"Shot? By what?"

"By a big fucking arrow. Get down here. Now."

He yanked the arrow from his leg and flung it to the forest floor. "Or you're fired," he added and shut off the connection.

His pursuers were close now, so close he could hear the fierce crackle of flames mixed with the rise and fall of excited voices. He ignored the pain in his leg and took off through the trees again. A few minutes later, he skidded to a halt.

Straight in front of him, the land fell away abruptly. He peeked over the edge. A long way below, water roared. A lot of water. A lot of *cold* water. He hated cold water. He searched the sky for any sign of Tannis, but a thick layer of cloud obscured the moons and he saw only darkness. He jammed his finger onto the comm unit. "You here yet?"

"Have a little patience. I'll be there in five minutes."

"Great, just great. The problem is, *I* might not be here in five minutes."

"Don't be so melodramatic. Just hold on."

He stared over the edge into the dark, turbulent water. "Hold on to what?"

A low snarl sounded behind him. With a sigh of resignation, he turned to face his pursuers. They emerged from the shadowy tree line, torches held in front of them, before fanning out to form a semicircle around him.

One of the hounds crept toward him, belly close to the ground, growling softly. It reminded Rico a little of the dogs back on Earth, probably even had some real dog DNA in there somewhere. Rico growled back, baring his fangs. The animal got the message, turned tail, and ran.

A tall man stepped forward to stand at the center of the group. He wore the long black robes of a priest, and Rico groaned. Not heathens after all. Bloody religious fanatics. He should have expected it.

When man had fled to the stars nearly a thousand years ago, the old religions had gone into an abrupt decline. By the year 2600, they had all but vanished from the universe, and good riddance as far as Rico was concerned.

But that had changed with the discovery of Meridian.

A rare, radioactive element with the ability to bestow immortality on those lucky enough to afford its exorbitant price, Meridian heralded the evolution of a new class — the Collective. Super rich and virtually indestructible, the Collective quickly gained power. Now, they ruled most of the civilized universe.

But while not everyone could afford Meridian, everyone wanted immortality, and the old religious beliefs had gained a new popularity. The Church of Everlasting Life offered a cheaper, if less reliable, alternative with its promise of an afterlife in paradise.

On these isolated outer planets, the Collective's influence was slim and the Church took advantage of that and jumped in to fill the gap. A shudder of loathing ran through him. Rico had no feelings either for or against the Collective, but he hated the Church as only someone who had lived through the Inquisition could.

"Son of Satan," the priest cried, and the mob behind him roared.

Rico rolled his eyes. "We're not actually related."

A second man stepped forward, dragging a girl with him, and the priest grabbed her hair, tugged back her head. In the flickering light, Rico saw the puncture wounds in her ivory neck and had a flashback to the sweet taste of her blood.

"I have been ordained by God," the priest said, "for the punishment of the wicked and the eradication of evil."

"Get a life," Rico muttered. "Look, it's honestly no big deal—the marks will heal in a couple of days. You won't even know I was here."

His words didn't seem to impress them. Of course, the Church was rarely impressed unless they were slaughtering innocents, and Rico was the first to admit he hadn't qualified as an innocent in numerous lifetimes. If ever.

Five men stepped forward, and Rico watched them warily. They raised their bows, cocked their wooden arrows. Drew them taut and aimed them straight at his heart.

Rico glanced over his shoulder at the icy water below. He was going to have to jump. "Shit."

He tensed himself, ready to dive over the edge, just as the sky filled with noise and light. His gaze shot upward. He released his breath. The shuttle hovered above them, and a laser beam shot out, cutting the ground between him and the archers. A voice boomed from the open hatch.

"Lower your weapons."

But they were already edging backward. The shuttle flew lower, almost touching the ground, and Rico lunged for the open hatchway. "About bloody time."

The mob was almost back in the trees now, but at the last moment, the girl pulled free and raced toward the shuttle. She stared up at them, imploring. "Take me with you, Rico."

He looked at Tannis, raised an eyebrow.

"No freaking way." She reached across and slammed her palm to the door panel.

Rico had a last brief glimpse of the girl. He hoped she'd be okay, that her people would treat her as a victim, though she'd hardly been reluctant.

"What took you so long?" he growled as the hatch slid shut behind him and the shuttle sped away from the planet.

Tannis swiveled her chair to face him. She ran a hand through her short, dark hair and raised one brow in accusation. "Been eating the natives, Rico?"

"*Dios*, I go out for a snack and all I get is hassle. I've got to eat."

He hobbled across and sank into the seat next to her, rubbing his leg and tossing Tannis a wounded look. His ship's captain was no Florence Nightingale, but dammit, his leg hurt. "They shot me."

"Aw, poor baby." She uncoiled her lean body from the chair and came to stand over him, her cold, yellow eyes looking him over. Reaching down, she tore open his pants leg. The bleeding had already stopped, the wound healing over. "You'll live."

He frowned. "So what kept you?"

"While you were down there playing, *I* got us a job."

"Legit?"

"Shit, no."

His mood lightened. "Dangerous?"

"For this sort of money, it's probably going to kill us."

He grinned. "Sounds like my sort of job."

CHAPTER TWO

Lasers blasted from all sides, and the stench of scorched air burned her nostrils. Skylar had passed beyond exhaustion, to where her body reacted automatically, whirling and countering, her own pistols deflecting each incoming shot.

It wasn't enough. At the thought, the speed of the shots increased until the area was a blur of flashing lights. Off to her right, a blaster roared and Skylar dived for cover. A laser beam slammed into her while she was midair, hitting her directly in the chest. She crashed to the floor, and the breath left her lungs in a whoosh.

Ignoring the searing pain, she rolled, came up on her feet, legs braced, a pistol still gripped in each hand.

"My office, now, Lieutenant."

The words sounded in Skylar's mind. At the same time, the shots ceased, and the room lights came on as the simulation unit shut down. Skylar stood for a moment, head hanging, her breathing short and fast as she came down from the adrenalin high. Sweat stuck the material of her jumpsuit to her skin, rivulets ran down her forehead, stinging her eyes, and her chest ached viciously from the laser blast. She needed a shower, and a few minutes to get her shit together before she faced the colonel.

"I'll be there in five, sir."

"I said now, Lieutenant."

"Crap," she muttered under her breath.

A group of trainees stood around the edges of the room, their expressions ranging from awe to fear. None of them spoke, but a tall young man tossed her a towel as she passed. She nodded her thanks and wiped the sweat from her forehead.

The suns were high overhead as she crossed the courtyard from the training center to the office block, and it was a relief to enter the relative coolness of the corridor. Pausing outside the colonel's office, she rubbed her hands down the sides of her jumpsuit and ran a calming mantra through her mind. If she wasn't careful, the colonel would pick up her inner turmoil and he'd terminate her first solo mission before it even began. The mantra completed, she tapped on the door and pushed it open without waiting for an answer.

The colonel stood at the far side of the large room, hands behind his back, staring out of the window to the courtyard beyond where a group of new recruits were being put through their paces. He turned as she entered the room, and she saluted.

He was dressed identically to Skylar in a black jumpsuit, with the violet insignia of the Corps on his chest, long boots, and a weapons belt strapped at his waist. Although he was tall, he always reminded Skylar of a boy dressed up as a soldier, until she looked into his eyes and saw the centuries reflected there.

She'd heard he'd only been eighteen when he'd taken the treatment, and while some people changed over the years, the colonel hadn't aged at all. His gaze wandered over her, his eyes narrowing as he took in her disheveled state.

"You were hit?" he asked nodding at her chest.

She glanced down and saw the rusty scorch mark where the blast had caught her. "I was training, sir."

"I know, Lieutenant. I asked if you were hit."

"Yes, sir. I was careless."

"Either that or you raised the simulation unit to level eleven, when the maximum recommended level, even for trained operatives, is eight."

Crap. Had she? No wonder those newbies had been giving her odd looks. She kept quiet; there wasn't much she could say.

The colonel pursed his lips, then shrugged. "At ease, Lieutenant. Take a seat."

Skylar sank down into the hard upright chair in front of the desk. The colonel took the seat opposite and leaned back watching her for a moment. She tried not to squirm under the intensity of his stare.

"Your recent psych profile threw up a few concerns."

More crap. "It did?"

"The consensus is that you're becoming less integrated into the whole. Any idea why that might be?"

What could she say? That recently she'd felt so alone. That all the voices in her head just made her feel more disconnected. That she was worried she'd made a huge mistake and was going to have to live with it. Forever. The concept of forever filled her with fear.

But if she said any of those things he'd bust her out of his army so fast she'd be spinning. And this was better than before; over the years, she had found some respite in the action. And if she just got this mission and got away for a while, then maybe she could work her way through her problems.

"No, sir. I'm fine, sir."

"What about Aiden's death?"

"We weren't close."

But his death had unsettled her. Maybe because she had been thinking they were indestructible, but Aiden's assassination had proved that a lie. So maybe 'forever' wasn't quite so long after all.

"Hmm. Well, in the end, it was considered your particular…issues would be an advantage for this posting, as you'll be working alone. Afterward, we'll review your case."

"So the mission is on?"

"It's on."

She maintained her rigid control, but a smile tugged at her lips. She had tried not to think about it, but as relief flooded her system, she knew she might have gone crazy if she had to go back to her old command. Or even worse, if she was kicked out of the Corps altogether. Then she wouldn't belong anywhere.

"Tell me what you have so far."

She forced her mind back to the mission. "I've made initial contact with the captain of a ship I think is suitable—"

"Show me," he interrupted.

Skylar reached across the desk and flicked on the monitor.

She brought up her mission files, then sat back as the colonel perused them, his brows drawing together in a small frown.

"Why this ship? This crew?"

Skylar considered what to say. The truth was, she wasn't sure. She'd reviewed over twenty possible ships looking for a suitable candidate. But she'd always come back to this one. Something about *El Cazador* tugged at her interest, and little did that these days.

"Gut instinct, mainly," Skylar said. The colonel was a big one for his officers using gut instinct provided they could back it up with logic. "But the ship has everything we need. The crew is a motley bunch of misfits with moral flexibility and mercenary tendencies, but they're also good at what they do."

"Which is?"

"Mainly low-level smuggling jobs which keep them just below the scanners. Plus the odd misappropriation of property—but to order, not random robbery."

"Sounds good."

"And something else. The owner has a reputation as a womanizer—I thought I might use that, go in as some sort of bimbo, try and get him off balance."

The colonel considered her, his eyes running down over her figure, making her want to fidget in her seat. Okay, so she wasn't exactly bimbo material, but she was sure with a bit of effort she could clean up okay.

"And you're good with that?" he asked.

"I can control the situation."

"I'm sure you can. You have an impressive reputation for keeping men at arm's length, Lieutenant."

She bit back a scowl. Was that a good thing? Anyway, it

didn't matter. She would use the womanizer aspect to get in there, maybe distract him a little, but the real hook would be the money.

The colonel rose to his feet, and she knew the meeting was over. "I'm sure you have arrangements to make. I'll speak with you again before you leave. And Lieutenant…"

"Yes, sir."

"I'm sure you'll make an excellent 'bimbo,' but maybe you should get a little outside help with the disguise."

Skylar gritted her teeth and kept her thoughts to herself. "Yes, sir. I'll be sure to do that, sir."

She managed to maintain her blank expression until the door closed and then she grinned. The mission was on.

• • •

The star cruiser grew smaller in her monitor until it vanished, leaving her alone in the vastness of space. Inside, some of her inner tension relaxed, and she sensed the first stirrings of anticipation. Finally, she checked her coordinates and brought the small shuttle to a standstill.

"Are you ready, Lieutenant?" The colonel's words sounded in Skylar's mind.

"Yes, sir. I've arrived at the rendezvous point."

"You know how important this mission is to us?"

"I do, sir."

"Could you put me on visual?"

She wanted to ask why, but she already knew the answer. She flicked on the monitor and tried not to scowl as the colonel's face filled the screen. He scrutinized her for a minute, his lips twitching in obvious amusement.

"You'll do."

"Thank you, sir." Despite the sarcasm in her tone, the colonel just nodded.

"Okay, then I suggest you lock down the link. Good luck."

"Thank you, sir."

Skylar switched off the monitor, sent a message to her internal AI unit to break all contact, and blinked in the sudden silence. For the first time in many years, she was alone inside her head. It was a strange feeling and not entirely unpleasant.

She'd spent most of her life on active combat duty, but always as part of a team, never alone. Then she'd been promoted to a more strategic planning position, and she'd missed the fighting, but not the barracks life. Now she'd moved on, volunteered to be part of the elite intelligence division in the hope that she would find some challenge in the job to stave off the restlessness that seemed a constant companion these days.

She'd planned this job carefully. She'd factored in everything she could discover about the *El Cazador* and its crew, put that somewhat scanty information together with all possible permutations of events, and added a probable fuck-up factor of ten, the highest level available. And this had been calculated as her best-chance-of-success scenario. Still, she wished she'd come up with a plan that didn't involve her looking quite so ridiculous.

Tugging at the neckline of her silver tube dress, Skylar tried to ignore the fact that even staring straight ahead, she could still see her breasts. She'd never considered herself particularly well-endowed, had never given the whole breast thing much thought, but this dress had the effect of making them impossible to overlook.

Christ, she'd give anything for a jumpsuit and a laser gun.

But there was no point in putting this off. Taking a calming breath, she reached across and opened the comm link.

"Kestrel 617, calling *El Cazador*."

A woman's voice came over the comm, cold and clipped. "This is Captain Tannis of *El Cazador*."

"I'm at the rendezvous point, Captain. When can I expect you?"

"We'll be there in an hour."

The link went dead.

Skylar sat back in her seat as the adrenalin surged in her veins. The game was on.

• • •

"Rico, get your lazy ass out of bed. Our client just called. We're on our way."

Rico had been aware of Tannis the moment the door glided open, but maybe, if he kept his eyes shut, she would get the hint and go away. When her booted feet stomped across the cabin, he knew it wasn't going to happen. He buried his face in the pillow.

"Rico!"

Something sharp prodded him in the lower back until he rolled over and opened one eye. Tannis stood, legs braced, staring down at him, his sword dangling from her fist.

He frowned. "Hey, put that down—it's dangerous."

"Actually," she said, holding up the sword, "*this* is a toy." She opened her fingers, and the sword clattered to the floor. Tannis drew the laser gun from the holster at her hip and pointed it straight at him. "Now *this* is dangerous."

"*Dios*." He went up on one elbow and regarded her balefully through half-closed lids.

They'd docked last night at a spaceport close to the rendezvous point, waiting for the client to make contact, and Rico had taken the opportunity to indulge in a little recreation. He felt good, sated with food and sex, but the one thing guaranteed to spoil that mood was a laser shot in the backside. And he knew from experience she'd do it.

He opened his eyes fully and glared. She stepped back, and he knew they must still be glowing crimson from his recent feeding.

"Shit," she muttered.

Reaching down, she flipped over the corner of the black silk sheet, revealing the naked woman beneath. Rico followed her gaze. The woman's eyes were closed, her skin pale with the waxy perfection of a lily.

"Is she dead?" Tannis asked.

He frowned. "Of course she's not dead. What do you take me for—some sort of monster?"

Though he *had* taken a lot of blood, and the woman was rather quiet. He nudged her with his toe. She rolled onto her side, snuggled into the pillow, and Rico sighed in relief. He was willing to kill if he had to, but he had nothing against this woman—she was only doing her job. Besides, killing by accident was just plain careless.

Tannis reached down, running a slender finger across the woman's throat. The puncture wounds were already closing.

"Neat," she murmured. "But what have I told you about bringing whores on board my ship?"

Rico pulled himself up and swung his legs out of bed. "Whose ship?"

She raised an eyebrow. "*You* asked me to be captain. So *you* do what *I* say."

"Yeah, like that's going to happen."

Her finger tightened on the trigger of the laser gun, and he held up a hand. "Okay, Okay. I'll get rid of her."

He reached across and punched the comm unit next to the bed. "Al, get in here."

Rolling to his feet, he stretched, raking a hand through his hair and scratching his scalp where the skin tingled. He could still feel the residual buzz of the blood in his system, and he closed his eyes to savor the feeling.

When he opened them, it was to find Tannis, propped against the wall of his cabin, arms folded across her chest. At least she'd holstered the pistol. Her gaze dropped to his naked body. She didn't look impressed.

"Shower," she snapped and pointed to the cubicle.

"What are you—my mother?"

"I just don't want you smelling like a brothel when we meet the client."

Rico decided compliance was the easier option. Besides, she was right, he reeked of cheap perfume.

He showered quickly, using the air blaster to dry himself afterward. When he came out of the shower cubicle, Tannis was still leaning against the wall, tapping her foot on the metal floor. Al's slight figure hovered in the open doorway. The boy peered warily into the cabin. His huge, gray eyes widened as he took in Rico's naked figure, then shifted quickly away. *Dios*, the boy was skittish, always acting as if he expected Rico to bite. It irritated the hell out of him. The scrawny bag of bones wouldn't be worth the effort it took to catch him. He was one of Tannis's strays, picked up starving on some backwoods planet.

"Get in here," Rico snapped.

Al sidled into the room, keeping close to the wall and as much distance as possible between them, and Rico narrowed his eyes. If Al wasn't careful, Rico would give him something to really worry about. He flashed his fangs, and the little remaining color drained from the small face. Al stared at Rico as though mesmerized. Rico stared back. Come to think about it, the boy was quite striking, with that pale flawless skin and shock of dark red hair.

"Rico!" Tannis glared at him.

"What?"

"Leave him alone."

He shrugged. "What did I do?"

Tannis didn't answer. Instead, she turned to Al, her expression softening. "There's a woman on the bed," she said. "Make sure she's off the ship in the next five minutes."

Al took in the naked body on the bed. Rico hadn't thought the boy's eyes could widen any further, but they did, until they almost bulged out of his head, and Rico had to catch himself before he laughed at the kid and pissed Tannis off even more. Tannis was protective of her crew. *He* could get an arrow through the leg and all he'd get from her was a load of sarcasm, but if one of her precious little charges was threatened...

Al took a tentative step closer. "Is she dead?"

"No, she's not bloody dead." Rico ran a hand through his hair. "Jesus, why does everybody think I go around killing people?"

"Well, it has been known," Tannis said mildly.

"Only when they deserved it." He glanced at Al and couldn't resist adding, "Or when I was *really* hungry."

Hiding his grin, Rico turned away and hunted for his clothes. They were scattered around the floor of the cabin where he'd dropped them. He picked up his pants and pulled them on, then found his gun belt lying on the chest by the bed, fastened it around his waist and strapped it down to his thighs. He shoved the laser pistols into the holsters just as a faint vibration from the ship pulsed up through his bare feet.

"What's that?" he asked Tannis.

"I told Daisy to fire up the engines."

He scowled. Daisy was yet another stray. They'd picked up her damaged escape pod floating aimlessly in deep space after the experimental station where she was living had been attacked and her family massacred. She was crazy about flying, and grabbed every opportunity to take the controls of *El Cazador*. She was okay—a good flier—though her tendency to follow him around like a lost puppy could be irritating. "Well, she'd better not be in my seat."

"I'm sure she wouldn't dare." Tannis didn't even try to keep the sarcasm from her voice. *Smartass.* "But we're rendezvousing with the client in orbit, and we should have been there five minutes ago. I don't want to lose this one. We need the money."

"You're *so* mercenary."

He pulled on his tall black boots and black shirt, then strapped on the leather shoulder holster. He picked up the sword from the floor where Tannis had dropped it and slid it into the scabbard so it hung down his back.

Finally, he pulled his hair into a ponytail. He glanced up to find Tannis and Al watching him and raised an eyebrow in query.

"Poser," Tannis muttered.

Rico caught a grin on the boy's face, which was quickly wiped away when he saw Rico watching. The kid wasn't as downtrodden as he pretended to be, which begged the question—what was he hiding? He made a mental note to find out, but not right now. He turned to Tannis. "You just wish you could look half as good."

"Yeah, right. And put some dark glasses on. We don't want you frightening off the client. She sounded the nervous type."

"Aye, aye, Captain."

CHAPTER THREE

Skylar peered out of the viewer as her shuttle drew close to the larger ship. A Star Cruiser Mark 3. She was very impressive and very beautiful, with elegant lines. Wide at the rear, tapering to a sharp point at the front, the sleek shape was mirrored by twin propulsion units, which sat on either side. She was also entirely black, except for her name painted in silver script along the hull: *El Cazador de la Sangre*.

She'd never heard the ship referred to as anything other than *El Cazador*. Skylar didn't recognize the language, and she quickly accessed her AI system. She blinked her eyes as the information came up on her internal monitor.

"El Cazador de la Sangre": The language, Spanish, originated on Earth and hadn't been used in nearly a thousand years. The words translated as *Blood Hunter*.

A shiver of unease rippled through her. She'd come across some strange, dark rumors regarding the owner and pilot of *El Cazador* while doing her research, but nothing that could be substantiated. If she was honest, those rumors were what had piqued her curiosity enough to select this ship and crew over others who had been just as suitable. Now she couldn't help but wonder if giving in to that curiosity had been wise.

She mentally shrugged. It was too late to change her mind now. She had ten days to complete this mission, and it would take at least eight to reach Trakis One. No time to find a replacement.

But she hadn't realized how isolated she would feel once she cut the link to the others. Mostly she liked it, and she knew that when the time came to re-mesh, she would regret the loss of privacy. All the same, she occasionally missed the sense of being part of something larger, and at times like these, it would have been nice to know she wasn't entirely alone.

The shuttle gave a small shudder as it locked into the docking bay of the ship. The hatch closed behind her. Skylar unstrapped her harness and stood, wobbling precariously on her high heels.

"Goddamn, stupid shoes," she muttered. They were silver to match her dress, with four-inch platform heels. Why would anyone voluntarily wear such things? She caught sight of her reflection in the blank screen and scowled—she bore a remarkable resemblance to an unregistered pleasure provider from the dark side of Trakis Two. Not that she'd ever actually been to Trakis Two, but she'd heard plenty about it—the planet where 'you can party forever, because the night never ends,' with more pleasure providers than the rest of the universe put together. No doubt all looking just as ridiculous as this.

But wasn't that exactly what she'd been aiming for?

Grabbing her small silver bag, she pressed her other hand

to the door panel and stepped out, the tap of her heels on the metal floor echoing in the cavernous docking bay.

This was her first time on a pirate ship, and she was impressed despite herself. She'd been expecting something a little bit seedy. Instead, the area, empty but for a medium class shuttle and a small pod parked against the far wall, was spotless, the ship gleaming silver and black, the air fresh—no stinting on recycling here. No one came forward to meet her, and she stopped in front of a security camera angled over the doorway, almost twitching with nervous tension. She'd planned this for so long and now she just wanted to get things moving.

"Follow me, please."

At her feet, an automated guide hovered just above the floor, spherical and matte black with no markings.

Skylar had been on a Mark 3 cruiser before and knew the ship consisted of three levels. The lower level housed the cooling and recycling systems as well as the engines. The middle section held the docking bay and a small cargo area— though this ship wasn't built to carry cargo. She was a fighting machine, sleek and deadly.

The upper level housed the bridge and the crew's living quarters. She guessed this was where they were heading as she followed the guide through the bay, up a ramp, along a narrow corridor, ever deeper into the heart of the ship. With each step, Skylar's sense of isolation grew, as though she'd been swallowed whole by some great beast. She could only hope it would dislike the taste and eventually spit her out again.

Finally, the guide led her into a conference room. "Wait in here, please."

Skylar surveyed her surroundings. More silver and black. The walls were bare with no portholes this far inside the ship. At the far end, a group of low, comfortable chairs beckoned to her. She tottered across and sank into one, sighing with relief. It was short-lived. The door slid open, and a tall woman entered.

"Welcome to *El Cazador*," she said.

Skylar jumped to her feet. She quickly cross-referenced the woman against the crew list she'd memorized—this must be Captain Tannis.

She was striking, her body long and slender—sinuous— beneath the tight black pants and scarlet T-shirt. Her skin glowed, a pale, luminous ivory run through with shimmering iridescent lights. Skylar raised her gaze to find the woman watching her coolly out of yellow eyes, almost a solid color and only broken by a black slit down the center.

From her intel, Skylar knew the Captain of *El Cazador* was genetically modified, or a GM as they referred to themselves, and it didn't take a close look to see the effects on this woman. She'd obviously made no attempt to hide what she was, which was unusual. Most GMs tried to conceal their heritage, and with good reason. When the Church's influence had risen in the aftermath of the Meridian discovery, the high priests had called for a purge of any with mixed DNA, claiming they were abominations against God.

"Seen enough?" the woman snapped.

"Sorry, I've never—" Skylar trailed off as a second figure entered behind the captain. She'd studied the files on the owner and pilot of *El Cazador* while planning this mission, but still her mouth fell open in shock.

Holy Meridian.

Nothing in the files had prepared her for this.

He was tall, with a lean body dressed in black pants and a black shirt. Real leather boots up to his knees, silver pistols at his hips, and an honest to goodness sword at his back.

His midnight-black hair was pulled into a ponytail, revealing olive skin and perfect bone structure. Dark glasses covered his eyes, but even so, Skylar was quite aware they hadn't yet risen above the level of her breasts. A slow, lazy smile lifted the corners of his sensual mouth, and her hand twitched with the need to tug up her dress.

"Hello," he murmured, his voice like warm honey. He held out his hand. "I'm Ricardo Sanchez—Rico to my friends. And I'm sure the two of us are going to be *very* good friends."

Beside him, the captain snorted, but Rico's gaze never left Skylar.

"Skylar. Skylar Rossaria," she said, sliding her hand into his much larger one. His felt cool against her skin, and he stroked little circles on her palm with the pad of his thumb.

"Delighted to meet you, Skylar."

His eyes behind the dark shades finally left her breasts to wander up and down her figure. A ripple of awareness prickled across her skin. She shifted, then reminded herself that there was a reason she'd dressed like this. The information on the crew had been incomplete; somehow, they had managed to stay beneath the Collective's radar—that wouldn't last for long if they took on this job. The rumors surrounding the owner of *El Cazador* had ranged from rogue immortal to spawn of Satan, depending on whom she'd asked, but all agreed on one thing—Ricardo Sanchez was a womanizer, and he liked his women obvious.

Skylar sighed but straightened up, tossing her long blond mane, drawing back her shoulders, and thrusting her breasts out a little farther.

"Really delighted," he added.

The woman at his side groaned. "Cut the crap, Rico."

He grinned but released Skylar's hand, crossed the floor, and sank into one of the chairs, his booted legs resting on the table in front of him. He patted the seat next to him. "Come and sit down, Skylar, and tell me exactly what I can do for you." His voice sank to a low drawl that caressed her ears. She stared at him, mesmerized.

The captain shook her head before sitting down next to Rico, gesturing to the chair opposite. "I'm Tannis, captain of *El Cazador*," she said as Skylar took her seat. "So what is this job you have for us?"

Skylar's gaze flickered from one to the other. She nibbled on her lower lip and tugged at a strand of hair, twisting it round her finger. She'd listed all the possible methods of approach, but until she'd met the people she was dealing with it had been impossible to know which one to go with. Now, looking at Tannis, her foot tapping impatiently on the floor, she decided on the most direct approach.

"I want you to break a friend of mine out of the Collective's maximum security facility on Trakis One."

She watched intently for their reactions. Rico's she couldn't tell. His face remained blank, his eyes still obscured by the dark glasses, but Tannis showed a faint flicker of shock, quickly hidden.

"A friend?"

She nodded. "A very good friend."

Tannis studied her through narrowed eyes. "You are aware that nobody has ever escaped from Trakis One?"

"I know, but I have to try." She bit her lip, forced a pleading look into her expression. "He's scheduled for transfer to the Meridian mines on Trakis Seven in ten days' time. After that…" She trailed off. There was no point in saying more. Everyone knew entry into the atmosphere of Trakis Seven meant instant contamination for which there was no cure. Once there, any rescue would be pointless—unrefined Meridian was a radioactive poison that permeated the cells instantly on exposure. Wherever he ran to, he'd be dead within two years.

"So why is he being held?" Tannis asked.

Skylar had given this one a lot of thought. She didn't want to put them off totally, but on the other hand, it had to be believable.

"He was obsessed with getting enough credits for us both to have the Meridian treatment. He could have paid for himself years ago, but he loved me and wanted us to be together."

The two people opposite remained silent, and she forced herself to continue. "Jonny didn't mean to kill anyone. It was an accident. He'd been contracted to steal a shipment of raditron from a storage facility on Trakis Five, but the explosives went off prematurely and a lot of people died."

"Hmm." Tannis sounded skeptical. "And your friend wasn't harmed?"

"He had protective gear, but the blast knocked him out and they caught him. They sentenced him to life in the mines, which everyone knows is a death sentence."

Tannis eyed her as though not quite believing her story. Which wasn't completely unexpected. Maybe it was time to get away from the story and onto what really mattered.

"I have money to pay you," Skylar said. "Lots of money."

"The money saved for the treatment?"

"Not all, but some of it."

"Can you prove you have access?" Tannis leaned forward.

Skylar nodded. "I have the account codes. Verification is code-level one."

"Give it to me."

Skylar reeled out the list of numbers while Tannis pressed the button on her wrist console, opening a hologram palm screen on her left hand. She punched in the numbers and waited, humming under her breath. After a minute, a slow smile spread across her face. She nodded to Rico, and then turned back to Skylar. "That's a lot of credits—not tempted to use them yourself?"

Skylar shook her head. "It's pointless now. I'd rather have one lifetime with Jonny than eternity without him." She was worried she'd gone over the top, but what the hell—she couldn't back down now. Might as well go the whole way. She'd been practicing for this moment. She concentrated hard, remembering the laser blast she'd taken in the face during a training exercise last month. The pistol had been set to stun, but, shit, it had still smarted. She blinked once, and a tear rolled down her cheek. "Please, you're my last hope. You have to help me."

Rico rose, crossed the narrow space between them, and crouched down in front of her. He reached out and wiped away the tear with the tip of his finger, surprisingly cool against her cheek. A tingle ran through her skin from the point of contact.

"Hey, don't cry," he murmured, his voice husky. "We'll get your boyfriend back for you."

Wow, the guy was a pushover. His file hadn't said he was a big softie. How had he survived this long?

Skylar stared into his face and saw her own reflection in the dark shades. She widened her eyes a little, batted her lashes once or twice.

He smiled and bent his head toward her so his breath feathered against her skin. "Just give me a few minutes to convince the captain, and we'll be off after your boyfriend. We'll have him back in no time."

"You can do it? It's never been done before."

He snapped his fingers. "Piece of cake."

She frowned, and his smile broadened. "Old Earth saying. It's a hobby of mine." Reaching out, he patted her hand. "Try not to worry. Tannis?" He gestured to the doorway.

Tannis was still seated, an expression of complete disgust on her face, but she got up when he spoke her name. They crossed the room, but Tannis paused in the open doorway. "Just one thing. You could get anyone for that sort of money. Why us?"

Skylar fixed her gaze on Rico as she answered. "I heard you were the best."

"Hmm." Tannis didn't sound entirely convinced, but she gave Skylar one last searching look and strode out of the room. The door closed behind them, and Skylar's shoulders sagged. After a minute, she straightened her spine. She doubted they'd be watching her, but she should stay in character just in case.

They'd obviously bought her story. She'd known they wouldn't be able to resist the lure of such a huge sum of money. Skylar prided herself on her pre-mission research and she was rarely wrong.

She got out a mirror from her small bag and studied her reflection. She looked like a stranger, her eyes no longer her own. Her lipstick had vanished, nibbled away during her award-winning performance. She pulled out her makeup and swiped the bold red tube across her lips, in what she hoped appeared a practiced movement, before returning it to the bag. Smoothing down her hair, she assessed her situation.

She couldn't believe how well the meeting had gone. It was comforting to know that if this did go wrong, she could always get a job as an actress. Though she doubted she would ever find an audience quite as gullible as Ricardo Sanchez.

. . .

Rico poured them both a whiskey from his flask and threw himself on the red brocade couch. Tannis's cabin was one of the few places on the ship where the black and silver décor didn't prevail; she'd added bold splashes of crimson and scarlet. He liked it.

Tannis took her glass and sat opposite, stretched her legs out, and crossed her ankles. She gulped the drink in one go and slammed the glass on the short table next to her. "That was revolting. The horny little bitch couldn't stop fluttering her false eyelashes at you. *I heard you're the best,*" she mimicked.

Rico grinned. "Jealous?" He knew she wasn't—they'd never had that sort of relationship, but he enjoyed winding her up. Once or twice, in the early days, he'd been tempted to try, but he'd always backed off; lovers were easy to come by, friends almost impossible. Besides, he wasn't entirely convinced he'd succeed.

"No," she replied. "I just didn't fancy losing my breakfast." She cast him a look of disgust. "And you were no better. Tell me, have you always been…" She paused as if searching for a word, then gestured in the general direction of his groin.

He raised an eyebrow. "Extraordinarily well-endowed?"

"Ha ha. I meant a sex-crazed womanizer."

He considered ignoring the question. There had always been an unspoken rule between them that they never discussed the past, but she appeared genuinely curious. "No, I wasn't always a womanizer. In fact, I married when I was seventeen and was faithful for the next twenty years."

"You were *married*?"

His lips curved at the incredulity in her voice. "A long time ago in a faraway place."

"Wow, so what changed you?"

He gave her a look of complete amazement.

"Yeah, right," she muttered, "the whole vampire thing. So do all vampires like sex as much as you?"

"I don't know about all vampires—we're not exactly a chatty bunch. But I've found it's the best way to keep the hunger at bay."

"The hunger? You mean for blood?"

"Not only blood."

While he was quite capable of feeding and leaving his victim virtually unharmed, there was a dark place inside him that craved death. A place that urged him to drain the last drop of blood from his prey, until their life force belonged to him. Rico lowered his dark glasses and allowed a little of that darkness to bleed into his eyes.

Tannis stared, mesmerized, then swallowed. "Right then. You know that 'no whores on board' rule? I've changed my mind—have as many as you like."

Rico grinned and pushed his glasses back in place. He settled back and sipped his drink. He could almost see the thoughts whirling in her head and the moment she decided to change the subject.

"So, this job—can we do it?" she asked.

"Maybe. Maybe not. As you said, no one's done it before, but I like a challenge."

"Hmm. And the money's good."

"There's only one problem—"

When he didn't continue, she frowned. "Are you going to tell me what that is?"

"Well, at a guess, I'd say that not one word that came out of those pretty little lips was the truth."

Tannis's jaw dropped open. "What?"

Rico shook his head. "You are *so* gullible."

"But you were drooling all over her."

He licked his lips, breathed in deeply, and smiled. "She smelt divine. I'm not saying I wouldn't like a taste, but that doesn't mean I believed a word she said."

He tapped the control pad on the couch's armrest, activating the monitor on the wall to the right. Skylar Rossaria's face filled the screen, and he changed the setting so they could see all of her. She appeared quite relaxed. Which was odd in itself. *El Cazador* had a reputation and not a good one—he'd made sure of that. It encouraged the rest of the bad guys to keep their distance. She also had a self-satisfied smirk on her face.

"She looks legit to me." Tannis sounded disgruntled—she hated to be wrong about anything.

Skylar stood up and wandered round the room, wincing as though in pain. She slumped down in one of the chairs and slipped off her shoes, gently massaging her feet. A look of relief washed over her face. She peered down at herself, and a frown of disgust replaced the relief as she attempted to tug the silver dress over her very impressive breasts. Rico felt his cock stir in his pants and shifted in his chair, savoring the feeling.

But he recognized there was more to Skylar than his usual attraction toward a beautiful woman. Maybe it was the mass of contradictions he sensed seething just below the surface. A beautiful woman who'd appeared almost surprised at the effect she had on him. She'd obviously dressed to impress, but wasn't entirely comfortable with the results. Whatever—he knew he wanted the chance to explore it further.

Tannis made a low noise beside him. "Hungry or not, could you get your mind off your dick for one second and tell me if you have any proof. She's offering good money. Better than good—brilliant, and I need that money."

"My guess is, she's never worn high heels in her life. She's not at all comfortable in that dress, and she's got calluses on her palm from holding a laser pistol. I'd bet my right fang she's more at home with a gun than a lipstick."

"Christ, I wish you were wrong. I'd love your right fang. I'd wear it on a chain around my neck." Tannis sighed. "But much as it pains me to admit—you're never wrong."

He grinned. "And don't you hate that."

"Yeah. Damn, but I wanted that money." She punched the comm unit on her wrist. "Daisy, fire up the engines, we're out of here as soon as the power's up."

Tannis listened to Daisy's reply, a frown forming on her face. "I don't care where. Just away from here."

Rico waited until she'd closed the connection. "You know, there's no guarantee we could have done the job anyway. As you pointed out, no one has ever been broken out of Trakis One. Though it might have been fun trying."

He turned back to watch the woman on the screen. It had been a long time since he'd felt a hunger like this. He licked his lips as he considered the options. "How about she gives us the money anyway."

Tannis's eyes lit up at the prospect.

"Give me an hour alone with her," he continued, "and she'll be begging to give you every credit she's got."

Heat stirred in the pit of his belly at the thought. He didn't kill often; he kept that particular hunger tightly leashed, but it was always present. He had his own set of morals and he did his best to stick to them, but this woman had crossed the line. She obviously had another agenda, which no doubt involved double-crossing them in some way, and that made her fair game.

Tannis narrowed her eyes, but he could tell he'd piqued her interest. "You're a sick bastard, Rico."

Rico didn't try to deny it, and he waited while Tannis mulled the idea. She *was* captain, after all. Finally, she shook her head. "No, it wouldn't work. Not with level-one verification protocols in place. You could get her to make the transfer, I'm sure, but it would never pass the screening. The voice recognition sensors would pick up any signs of coercion."

She sat back, drumming her fingers on the arms of her chair, deep in thought, watching the woman on the screen while Rico watched her. He liked to watch Tannis, liked the clean lines of her face and body, the luminous skin with a hint of scales. Her cold, reptilian eyes. There were very few people he counted as friends, and he'd mostly been happy to keep things that way—people had an unfortunate tendency to die on him—so he'd found it better not to get too close. But once, long ago, Tannis had rescued him from a prison and certain death. She'd no doubt regretted the impulsive action a few times in the years since, but he was equally sure she'd do it again. At heart he was a loner; it was the nature of the beast as well as a personal preference. But lately Rico found it strangely comforting to know that there was at least one person in the world who would care if he ceased to exist. He was getting maudlin in his old age.

They both sat in silence, watching the screen. Skylar still had that smug, self-satisfied smile on her face. Tannis reached across, punched the off switch, and the screen went blank.

"Don't look so disappointed," she said. "If this is some sort of scam, she's going after the wrong people, and she's all yours. You can do what you like with her. But first I suppose we should find out exactly what she's after." She ran a hand through her short, spiky hair. "It's got to be a setup. Maybe you'd better get me a list of people you've pissed off recently."

"How long have we got?"

"Good point—probably not long enough. We should talk to her again. Soften her up a little. See if she'll tell us what she's after."

He liked the sound of that. At the thought of softening her up, his gums ached, and the bloodlust uncoiled inside him. He lowered his dark glasses and regarded Tannis. "Let me go in there alone, and I'll get her to spill everything she knows."

Tannis studied him for a moment, lips pursed. "Fine, but I'll be watching."

"Pervert," he drawled.

"Not at all. I just don't want you finishing her off until she talks. If there's someone coming after us, I want to know exactly who it is."

Rico rose to his feet and rolled his shoulders, his body tight with anticipation. "She'll talk."

CHAPTER FOUR

Skylar wondered how much longer they would keep her waiting. She tapped her foot, impatient to get moving.

Excitement fizzed in her blood. This was actually going to work. She would do it. She had to. The colonel had impressed upon her how important this mission was. She couldn't fail — her future depended upon it. Even this short time away, it was as though a weight had lifted from her mind. She felt alive, excited about the mission ahead of her. She couldn't go back to her old life.

The door slid open. Ricardo Sanchez — Rico — stood in the opening. He didn't enter but lounged against the frame, watching her. He was alone this time, and Skylar forced what she hoped was a bimbo smile onto her face.

He didn't return the smile. He still wore the shades, so she couldn't see his eyes, but his mouth remained a compressed line.

She got to her feet, needing to move. Maybe the plan

wasn't going so well after all.

"Mr. Sanchez—Rico—"

"Sit."

Had she really thought his voice sounded like warm honey? That one word cut through the air like ice. She didn't even have to think about it. She sat right down. Her lips were suddenly dry, and she ran the tip of her tongue over them.

"Is there a problem?" She decided that the squeak in her voice was quite allowable within the parameters of her character.

He strolled into the room, one hand resting on the laser pistol at his thigh, and came to a halt in front of her chair, far too close. He was tall. And broad. And menacing. She licked her lips again.

"Just a small one."

"Well, I'm sure we can sort it out." When Rico didn't rush to agree with her, she decided to give the bimbo smile another try. Her dry lips stretched across her teeth in what she hoped would bring an answering smile from Rico.

He grinned, but for some reason it didn't make Skylar feel any better at all. "Oh, I'm sure we can." His smile broadened and the tip of one white fang showed briefly.

Skylar's heart stopped. Then started again, so loudly she could hear the blood thundering in her veins.

Holy Meridian. What the hell was this guy?

Her mind flashed back to the rumors she'd heard about him, rumors she had ignored as too ludicrous to even consider. Just legends dredged up from the past.

She forced herself to take a deep breath. He could be any number of things. One rather large tooth did not mean he was a….

He reached up and slipped the shades from his eyes. His gaze locked with hers, and ice-cold prickles skittered down her spine. She'd been in some perilous situations in her time in the military, had faced off against some of the scariest badasses in the known universe. But they'd all been human—or mostly human. Nothing had ever chilled her like the darkness she sensed lurking behind his eyes.

"Er—I just have to pop back to my shuttle for a moment." She stumbled to her feet. "I forgot to—"

She closed her mouth as he continued to stare at her out of those crimson eyes. Who, or rather what, had eyes the color of blood?

He reached out a hand, placed one finger on her shoulder, and pushed her down.

Skylar collapsed onto the chair but decided that wasn't so bad. She doubted her legs would have held her much longer anyway.

Closing her eyes, she tried to remember her training. What to do if caught. What to do if facing torture. Unfortunately, nothing was coming to mind.

Concentrate.

She could turn off her pain receptors, but not many people were capable of that sort of neural control and it would give her away. Unless she could pretend she was feeling pain, but somewhere along the way, she'd lost faith in her acting abilities.

So, keep the pain receptors on? That didn't seem such a good option either, but probably the higher chance of success. While she didn't like pain, she could deal with it.

Taking a few deep breaths, she pushed her fear to the back

of her mind.

She knew they wanted the money. She'd seen the greed in the captain's eyes. She just had to hope that they wanted the money more than Rico wanted—

Again, her mind refused to finish the sentence. After all, she didn't actually *know* what he wanted.

He licked his lips, ran his tongue over one sharp white fang, and stepped toward her.

Okay. She didn't know, but her mind was doing a good job of guessing. Or a bad job.

She shook her head, took another deep breath, and sat up straight. She studied him quickly. His whole figure radiated tension, and a predatory hunger lurked behind his eyes. She was sure he wanted her. She had to find a way to use that and diffuse the situation. What would work?

"So," she said and was proud of how normal her voice came out, "this problem… Are you going to tell me what it is, or are you just going to stand over me and drool?"

Surprise flashed across his face. He grinned again, and this time some of the lethal energy eased from him. The atmosphere in the room changed instantly, and he stepped back, sank into the chair opposite, and rested his booted feet on the small table between them. He didn't put the glasses back on but sat regarding her, head cocked to one side.

She held herself still, running a relaxation mantra through her mind, and finally her fingers uncurled and her breathing returned to normal.

He raised an eyebrow. "You're a cool one."

"Is there any reason I shouldn't be?"

"Oh, plenty of reasons."

A shiver ran through her at the dark promise in his voice. "The problem?" she prompted.

He shrugged. "I don't believe a word of your story."

"Why?"

He ignored her question. "And you're way too cool for someone who must suspect she's in big, big trouble."

Cool? She couldn't remember being this frightened— ever. Maybe she was a good actress after all.

"What makes you think I'm lying?"

His eyes ran over her, lingering on the swell of her breasts. "Believe me, I've met a few space tramps in my time, and you do not fit the mold."

What's wrong with me?

She bit her tongue to keep from asking the question.

He sat up and leaned toward her. "Who are you working for?"

"I'm not working for anyone."

He sighed. "Look, we can make this relatively pain-free. Or—"

He paused dramatically, and Skylar rolled her eyes. "Or what? You'll torture me?"

"Actually, I was thinking more along the lines of eating you."

Instead of fear, that thought conjured up some rather interesting possibilities, and she squirmed in the seat. "Ugh," she said in case he'd noticed.

He laughed and relaxed back in his chair. "Who are you working for?"

Skylar sighed. There were some occasions when only the truth would do—but was this one of them?

"Okay, I lied," she said. "But not about everything."

She hesitated. She knew interrogators were more likely to believe you if they had to work for the information.

"Yes—?" he prompted.

"I do want you to extract a prisoner from Trakis One. And they have scheduled him for transfer to the mines in ten days. But he's not my boyfriend."

"Who is he?"

"My brother."

He frowned. "Why would you lie about that?"

"Because I didn't think you would take the job if I told you the truth."

"Honey," he said, "boyfriend, brother, it makes no damn difference to me. And you're making no sense but you'd better start soon."

"He's not a bank robber." She paused again.

"*Dios mio*," Rico muttered. "I think I might torture you after all. Will you get on with it?"

She bit her lip. "He's a member of the Rebel Coalition, and he's being held for the assassination of Collective member Aiden Ross. You must have heard about it."

"Ahh."

She was certain, from that one word, that she had him. The Rebel Coalition usually had no fight with the Collective. Their goal was to bring down the Church of Everlasting Life. But Aiden Ross had been an advocate of the Church and a supporter of some of its more radical activities, including the slaughter of millions of 'abominations,' as the Church referred to anyone with less than 100 percent human DNA. By destroying him, the rebels hoped to discourage any future collaboration. Skylar doubted they'd done any such thing. More likely, the Collective would now go all-out to exterminate the rebels, but that was beside the point. "I knew you wouldn't go up against the Collective. Nobody will."

"So why don't his rebel buddies break him out?"

"I went to them, but they wouldn't do it. They said that nobody had ever broken out of Trakis One, and they weren't going to waste good credits trying."

"Nice friends." He regarded her closely. "I'm suspecting there's more."

She nodded. "I had to find a way to get Jonny out. He's my baby brother, and I've always looked after him." His eyes were no longer crimson but had darkened to the color of bitter chocolate. She was sure he believed her. "I've got good contacts. We've been part of the Rebel Coalition for years— ever since our parents were murdered during the Purge." She wondered whether a few tears would go down well at this point, but decided against it. "We gave them our whole lives and they abandoned Jonny. I knew I couldn't rescue him alone, that I'd have to pay somebody to help me. So I stole some money from them."

"How?"

"It was easy. I'm quite high in the hierarchy—I have access to funding."

"That's where the money in the account came from?"

She nodded again. "Now the Coalition is after me, so I couldn't go to anyone I know. I had to find someone who wasn't tied to either the Collective or the rebels."

"What about the Church of Everlasting Life? The high priests will often go against the Collective just to piss them off."

She shook her head. "Not this time. Aiden Ross was their strongest supporter in the Collective. Anyway, they won't work overtly against the Collective. The Church is powerful, but only because the Collective allows it to be—they know that. Besides, they wouldn't help Jonny. He's a known rebel and a GM. You know how the Church feels about the experiments. They'd put him down rather than save him."

Skylar held his gaze, willing her features into a pleading semblance. When his shoulders appeared to soften, she was careful not to let the corners of her mouth turn up.

· · ·

She gazed up at him with those huge eyes, and Rico frowned. The interview hadn't gone as expected.

The problem was—he liked her.

He'd expected her to fold immediately, maybe cry, but he'd been basing that presumption on her appearance. Stupid, when he'd already concluded she was not the tart she'd portrayed. She was tough, and toughness was one of the few traits he admired.

The other problem was—he believed her.

Her story made sense. The vast majority of people would not go against the Collective. A black mark in its books meant absolutely no chance of the Meridian treatment even if you could afford the exorbitant prices. And everyone lived in hope of somehow finding the money and gaining immortality.

Everyone except him, of course.

Rico spoke into the comm unit. "Tannis?"

"What?"

"Are you getting this?"

"No. I've gone deaf all of a sudden. Of course, I'm getting it. You want me down there?"

He sighed. "Yeah."

"Aww, poor Rico. Fun time over?"

"Maybe." He glanced across at Skylar where she sat nibbling on her succulent lower lip. He'd known she was afraid, but he was also aware it wasn't only fear she felt. He could scent her arousal, the sweet muskiness making him shift in his chair as his body hardened in response. "Or maybe not."

He sat back and tried to detect any flaws in her story while he waited for Tannis to join them.

Anyone deciding to help a rebel assassin would be risking the wrath of the Collective *and* the Church.

There was one thing about the story he didn't understand. "Your brother," he said to Skylar, "how did he do it? No one's ever managed to kill one of the Collective before."

"I don't know. He never shared the details with me."

"Hmm, very convenient. I heard he managed to completely destroy the DNA, making reconstruction impossible. I'm betting the Collective weren't too happy about that."

He'd also bet they'd be sending their own private army after anyone attempting to free the killer. And nobody wanted to be targeted by the Corps, not even Rico.

Tannis strode in before he could ask any more questions. She ignored Skylar and perched on the seat next to Rico. Her eyes shone with excitement—the prospect of money always had that effect on her.

"I think you're going soft, Rico."

He grinned. "Honey, if you can find one soft spot on my

body right now, you get another chance at that right fang."

Her eyes drifted over his body, lingering on the bulge in his pants. She rolled her eyes. "Don't you ever think of anything else?"

"Sometimes. But not often. So, what do you think?"

Tannis studied Skylar. "Do you believe her?"

"It makes sense. Not many people would go up against the Collective. Hell. Are you sure *you* want to? It'll end your chances of getting the treatment if they find out."

He knew Tannis's ultimate aim was immortality, though he had serious doubts about how she would fit in with the Collective. No one, outside the Collective, knew how Meridian worked. The treatment appeared to have no outward physical effects other than turning the eyes a deep, inhuman violet, but it altered something fundamental inside the mind, forming a tight bond with the rest of the group. And Tannis was a loner.

She'd actually make a much better vampire than a Collective member. He bit back a grin as he attempted to visualize Tannis as a sex-crazed predator. It would almost be worth the risk of changing her just to see how she'd cope with that. In all the time he'd known her, she'd never taken a lover.

But Rico hadn't changed anyone in over a thousand years, and he had no intention of doing so now.

"That might be true," Tannis said. "But I'll have no chance of getting the treatment if I don't get the money. So we'll just have to make sure they don't find out."

"The job's still virtually impossible."

As far as he was aware, no one had ever escaped the prison on Trakis One. Security was top of the range since the prison held the Collective's prisoners, many of whom were incarcerated for attempting to break into the Meridian stores. It seemed ironic to Rico that most of them ended up surrounded by the stuff, laboring in the mines on Trakis Seven. Instead of the immortality they sought, they got a reduced lifespan due to overexposure—if they were lucky, they lasted two years. Though maybe lucky wasn't the right word to use—he'd heard their slow death was far from pleasant.

Tannis interrupted his thoughts. "No job's impossible. I say we go for it."

Rico got up and paced the room. The prospect of an impossible job at least sounded a little bit more interesting than the smuggling jobs Tannis normally took on.

Skylar sat in her chair, hands clenched on her lap. "So you'll do it?" she asked. "You'll get Jonny back for me?"

Rico came to stand over her. This position gave him the perfect view of her cleavage, and the hunger rose inside him. The darkness had drawn back, the need to feed and kill receding until it was no more than a background buzz. But that didn't mean he no longer wanted to taste her.

"Under certain conditions."

Her eyes narrowed. "What conditions?"

"Well, you see, the problem is—money alone doesn't interest me. So if I do this I want a reward."

Tannis coughed behind him. He was quite aware how much money interested her. "A reward as well as the money," he added.

"What do you want?" Skylar's eyes narrowed.

"You, of course."

"Me?" It came out as a squeak. She cleared her throat and tried again. "Me? I'm not sure I follow. Just how do you want me?"

He smiled with a flash of fangs. "Every way there is, darling."

. . .

Skylar licked her lips and stared into his eyes. She knew what he meant, but instead of the expected fear and revulsion, heat curled in the pit of her stomach. She took a deep breath. "Isn't that sort of fatal?"

"Not necessarily."

Not exactly a comforting answer, but did she have a choice?

"You get little Jonny for me first. Afterward…" she trailed off.

"Afterward," he agreed, and she relaxed.

A small flicker of apprehension nudged at her mind, but she ignored it. She'd promised herself she would do whatever was needed to get the job done. Besides, his crude demand for a "reward" eased her conscience slightly; once 'little Jonny' was out she doubted Rico would be in a position to collect anything.

Minutes later, they left, and Skylar stood alone, staring at the closed door. It seemed the job was back on track. If not quite as originally planned.

At least this way she could get out of this dress and these ludicrous high heels. The sooner the better. She crossed to the door and pressed her palm to the pad, but it didn't respond. She had a momentary flash of panic, but she forced it down. They were just being cautious—they were unlikely to give her a free run of the ship until they trusted her a little more.

She went back to her seat and pressed the comm link. Tannis answered. "Yes."

"I was wondering if I could go back to my shuttle. Pick up some stuff. Get changed."

"No problem. I'll send someone to escort you."

· · ·

Skylar frowned down at the small figure standing in the open doorway, hands shoved in the pocket of his baggy pants. He wasn't what she'd expected. After all, so far she'd met a hybrid and a—she stopped short, her mind still refusing to say the word. Anyway, this one appeared almost normal, like an ordinary young boy, though with his mop of dark red hair, skinny figure, and huge gray eyes, he seemed far too young to be on this sort of ship, exposed to these sorts of *people*.

"He's a vampire, you know." The boy spoke for the first time.

Skylar scowled. "Actually, I was sort of in denial about that bit, but thanks for spelling it out for me."

The boy cocked his head to one side and examined her. "I just thought you should know. There might still be time for you to get off before he eats you."

"I'm sure he's not going to eat me," Skylar replied. Actually, she wasn't sure at all. Hadn't she just agreed to let him?

"He always eats the pretty ones."

"Always?"

He nodded solemnly. "I can stay outside when you get to your shuttle. I'll tell them that you overpowered me. Maybe you could hit me or something, make it look like you knocked me out. You might get away."

"Just who are you?"

"I'm Al, the cabin boy."

"Well, Al, I don't want to escape. Your captain's going to help me save my little brother."

"Oh. Well, maybe the captain will keep you safe. She keeps the crew safe."

"And who keeps Tannis safe?" Skylar couldn't help the question. She'd been wondering about Rico's relationship with his captain ever since she'd met them.

"Nobody," Al replied. "Tannis can beat any old vampire."

She could detect a good measure of hero worship in his words.

Skylar shook her head. "Thanks for the offer, but no can do. I told you, they're going to help me save my brother."

"It must be nice having a brother," Al said, his tone wistful.

She heard the longing in his voice. "Do you have any family? Do they know where you are?"

"No. I'm an orphan."

He sounded so forlorn that Skylar had to resist the urge to hug him. Instead, she followed him back the way she'd come.

"I'll wait for you out here," Al said at the entrance to her shuttle. "I'm to take you to the bridge afterward. The captain wants to talk to you."

In the privacy of her shuttle, Skylar kicked off the ridiculous shoes and stripped off the dress, tossing it on the floor while heaving a huge sigh of relief. She pulled on a black jumpsuit made of a strong yet supple material and long boots, strapped a laser pistol to her waist, and began to feel almost normal. Finally, she pulled off the wig and ran a hand through her short blond hair.

When she came out of the shuttle, Al peered behind her as if looking for the 'pretty' one, and she grinned.

Skylar had never been anyone's idea of a 'reward' before, and while her mind balked at being treated like a pleasure provider, another part of her—mainly the part between her breasts and her knees—was secretly thrilled. With her no-nonsense, military demeanor, she'd always had a tendency to intimidate men, and she'd found that useful. The laser pistol didn't hurt either. Now, Skylar couldn't wait to see if the sexy pilot was as easily frightened off.

In all likelihood, Rico would take one look at her and decide he didn't want that reward after all.

CHAPTER FIVE

"You might want to change your mind about that reward," Tannis murmured from beside him. "This one looks like she might fight back."

"I don't mind a good fight," Rico drawled. "As long as I win."

He swung his chair around and his gaze followed her line of sight, settling on the tall figure in the doorway. He wouldn't have recognized her if he hadn't known what to look for.

The silver dress was gone and a black jumpsuit now hugged her tall, toned body. She walked with the lithe grace of a predator, one hand resting on the pistol at her thigh. The long, blond hair, which had done a lot to soften her features, was also gone. In its place was a severely short, almost military cut that emphasized the sharp cheekbones, and the large, almost beaky nose. Her dark blue eyes were the same though, as was the wide, red mouth. He dropped his gaze. There was no disguising the lush curve of those breasts either, and his body tightened at the sight.

She'd come to a halt in front of them, and he raised his eyes from her breasts to her face to find her frowning at him.

"Skylar," he said, kicking out a chair and patting the seat. "Take a seat."

She regarded him suspiciously for a moment and then sat.

"Quite a disguise you had there."

"Part of my training," she replied.

"Your *rebel* training?"

She nodded.

"Tell me. Why were you with the rebels? You seem a little too…" He studied her, trying to think of the correct word. Normal maybe, but he had an idea that Skylar was far from normal.

"Human?" She supplied for him. "I am. But my parents worked for one of the genetic engineering companies. They really believed humans could be improved by gene modification. They were killed in an attack on the facility. My brother and I escaped and were picked up by a rebel patrol— we've been with them ever since."

"Hmm. So what else did they train you to do? What were you exactly?"

"Does it matter?"

"Humor us."

He watched her closely. She appeared relaxed now, no hint of tension in her body or face. Either she was a very good actress, or she was telling the truth. After the failed bimbo disguise, he was pretty certain she must be telling the truth.

"I was a fighter pilot first, then a division leader."

"Impressive."

And it was. Those rebels were a tough lot; they had to be to survive with both the Collective and the Church after them. To get to division leader she had to be very tough herself. He liked that. It made the idea of her squirming beneath him, begging him to take her, all the more enticing. Maybe she'd try to shoot him. He'd have to restrain her—

"Rico!"

He came out of his daydream to find Tannis staring at him in exasperation.

"Get your mind out of your pants."

"My mind wasn't in *my* pants."

She rolled her eyes. "Concentrate for just a few minutes." She turned to Skylar. "Okay, what do you know?"

Skylar took a deep breath. "Jonny was taken just over a week ago. He was on Trakis Five. He did the job, but something went wrong. I don't know what, but they caught him. He was classified as high priority—because of the Collective death— and they shipped him straight to Trakis One. I tried to see him before they took him, but—" She broke off and bit her lip. For the first time, Rico saw a hint of the vulnerability she had masqueraded earlier. Maybe it hadn't all been an act. "They must have rushed him through the system—he didn't even get a proper hearing."

"They never do with Collective cases," Tannis said. "Do you know anything about where he's being held?"

She nodded. "The rebels researched any possibility of getting him out. But when they learned he was in the high-security section, they said no way."

"Great," Tannis muttered. "The high-security section of a maximum-security prison. Maybe it *is* impossible."

"Just think of the money," Rico murmured.

"Oh, I am." She turned back to Skylar. "That reminds me. I need you to set up the payments—I want half of the fee now and the other half set up on a timed transfer for ten days' time. We'll be done by then—either that or locked up with little Jonny on Trakis One, headed for the Meridian mines."

"Or dead," Rico added cheerfully.

"Wow," Tannis said. "I really hadn't thought of that option." She rose to her feet. "I'm going to talk to Janey. Get her working on the systems, see if we can't find some intel on Trakis One. There has to be a weak link somewhere. We've got ten days to find it." She glanced from him to Skylar. "You'll look after our guest, Rico?"

"I'll see to her every desire," he replied.

"Yeah, I bet you will." Tannis cast one last look at Skylar, shook her head, and headed for the door, muttering something not particularly complimentary about men as she stalked away.

· · ·

Skylar waited until the captain left the bridge before turning to Rico. He settled back in his chair, watching her from hooded eyes. He appeared relaxed, but the air throbbed with tension, and a little trickle of apprehension washed through her.

She'd been so sure he'd lose interest once she was out of that stupid dress. But the expression on his face wasn't intimidated or disinterested—it was hungry.

Nervous energy thrummed along her skin, and she jumped to her feet. "I'm going back to my shuttle to make that transfer."

His lips curled into a lazy smile. "No need. We have guest quarters on board—you can do it from there."

"But I—"

"I insist," he said smoothly. "You'll be much more comfortable than in your cramped little shuttle."

She gritted her teeth and nodded.

"Just give me a minute." Rico pressed the comm unit at his side. "Daisy," he said. "Get up here. You're driving."

Skylar waited. She didn't know whether to sit down again or remain standing. She wasn't used to indecision; it wasn't part of her nature. Rico appeared totally relaxed, if a little amused, and she shifted restlessly under his intense gaze. She admired the up-to-date equipment on the bridge and the gleaming black and silver décor, then she peeked sideways at Rico with his black clothes and silver weapons.

"Tell me," she couldn't resist asking, "do you dress to match the ship, or did you decorate the ship to match your wardrobe?"

He gave her another lazy smile and opened his mouth to answer when a woman appeared in the doorway. Skylar stared. The woman was *green*.

She hurried across to them as Rico rose to his feet. Skylar hadn't realized earlier, but without her high heels, he loomed a good six inches over her.

"This is Daisy," he said by way of introduction. "And this is Skylar. Skylar is our new client."

Daisy appeared young, barely out of her teens, and she was dressed in all black, a sort of mini version of Rico, down to the knee-length boots. Her hair was pulled back into a ponytail. She nodded at Skylar then turned to Rico. "You want me to drive?" Skylar could hear the suppressed excitement in her voice.

"I want you to sit in *my* chair and stare at that screen. Comm me if anything changes."

Daisy grinned. "Sure, boss."

Skylar glanced back over her shoulder as they left the bridge. She hadn't wanted to stare, but she'd never seen anyone quite that green before. Skin like new leaves, hair of jade, and eyes the color of emeralds.

"She's a plant hybrid," Rico said as the door shut behind them.

"I've never seen one before."

"There aren't many left. The Church destroyed most of them in the Purge. Daisy escaped from a GM station just before religious fanatics attacked it. The rest, including her family, were murdered. By the time we picked up her pod in deep space, she'd been in cryo for years."

"And you took her in?"

"Tannis took her in." He shrugged. "Tannis is captain—the crew is her responsibility."

Skylar raised an eyebrow. "So how come, if this is your ship, you're not the captain?"

"I don't want to be captain. I like living in space; I don't have to worry about hiding in the daytime. Plus, *El Cazador* provides me with a safe haven and a quick escape if I need to get out of somewhere fast—"

"I bet that happens quite a lot," she interrupted.

He smiled. "Occasionally, but I don't want the responsibility. This works well for both of us. I like to keep my distance from the crew."

"Why?"

"In case I ever have to…" he paused as he came to a halt outside a door and pressed his palm to the panel.

"Eat them?" she finished for him.

He flashed her a grin. "I don't eat everyone I come into contact with—I'm very selective. But humans are fragile, and I've learned not to become too attached."

The door slid open. Skylar hesitated, and Rico put his hand to the small of her back.

She jumped and forced a smile. "Thank you."

His lips twitched. "I'll come in for a minute and show you where everything is." He applied a gentle pressure.

Skylar stood firm. "I'm sure I can find everything I need."

He ignored her. "And make sure you have no problems with the transfer."

"There won't be any problems."

The pressure increased. For a moment, Skylar resisted then gave a mental shrug and stepped inside.

Rico followed, and the door shut behind them. When she stepped away from him, his hand dropped to his side.

The cabin was big, luxurious even, with a large bed dominating the center of the quarters, a chair, and a desk. This was the first place on the ship she had seen any color—the room was decorated in shades of blue. Her favorite.

"Nice," she said.

"It matches your eyes."

Her gaze flew to his face. "How original," she muttered.

"But true."

For a minute, their eyes locked. His were dark, still amused, but with more than a hint of heat in their depths.

A small fire blazed into life in her belly, and she started with uncomfortable shock. What was it with this guy? She'd never had problems like this before. She tore her gaze from his and took a deep breath. "Right then, I'll do the transfer."

He lounged, one shoulder against the wall, arms crossed, and watched while she took a seat at the desk and switched on the external comm unit.

It took only a few moments for the transfer to be completed, and she sat staring at the holographic screen. "There," she said. "Done. You want to check?"

"I trust you."

She glanced up in surprise. "You do?"

"Sure. We're a team now." Rico pushed himself from the wall. "Which calls for some sort of celebration."

"The time for celebrating is when the job is done."

"Aw, come on. Have a little drink with me."

"A drink of what?"

• • •

Rico bit back a laugh. She clearly expected him to jump on her at any moment and latch onto that pretty neck. Not that the idea hadn't occurred to him. With that thought, he had to push down the hunger. He didn't want to scare her.

Well not just yet. He always found a little fear spiced up the blood.

It had been a long time since he'd wanted something this much. Maybe it was because she was an interesting combination of toughness and vulnerability. Earlier, he'd sensed her attraction and her confusion. She obviously wasn't used to either feeling, and that intrigued him.

An impossible job and an intriguing woman—what more could a man ask for?

He unbuckled the strap that held his back scabbard and pulled it off, placing the sword on the floor.

Skylar stared at him suspiciously.

"Just getting comfortable," he said.

He reached into his pocket and drew out a silver flask, held it up to her, and shook it so the liquid inside sloshed from side to side.

"Oh," she muttered.

"You sound almost disappointed."

She frowned. "Of course not."

He pulled two glasses from the cabinet above the desk and poured them both a shot. Picking up his, he gestured to Skylar to do the same. She inspected the amber liquid as though she suspected it might be poison but lifted the glass to her lips and took a small sip. She blinked and put the glass down, her eyes watering.

"What is that stuff?" There was a slight catch in her voice.

"Whiskey," he said. "An old Earth drink. I get it made specially."

He drained his glass and poured himself a second. Sinking onto the sofa opposite her, he watched as she took another tentative sip and licked a bead of whiskey from her lips. His gaze fixed on her mouth as the hunger stirred inside him. Leaning closer, he breathed in the scent of warm woman. "Tell me all about yourself, Skylar Rossaria."

"There's nothing to tell."

She was such a mass of contradictions, obviously trying hard to seem nonchalant and cool-headed—the hardened soldier, but Rico could hear the blood pounding in her veins. He leaned forward, and her rapid heartbeat rocketed.

"There's always something to tell."

She shrugged. "I told you everything you need to know."

He angled his head to one side and studied her face. *Dios*, she was pretty, but her expression was blank, and he wondered what she was hiding and how hard he would have to press her to get the truth. He realized he didn't want to force her. "Well, tell me something I'd like to know."

Her arched brows drew together, and Rico got the distinct impression that social conversation was not something she indulged in often. Curious.

"Like what?" she asked.

"Hmm. How about, what did you like best about being in the rebel army?"

She thought for a moment. "The planning. I liked planning the operations."

"Not shooting people? My guess is you've done quite a bit of shooting."

"Why do you say that?"

He nodded at her hands clasped on her lap. "You have calluses on your palm and fingers."

She squeezed her hands tighter. "How do you know?"

"I felt them straight away when we shook hands."

"That's what you were doing. I thought you were—" She trailed off, sounding almost disappointed.

Rico grinned. "Holding your hand? I was doing that as well, sweetheart."

She ignored the endearment and shrugged again. "I've been well-trained. I'm good."

"I bet you are." He tapped the seat beside him. "Why don't you come and sit next to me and tell me what else you're good at?"

Her gaze shot from the seat, to him, and back again. "I'm quite comfortable here, thank you." Reaching out, she picked up her glass, swallowed the liquid in one gulp, and coughed. "Wow." She picked up the silver flask, poured herself another measure. "Whiskey? From Earth? Another hobby of yours—the study of ancient human beverages?"

"Something like that," he murmured, watching in amusement as she swallowed the second glassful. To someone not used to alcohol it could be potent stuff. He sat back and sipped his own drink, anticipating the exact moment the alcohol hit her bloodstream. She rose unsteadily to her feet, her gaze narrowing on the flask as if it were a gas grenade, primed and ready to explode. "Have you drugged me?"

"Not exactly."

Her brow furrowed. "What does *not exactly* mean?" She reached out a hand and rested it on the desk, swaying a tad leeward. "I feel a little odd."

Very few people had encountered alcohol—it had been banned in the early twenty-first century as detrimental to human life. Still, he'd never seen quite such a dramatic effect before. But then, he normally drank with Tannis, who could drink even him under the table. He got up and strode to where Skylar stood. She didn't protest as he lifted her in his arms and carried her to the bed. He sat down, settling her in his lap. The curve of her bottom pressed against his groin, and he rested his back against the wall, savoring the feel of her, hard yet soft in all the interesting places.

"Lie still," he murmured. "You'll feel better in a minute."

She opened her eyes and blinked up at him. "What have you done to me?"

"Nothing on purpose. Don't worry, the effect will pass."

"It's quite nice. I close my eyes and the world spins."

"Haven't you ever taken recreational drugs?"

She shook her head. "Never. My family would not have approved, and once I was in the army, they were banned. "

"Well your family isn't here now."

"No, they're not." She sighed and wriggled against him. He was sure it was unintentional, but his body responded, his hips lifting.

She was drunk.

A better man wouldn't take advantage of that fact. Sometimes he was inordinately pleased he was not a better man. He ran a finger under her chin, raised her head, and kissed her. Skylar didn't move as he slipped his tongue between her lips. She tasted of whiskey and something else, something unique, but as divine as he'd expected. He leisurely stroked his tongue along the length of hers, feeling her shiver in his arms.

She wriggled again, and this time he suspected it was intentional. Shifting in his arms, she straddled him, a knee on either side of his hips, pressing herself down, rubbing against him until his cock ached with need.

He instinctively pushed up against her, and she moaned low in her throat.

At the throaty purr, desire burned in his belly, his gums ached. He wanted nothing more than to toss her on her back and take her in every way possible, but something held him back. Some crazy need to know this wasn't entirely because of the alcohol she had consumed. He went still as shock hit him in the gut.

What a goddamn stupid time to develop a conscience.

She scattered small kisses across his face and throat, her fingers cutting into his shoulders. It took her a minute to realize he wasn't responding, and then she drew back from him. "You've stopped."

Rico studied her. Her cheeks were flushed and a small pulse throbbed in her throat, but her eyes were clear. "How do you feel?"

She sat back on her heels, a confused frown furrowing her brow as she considered her answer. Her gaze wandered over him, and a slow smile spread across her face. "I feel wonderful."

CHAPTER SIX

His eyes widened in surprise at her answer.

She'd shocked him. Good!

But the truth was, she did feel wonderful. While the initial dizziness had passed, her blood still buzzed. She knew it was the aftereffects of the whiskey Rico had given her, but she wasn't sure she cared. It was as though her body had sprung into life after a long, deep sleep.

All the same, she ran a quick internal analysis, identifying the chemicals in her system. They would only take moments to eliminate.

But she hesitated.

Rico had made it clear he wanted her from the moment they'd met. And Skylar was honest enough to admit, at least to herself, that she wasn't totally immune to his charms. But she was a soldier, and she'd had every intention of keeping her mind, and the rest of her, firmly fixed on her mission.

Right up until five minutes ago.

Now, with this lovely buzzing in her blood and Rico's hard sex pressing against her, taunting her with delicious possibilities, she was rethinking her strategy. After all, she was working undercover. Maybe she didn't have to be quite so rigid in her attitudes. And wasn't that the key to being a successful operative—the ability to adapt your approach to changing circumstances?

As long as she stayed in control of the situation, why couldn't she have this one time? It wasn't outside the parameters of her character, and she could always say afterwards that she'd been under the influence. Perhaps she could even accuse Rico of taking advantage. Skylar had to bite back a smile at the idea. She had a strong suspicion he wouldn't mind the accusation, possibly even reveling in the slight.

How long had it been since she'd kissed a man? How long since she'd even wanted to? So many years she couldn't remember. But then, having a whole load of people in your head could be inhibiting.

Now she didn't feel self-conscious. She felt wild and hot, every nerve ending sensitized.

A vague doubt nagged at her, but she shoved it aside. Rico Sanchez was the most beautiful thing she had ever seen. Looking into that hard, handsome face sent frissons of pleasure shivering over her skin, tightening the hard knot of desire in her belly. The taste of him lingered on her tongue, her breasts ached, her sex swollen with need.

She shifted slightly, so the rigid line of his erection pressed more firmly against her core, and the knot unraveled, her insides melting.

She tried the movement again, and flames licked through

her, burning along her nerves, settling between her thighs. Closing her eyes, she concentrated on the sensations, rocking herself against him. So close.

"You don't feel light-headed?"

The question broke her concentration, and her lids fluttered open. Rico was watching her, his brows drawn together.

"My head feels fine." She moved in closer to kiss him, but his hands gripped her shoulders and fended her off.

What the hell? He'd come on to her strong; now he watched her as though he didn't quite understand what was going on. Maybe he was one of those guys who liked to make all the moves.

"How about the rest of you?" he asked.

Gritting her teeth, she forced a smile. "The rest of me is fine as well."

"You're not disorientated? You know what you're doing?"

She rolled her eyes. "Well I thought I did, though I have to admit it's been a while." A horrible idea occurred to her. "Is this some weird vampire shit? Do vampires even have sex? Everlasting Hell, don't tell me you're impotent."

"Impotent?" He repeated the word as though he wasn't sure what it meant.

"Please don't tell me the big come-on is all an act—you're overcompensating for the fact that you can't actually do it."

Skylar couldn't believe the disappointment that swamped her while her body still screamed for release. She tried to back away, but his grip tightened, squeezing her arms and holding her in place.

"Impotent?" His tone was incredulous, outraged. He

flexed his hips, pushing his erection against her as if to prove his point. "I am *not* impotent. I have sex. Hot, sweaty, *liquefying* sex. And I have it *often*."

Her body reacted predictably to each word, and she rubbed up against his hard body again. "Terrific news."

His hands shifted from her shoulders to the neck of her jumpsuit, and he pushed down the fastener. Swift fingers snagged on the weapons' belt at her waist, and she didn't protest when he flipped the catch and placed the belt on the table beside them.

He slid his cool hands up her ribcage, parted the material, and cupped her full breasts in his palms. He lifted them and lowered his head, drawing one nipple into his fiery mouth. Hard. Nipping and sucking with raw hunger. The sensation was exquisite, and a low whimper escaped her throat as pleasure exploded inside her, shooting from her breasts to her groin.

Her fingers burrowed beneath his silky hair, pulling it free from the band and pressing his head roughly against her chest, and everything fled her mind but his hot, wet mouth on her breasts.

After long minutes, he pulled back, his eyes dark with passion. In one fluid movement, he picked her up and swung her beneath his body, his weight pressing her into the softness of the bed. A low growl rumbled in his chest as he attacked her other breast with uncontrolled need, with single-minded focus, with a desperation she'd never known.

Her blood roared in her ears as he ran a hand from her breast to the mound at the base of her belly, then lower to cup her sex, massaging her through the thin material with the palm of his hand until her legs fell open for him. He withdrew, and she moaned. Ignoring the sound, he traced a path down over her inner thigh.

"Did you know, you have a vein, right here," he murmured.

"A vein?"

He rubbed his thumb over the spot. "Let me taste you, get to know you. I can tell a lot from a tiny sip of your blood."

She went still at his words. Fear forced itself beyond the pleasure-induced haze fogging her brain. "What—what can you tell?"

He shrugged, casually tracing his finger up and down her inner thigh. "How old you are, whether you're a hybrid or even a clone."

Panic flared.

"No, wait, I don't—"

"Shh, it won't hurt. You'll like it, I promise."

She scooted up the bed away from him. "We agreed—after the rescue."

For a moment, she thought he'd force the issue and she braced herself to fight. Instead, he stroked his hand back up her thigh, then slipped inside the open jumpsuit to caress her flat belly, his fingers gliding lower, dipping between the folds of her sex to tease lazy circles around her clit, never quite touching. She couldn't help herself, she lay back, her hips rising, her thighs widening. "Oh God, that feels good."

"This will feel even better." He leaned down to stroke her breasts with his tongue, hot wet velvet, while his fingers finally touched her where she needed him. She exploded with pleasure, her whole body arching off the bed. When the tremors eased, he bit down lightly on her nipple and squeezed her clit with a finger and thumb, and this time she threw back her head and screamed.

She must have blacked out. When she came around, he was crouched over her body, kissing her breasts, nuzzling her throat. Her limbs felt boneless, she never wanted to move again.

The sharpness of his fangs grazed her skin.

"No." The word came out as a yelp.

"You don't mean that," he whispered against her skin.

"I do." She cleared her throat. "Yes, I do."

"You'll enjoy it, I promise."

Skylar did her best to ignore the husky cajoling tone of his voice, as warm and intoxicating as the whiskey he'd given her earlier. Maybe she would enjoy it, but that was beside the point. If he was telling the truth, one taste of her blood and he'd know everything and the mission would be over. Her first mission in her new job—a total failure, and all her own stupid fault.

So much for staying in control.

She tried to concentrate, but it was impossible with Rico stroking her thighs and murmuring against her skin all the things he planned to do to her.

She had to get out of here, but she was no longer sure he would let her go. What did she really know of him? He was trying seduction right now, but that might change if she didn't give him what he wanted, and she couldn't risk him taking her blood by force. No, she needed a plan.

He nipped at the sensitive spot where her shoulder met her throat. "Relax, *querida*, and I promise you'll soon be begging for more."

No doubt she would, in fact the words hovered on her lips.

Think, dammit.

Why the hell hadn't they trained her to cope with situations like this back at the academy? Perhaps she'd suggest it if she got out of here in one piece—how to deal with a vampire who's just given you the most mind-blowing orgasm of your life and now wants to drink your blood.

A hysterical giggle rose up as she imagined the colonel's response. But at the thought of the colonel, a possible way out managed to dredge itself free from the primordial sludge her brain had been reduced to. It wasn't a perfect plan and might break her cover, but it was a risk she had to take. Opening her internal comm link, she sent out a quick message and prayed they'd respond before she started that begging.

Rico raised his head. His gaze met hers, his eyes glowing as he drew back like a coiled snake preparing to strike.

Holy Meridian. She'd run out of time. *Do something.*

Gathering her strength, she pushed against him. He was inhumanly strong but she managed to wriggle a hand between them and shoved him hard. He rolled off her onto his back, and she twisted quickly so she lay on top of him.

He growled low in his throat. "What—?"

"Just returning the favor." She ran her hand over his lean belly, flicked open the button on his pants and lowered the zip. Moving quickly, she pushed her hand inside and wrapped her fingers around the length of him. He was huge and hard, velvet and steel, and despite the imminent danger, a familiar pulse started between her thighs.

He wasn't fighting now. His eyes were half-closed, his breathing shallow. She slid off him to kneel at his side, still grasping him in her tight fist. He lifted his hips, and she pushed down his pants. Bending over him, she blew gently on the swollen tip of his shaft just as the whole ship leapt sideways.

The force flung Skylar from the bed. Rico landed on top of her in a tangle of limbs. For a moment, they lay there, then Rico twisted free and pressed the comm link on his wrist.

"Daisy, what the fuck is going on?"

Tannis answered. "Put your dick back in your pants and get up here. Now."

He frowned. "Are you watching us?"

"No, I'm making a calculated guess based on past experience. We need you up here. We've got company."

He sighed and got to his feet. Skylar still lay sprawled on the floor, and he reached down, picked her up, and dropped her on the center of the bed.

"I'll be back." And with that prophetic declaration, he jerked his pants up and left.

Skylar stared at the closed door. What the hell had just nearly happened?

She got to her feet and swayed, reaching out to balance herself.

Her body felt strange. It had been a long time. A very long time. Even so, how had she let things go so far, so fast? She shook her head and jerked the fastener of her jumpsuit up to her neck, then picked up the weapons belt—she couldn't believe she had let him strip her of her weapons. Her clothes perhaps, but her *gun*?

She strapped it back on and felt immediately better.

Her eyes settled on the glass on the table. She picked it up and sniffed, wishing she could blame the drink, knowing she couldn't. The whiskey was well and truly gone from her system now, and all she could think was she'd been an idiot, like some sex-starved vampire groupie. She slammed the glass back down.

No more cozy little drinking sessions with the vampire. She needed to make sure she kept her distance from now on. She wasn't sure what he would pick up from tasting her blood, but she couldn't risk letting her guard down again. However good it had felt. Her future depended on it.

She pressed her palm to the lock and, to her surprise, the door slid open. Al was leaning against the wall outside, obviously waiting for her.

"The captain said I was to take you to the bridge once you'd got your clothes back on."

Skylar ground her teeth together. "I did *not* take my clothes off." Only half took them off.

"The captain said sorry for interrupting your important business, but she needed to get hold of Rico fast and…." He shrugged one narrow shoulder.

"Shit." Did the whole crew know what she'd been up to with Rico? For a moment, her lashes fluttered closed, but things weren't going to get any better by putting them off. A wave of anger washed over her—she blamed this on Rico and his mojo lust drink. Had he planned to seduce her, maybe even boasted about it to the crew? And to think she almost gave in…

She squared her shoulders and stalked off, leaving Al to follow or not.

Another shot hit the ship, hurling her against the wall. She rubbed her elbow, picked herself up, and hurried to the bridge.

Everyone appeared amazingly calm considering they

were under attack. Rico lounged in the pilot's seat, talking to Daisy.

"It came out of nowhere," she said.

"Intergalactic space cruisers do not come out of nowhere."

"Well, this one did."

Skylar studied the monitor. The image of a ship nearly twice the size of the *El Cazador* and with ten times the firepower filled the screen. It was coming round on them once more, and she quickly found something to grab hold of. This time she managed to stay upright.

Rico swore loudly. "Don't let go of whatever you're holding on to," he said, and deftly maneuvered the ship with a hard bank down and left, darting around so he came up behind the space cruiser. He hit the fire switch and the laser guns blasted the other ship. It was a direct hit, and the ship veered away, disappearing from the screen.

"That should keep them for a minute or two." They waited in silence, but the screen remained blank.

"It's gone," Daisy said.

Tannis stepped up closer to stare over Rico's shoulder at the screens. "What do you mean 'gone'?"

"Vanished."

"Intergalactic space cruisers do not just vanish."

"Well, this one did," Daisy said.

"What's going on?" Skylar asked.

Tannis turned to look at her. "I don't know. We seem to have attracted the attention of a Collective cruiser. It came out of nowhere and now it's disappeared." She peered at Skylar suspiciously. "Is there something you're not telling us?"

"Like what?"

"Like the fact that you've got the Collective on your tail."

"I made no secret of the fact that I'm with the rebels and wanted by the Collective. But do you really think that if they knew I was on board, they would shoot a few times and then vanish?"

The yellow eyes seemed to bore through her. Skylar held her gaze, keeping her expression guileless.

"She's right," Rico spoke into the silence. "If they knew we had a rebel on *El Cazador*, we'd be boarded by now."

"I still don't like it."

Rico punched something into the console in front of him and shook his head. "They're definitely gone. Was there any damage?"

"None," Daisy said. "The shields took the impact. It's as if they were playing with us. As if they didn't want to do any actual damage."

"So what did they want?" Tannis asked.

Rico shrugged. "Get our attention maybe. Whatever, it's time to get out of here." Skylar stalked over to him and he swiveled in his chair and rose to his feet. "Hey, sweetheart— did you miss me?"

At the endearment, her fury rose again. She drew back her fist and punched him in the mouth.

"Ow," she muttered, shaking her hand.

She glanced into Rico's face and took a step back. A glint of ruby gleamed from behind his half-closed lashes. A drop of blood beaded on his lower lip. He licked it slowly with his tongue then rose to his feet to tower over her. His lips peeled back in a snarl to reveal razor sharp fangs.

The sight just made her madder. Those damn fangs had

gotten her into this mess in the first place, and it was about time he learned to keep them to himself. Skylar's hand went to the laser pistol at her hip, and his gaze dropped to follow the movement. She took a deep calming breath and kicked out with her booted foot. She connected with his thigh and swept his legs from under him so he crashed to the floor. Drawing the laser pistol in one fluid move, she stood over him, the pistol aimed at his heart.

He stared up at her for long moments before the tension oozed from his body. He reached up and stroked his finger over his mouth where her fist had connected.

"Hey, I promised to come back."

"Did you plan that?" Her eyes narrowed on him, and her finger tightened on the trigger.

"That?"

"To get me intoxicated and…" She became aware of the rest of the crew listening avidly.

He looked at the gun and back at her face. "No, it was a spur of the moment thing, but you were hardly fighting me off. And that gun won't stop me, but it will hurt, so I suggest you think twice before you piss me off any more than you have already."

She held her stance for a minute longer, just to prove she could, then lowered the pistol and shoved it back in the holster. Rico rose gracefully, brushing himself off.

His gaze settling on Tannis, who stood propped against the wall, grinning. "Thanks, Captain, it was good of you to jump to my rescue."

She lifted one shoulder carelessly. "You're alive, aren't you? Now do you think you could get us out of here before that space cruiser decides to come back and take us out after all?"

Skylar stepped out of the way, and they prepared to make the jump. Tannis came to stand beside her.

"Hey, don't feel bad about it."

Skylar scowled. "About what?"

"Getting all hot and sweaty with Rico."

"Thanks for reminding me."

"You'd forgotten?"

Skylar didn't answer.

"Mind you," Tannis said, "I've never known him to make a move quite that fast."

Skylar heaved a huge sigh of irritation. "Your point is?"

"I'm just saying he's a vampire." Tannis leaned in closer and lowered her voice. "Apparently, if he doesn't get sex on a regular basis, he goes all dark and scary."

Skylar stared at her hard, trying to tell if she was joking, but Tannis's face was as deadpan as usual.

"Also," Tannis continued, "they have this whole seduction thing going. Helps them catch their prey, apparently, if everyone's trying to jump their bones."

"I was not trying to jump his bones."

"No? Well you were sure wound up about something." She grinned.

Skylar resisted the urge to pull her pistol again and instead changed the subject. "Have you come up with a plan yet?"

"You're a cool one," Tannis murmured. "I'm not sure what to make of you. I don't quite trust you, but I have no clue what your angle could be. I can't even begin to guess what you might be after."

"I just want to free my brother."

"Hmm. Let's hope so, but double-cross us and Rico will be the least of your worries."

She gave Skylar one last long look then strode across the bridge, one hand resting on her laser pistol. At the door, she turned to face the room. "I suggest we get moving toward the Trakis system. We have ten days to make this happen."

"And where are you going, Captain?" Rico asked.

"I'm going to come up with that plan."

CHAPTER SEVEN

Skylar was hungry.

At least she presumed that's what the hollow sensation in the pit of her stomach was telling her. It was weird—as though her appetites, long suppressed, were coming to life.

All her appetites.

An image of Rico flashed through her mind, lying on the bed, his pants undone, his… She shifted, her thighs clenching as she remembered the feel of his mouth and hands on her breasts, between her legs….

Oh God. Maybe food would take her mind off sex.

But as well as food, she wanted company, real company.

There was no day and night in space, but *El Cazador* kept to a twenty-four hour cycle with regular sleeping and meal times—similar to the old Earth setup—as it had been found that humans responded best to this.

Skylar guessed it was close to supper time. Last night, her first night on board, she'd pleaded exhaustion, and Al had brought her a tray to eat in her room. Maybe tonight he would stay and talk while she ate. Tell her about Rico.

Rico again. She was obsessed. She had to get her mind off him and his hands and his mouth and his tongue and….

A light tap on the door interrupted her thoughts. She leapt up, crossed the room, and peered into the viewer. Al stood outside, shifting from foot to foot. Tonight he didn't carry a tray, and Skylar's stomach rumbled in protest.

She pressed her palm to the panel and the door slid open.

Al shoved his hands in his pockets. "Captain Tannis says if you want to eat, you have to join us in the galley."

"I—"

"She said that anyone who thinks they're too good to eat with her crew can go hungry."

"But—"

"So are you coming? The vampire won't be there. Vampires don't eat—not food, anyway."

Skylar made a swift decision, nodded, and followed Al down the corridor. He stopped before they reached the galley and turned to her. "You know, if you're worried about the vampire, I can protect you."

Skylar managed to keep a straight face as she imagined the boy going up against the vampire. "You can? Don't you have work to do?"

Al nodded. "But when I'm busy, one of the others could take over." He chewed on his lower lip. "You'd probably have to pay them though."

"You think it would be worth it?"

"Oh, yeah. He won't try anything when one of the crew is around. He promised the captain. You'll be safe."

Skylar wasn't really afraid Rico would snack on her against her will. On the other hand, after their previous up-close encounter, she wasn't sure just how much against her will it would be. Besides, it was clear Al wasn't going to be satisfied until he felt she was safe. "That's great. You organize it, and I'll pay."

The galley lay right at the center of the ship. The scent of food wafted from the room, and her stomach rumbled again. A large oval table took up most of the floor space, and a bank of food dispensers stood against one wall. Four people sat around the table. They looked up as Skylar hovered in the doorway.

"Good of you to join us," Tannis said.

Skylar managed not to wince at the sarcastic tone. Instead, she curled her lips in the semblance of a smile. "My pleasure."

Next to Tannis sat a woman Skylar hadn't met before. She was perfect, from her tawny gold hair to the elegant black dress to the silver high heels, which looked right at home on the end of her slender legs. Skylar bet this woman never tripped over her feet.

"I'm Janey," she said with an easy smile. "I look after the systems around here. Daisy you've already met, and"—she waved her fork at the man next to her—"this is the Trog. He's our engineer. He doesn't talk much, so don't try and engage him in conversation."

The Trog lifted his head and grunted. He appeared wholly human, but it was hard to tell anything beneath the shaggy mop of dark blond hair. He gave her a shy smile and continued eating.

Skylar smiled in greeting and slipped into a chair. Al

handed her a disposable tray of food, and Skylar kept her head down as she ate. After a few minutes, the conversation started up again, and she let it flow over her. The food was good, some sort of beef stew, and it tasted almost real. Finally, she put her fork down and sat back replete, to find everyone watching her. Everyone except Al, who jumped to his feet and started clearing the trays, depositing them down the recycling shoot.

Their gazes shifted to focus on something behind her. Skylar peeked over her shoulder, and the air seemed to leave the room. Rico's lean figure lounged in the open doorway, enticingly rumpled, still in his usual black pants and shirt, but his weapons were gone, his feet were bare, and his dark hair hung loose around his shoulders. A whole new kind of hunger rumbled in her belly.

His lips curved into a slow smile, and he sauntered into the room. He touched her lightly on the shoulder as he passed, and a shiver prickled across her skin, her breath catching in her throat. He held something in his hand—a small rectangular object that he placed on the table in front of him as he sank into the chair opposite.

Skylar pushed herself to her feet. "Thanks for the food," she said to the room in general.

Rico watched her sleepily. "Stay," he murmured. When she didn't move, he tilted his head to the side and studied her. "What can happen with everyone here?"

Tannis snorted, but Skylar ignored the sound, concentrating on Rico. He leaned in closer. "I won't bite, and I'm lonely and feeling nostalgic. I thought we might play an old Earth game." He glanced around at the others. "All of us."

Skylar realized she wanted to stay. Everyone else appeared relaxed; Janey and Daisy were staring at Rico with something approaching hero worship. Tannis was actually smiling.

What harm could it do?

"Come on, Skylar, you know you want to play with me." Rico's tone was low and dark and ignited a fire deep inside her.

The flare of heat reminded her that he was dangerous—that she couldn't trust herself around him and that she should get the hell out of there. Instead, she slowly sank into her chair. "What are we playing?"

He grinned. "Seven-card stud. A game I learned when I lived in the Wild West. Around a thousand years ago, give or take a couple of hundred."

"I've read about the Wild West," Daisy said, eyes wide. "Were you a cowboy?"

Amusement gleamed in his eyes. "I'm a vampire, honey, and there aren't too many cows that need chasing at night." He relaxed in his chair. "So this," he said, picking up the box in front of him, "is a deck of cards."

• • •

It was true, he was feeling nostalgic—a new experience for him. He suspected Skylar was the cause, but had no clue why she affected him so profoundly. After she'd punched him yesterday, he'd decided to give her a little space. But all day, he'd had to fight the urge to hunt her down—not for sex, or food—but just to spend time with her, to get to know her. A loner by nature, he couldn't understand what drew him to Skylar.

She was a mystery. A tough, highly trained soldier who occasionally revealed flashes of vulnerability. A beautiful woman almost unaware of her own sexuality.

He'd managed to resist until tonight, when he was lying alone in his cabin, restless, unable to settle, and suddenly craved company. One person's company in particular, but he'd put up with the rest of the crew if that's what was needed to put Skylar at ease.

He caught her gaze, and her lips curved into a sweet smile. He'd bet it was the first genuine smile he'd seen on her face, and it twisted something deep inside his chest. He had a sudden desire to see her laugh, to break down the natural reserve that hung about her like a protective shield.

"Gather around, children," he said. "I'm going to teach you everything I know—which is a lot—so pay attention." He shuffled the cards. "And if you're *really* good, tomorrow night, I might teach you a variation."

Daisy giggled. "What's that?"

"Strip poker—I'll leave the details to your imaginations. But for tonight we're going to bet with these." He took a worn leather pouch out of his pocket and emptied it onto the table. A stream of sparkling gemstones glittered against the matte black metal.

He picked up a stone from the glittering pile and held it up to Skylar. "Did you know, back on Earth, men would give one of these to the woman they wanted to marry, and she'd wear it on her finger for all to see."

She raised an eyebrow. "Another old Earth custom?"

"Yes." Reaching across the table, he picked up her left hand. "This is your ring finger. Folklore has it that the fourth finger of the left hand has a vein leading directly to the heart. The ring was supposed to symbolize eternal love." He held her gaze, as he rubbed the pad of his thumb across her palm. A shudder ran through her. She pulled her hand free and placed it on her lap, out of reach.

"Eternal love? How sweet." Tannis spoke from beside him, and he turned reluctantly to face her. "Did you give *your* wife a ring?" she asked.

"I did—an emerald—green like her eyes."

Daisy perked up. "Like mine?"

He bit back a smile. He doubted anyone had eyes or anything else quite as green as Daisy. "Just like yours."

He wondered whether Skylar would ask about his wife, wondered whether he would answer if she did. But except for a slight widening of her eyes, she made no response.

He toyed with the stone he'd picked up, rubbing it between his finger and thumb. It wasn't an emerald, but a deep purple amethyst, glowing with violet fire. He tossed it toward Skylar, and she caught it in her hand and closed her fist around it.

"Pretty," Janey murmured, picking up a diamond and holding it up to the light.

"And unfortunately, totally worthless. But these were once quite valuable—a souvenir from my days as a real pirate."

"A real pirate? On a ship sailing across oceans?"

"I was, and an excellent one. Unlike cows, it's quite easy to chase ships in the dark." He split the stones into piles, pushed one toward Skylar, his fingers lightly grazing hers as she took them. She jumped as though a shock had run through her, and a little glow of satisfaction warmed him—definitely not immune. "Let's play."

He dealt two cards down, one up. "Now, you can look at your cards, but don't let anyone else see them." He glanced across at Skylar. "And no peeking. Any cheating will be severely punished."

She smiled again, and the glow burst into flames. No, he didn't understand what attracted him to Skylar and he still had some serious reservations about her story, but they just added to the intrigue, made her that little bit more fascinating. He looked forward to unraveling the mystery, discovering what was beneath the lies and evasions.

But not tonight. Pushing the thoughts aside, he settled down to the considerable challenge of making Skylar Rossaria laugh.

CHAPTER EIGHT

Rico settled back in his seat, raised his arms above his head, and stretched. They'd been poring over intel on Trakis One for the last few hours. So far they'd found nothing of any use.

He looked up to find Skylar's gaze on him, and he stretched again, liking the way she ate him up with her eyes. She'd been on board five days, and somehow she'd managed to avoid being alone with him in all that time, though she was happy enough to spend the evenings with him and the rest of the crew. He'd even managed to make her laugh a few times.

He kept the atmosphere light during those games with the crew, but beneath the banter, he was surprised to realize he was telling her about himself, revealing things he hadn't thought about in years—if ever. He wanted her to know who he was. What he was. And he wanted to get to know her, too. She was relaxing, but she was still something of an enigma. And if he tried to get her alone, she'd vanish, or someone else would miraculously appear and demand her attention.

It was actually quite impressive.

She wanted him. He was sure of it. But she had amazing willpower. He would have pushed it, but he was interested to see how it played out, and he would get her in the end. A deal was a deal.

"If you could stop thinking about sex, you might manage to work out a way for us to get into this stupid prison," Tannis said from beside him.

He grinned, topped off her glass, and then held the silver flask up to Skylar. She shook her head, but changed her mind and nodded. Interesting, another thing she'd avoided since their encounter. Maybe she was willing to loosen up a little.

She sipped the drink, barely even grimaced. "It's impossible, isn't it?"

"Nothing's impossible," Tannis replied. "It's just difficult. There's a way. We just haven't found it yet."

Skylar rose to her feet and paced, running her hand through her short hair. Finally, she thumped into her chair, topped off her glass, and sat back. Tannis reached across to pour herself more but found the flask empty. She stood up. "Got any more of this stuff?"

"In my cabin. Do you want me to go?"

"No, you look far too comfortable. I won't be long." Her gaze darted between the two of them. "Be good."

Rico turned to Skylar as the door slid shut behind Tannis. "Alone at last." Skylar didn't respond. Instead, she gazed into space. After a minute, she looked at him, studying him closely.

"So what exactly are you?" she asked.

The question took him by surprise. Not many people wanted to know the details. Either that, or they never quite got up the nerve to ask. But the one thing Skylar did not lack was nerve.

"That's a broad question."

She rolled her eyes. "You know what I mean."

"I'll tell you what—I'll answer a question of yours, and afterwards, you answer one of mine."

She shrugged. "Why not? Me first. So—what are you?"

"You know what I am."

"You're a"—she paused, obviously still having problems with the word—"vampire." She thought for a moment. "Were you ever human?"

He nodded. "My turn. How old are you?"

She hesitated, which was interesting. "Thirty-two. How old are you?"

He had to calculate his answer; it had been many years since he'd given it any thought. "One-thousand, five-hundred and ninety-six."

Her eyes widened. "Wow, that's old."

"I was born in 1452 back on Earth. There, that was a bonus answer. My question now. Why are you avoiding me?"

Her brows drew together at the question. "I don't like losing control."

Rico was sure her answer was part of the truth, but not all of it. He shrugged; he would uncover her secrets in the end. "Your turn."

"How often do you need to drink? I mean are you hungry right now?"

"No, I'm not hungry. I can go a long time between feeding. That doesn't mean to say I wouldn't drink if it was offered."

She bit her lip. "And do you kill your victims?"

He smiled, his lips drawing back to give her a flash of fangs. "Sometimes."

• • •

The answer took Skylar by surprise. She'd been expecting him to evade the question.

"Well, that's honest," she murmured. She couldn't get over how old he was—far older than any of the Collective.

He rose gracefully to his feet, then crossed the room toward her. Every one of her senses went on high alert.

By careful planning, and a lot of help from Al and the rest of the crew, she'd managed to avoid being alone with him over the past few days. Perhaps she should make an excuse and get out of here now. But a reckless excitement was stirring inside her. She'd lived under such strict rules and constant supervision for so long, the last few days had been a revelation. Sometimes she felt as though she was a stranger, waking up from a deep sleep. She hadn't realized how repressed she had been. She'd thought she was doing what she wanted, but now doubts niggled at her subconscious.

Plus, and she was finally going to be honest with herself, she couldn't stop thinking about sex. For years, she hadn't given it more than a passing thought, but now it plagued her. Tannis had hinted that vampires had some sort of powers that made people want them—maybe that's all this was. Purely a predator-prey thing.

That didn't stop her nipples from tightening as he stepped around her chair and came to a halt behind her. She stared straight ahead, her body rigid with anticipation as his hands slid over her shoulders. His fingers dug deep into the knotted muscle.

"You're tense," he murmured, lowering his head so his cool breath brushed the back of her neck. Shivers of pleasure rippled down her spine, settling in the base of her belly, and she had to shake herself mentally in order to concentrate.

"Er, you've just told me you kill your prey—sorry—*sometimes* kill your prey, and now you're sniffing at me like I smell good enough to eat."

"You do smell good enough to eat." He breathed in deeply. "And while I do sometimes kill my prey, I very rarely kill my lovers." He kissed her ear, his moist tongue dipping inside, and she closed her eyes to savor the sensation. "So why don't we fuck now," he whispered, "and you can stop worrying about it."

Oh, God.

He kissed her neck, and it felt so damned good, tracing little patterns with his tongue across her sensitive flesh, his strong hands kneading her shoulders. Her head fell to the side to give him better access, and his hands slid down from her shoulders to cup her breasts. Her eyes shot open, and she stared at his hands, the skin pale against the black of her jumpsuit. His fingers brushed over her nipples, massaging her breasts until she was squirming in her seat, pressing her thighs together to intensify the craving burning through her.

"What do you say, Skylar?"

She couldn't say anything. His hand squeezed her breast as his mouth left her neck. She let out a little groan of dismay, but he kissed along her jaw line, small teasing kisses. At last, his mouth was on hers, and his tongue pushed inside as he took one swollen nipple between his finger and thumb and pinched it sharply. Pleasure and pain shot through her. Her hips rose from the seat, her head arching back as he swallowed her groan.

"Did you like that?" He soothed the sensitized nipple with his palm, before pinching again, harder this time. Wet heat flooded her core as a deep, scorching need flared to life inside her.

His hand slid over her stomach, his fingers flirting with her navel through the thin material, then lower, and everything inside her clenched up tight.

"Great," Tannis said from the doorway. "Nice to see you're being 'good.'"

Rico's hand went still against her. Skylar closed her eyes, fighting the urge to scream her frustration. When she opened them, Tannis was still there, staring at the two of them with irritation flaring in her yellow eyes.

Skylar reached up and pried Rico's hand from her body. She didn't move as Tannis crossed the room, sat back down, and filled up all three glasses from the flask in her hand. When Skylar was sure her own hand would be steady, she picked up her glass and swallowed the burning liquid in one gulp. The warmth spread through her, seeping into the cold corners, and she held out her glass for more.

"Right," she said, as Tannis poured the whiskey, "let's go through the intel one more time."

Tannis raised an eyebrow but didn't say anything.

Skylar avoided looking at Rico as he sat down next to Tannis. Instead, she opened her palm screen and scanned through the information, forcing her mind to function and hunt for flaws in the security. She was impressed by the amount of intel they'd managed to dredge up on a classified institution. There was obviously a whole load of leaks out there somewhere.

After a few minutes, she frowned. "You've plenty of information on the ordinary prison, but nothing on the maximum security section."

"We haven't located a source yet. The ordinary prison is easy—lots of ex-inmates. But we haven't found anyone yet who's been imprisoned in the maximum security section and got out to tell the tale."

"So what are you doing? We can't go in blind."

"Janey is trying to find anyone who might have actually been there—she's starting with ex-guards. We'll find someone."

"We'd better."

Skylar continued reading. "The security in the outer section doesn't look all that great."

"I don't think it's needed. From what I can see, there's not much danger in prisoners trying to escape. There's nowhere to go, and that takes us to the main problem, which is the planet itself. It's part of the Trakis system and close to the mines, but it's also almost impossible to approach." Tannis switched on the main screen, and a group of planets appeared, revolving in a complicated pattern of orbits around a number of suns. Skylar recognized them as the Trakis system—pretty much the center of the universe since Meridian had been discovered on Trakis Seven. Tannis narrowed the field until the image zoomed in on a single planet, circling a black star—Trakis One.

"There, you see—" Tannis stood up and pointed. "Trakis One is actually on an elliptical orbit around a black hole. Under normal circumstances a ship can't get close." She paced the room for a moment before coming to a halt in front of the screen. "Try and land at the wrong time and chances are you'll be sucked into that thing, never to be seen again. They don't even keep a ship on the planet. No point—even if there was some sort of disaster, they couldn't evacuate because of the black hole."

"So how do deliveries get made?" Rico asked.

"Very infrequently."

Skylar studied the planet, watching thc orbit closely. "My guess is that they coincide deliveries with shipping inmates in and out, when the single moon is aligned with the black hole. You could probably slip past without being sucked in."

"Probably?" Rico asked, and he didn't sound convinced.

"Well they must do it somehow," Tannis said. "And if they can, we can. After all, we have the best goddamn pilot in the universe." She grinned at Rico. "Or so he keeps telling us. Time we saw some proof."

"Do we know when the next alignment is due to happen?" Skylar asked.

"Well, if your brother is scheduled to be shipped out in five days' time then that would seem to be a good bet—they can't ship him out if the ship can't get to him."

"So we go in ourselves, get Jonny, and we're out of there before they even arrive."

"Unfortunately, I don't think it's going to be that easy." Tannis sat back down and took a sip of her drink.

Beside her, Rico shifted restlessly. "Are you going to tell us why?"

"I am. The radiation levels on Trakis One are off the scale. *El Cazador* would fry on entry into their atmosphere. They use special ships that are shielded. There's also a matter of getting into the prison once we're down. My guess is it will be top-of-the-range DNA recognition."

"There's a lot of guessing going on here," Rico said. "So we'll need the real guards."

"Yup. Or at least bits of them."

Skylar shrugged. "We hijack the transport ship, then."

"Looks like the only way."

Skylar thought about it for a minute. They might have to take out the crew. She didn't like the idea of any unnecessary deaths, but it was a risk she would have to take. This job was the highest priority—her boss had told her in no uncertain terms that failure was not an option. Anyway, with luck, the crew of the transport ship would see sense and surrender. Or they could stun them and lock them up. "Okay, sounds like a plan. When do we do it?"

"I'd say we wait until the ship is as close to Trakis One as we can make it," Rico said. "The security is going to be high, and the less time we have on board, the less chance we have of breaking one of the protocols. Any clue where the ship comes from?"

Tannis studied her palm screen for a moment. "Trakis Five."

"That's a two-day trip."

"And a two-day trip from here. Fits in well. We can intercept them." Tannis stared at the screen, a frown marring her face. "Almost too well." She shrugged. "I'm going to see if I can't scrounge up some more intel on the transport ship. Find out crew numbers and so on and get Janey working on breaking the codes. I reckon we're going to need some pretty hefty bribes. I'll leave you two to"—she paused and shrugged again—"whatever."

Skylar jumped to her feet. "I'll come with you."

"No," Tannis replied with an emphatic shake of her head. "I'm going to be contacting some people I'd rather you didn't know about. Stay here and keep Rico out of trouble. Besides"—she winked at her—"he looks hungry."

Skylar wanted to argue, but there wasn't a lot she could say. Rico was still seated when she turncd around, his arms clasped behind his head, a famished, almost sleepy look in his half-closed eyes.

"Now, where were we?" he murmured.

"I think I'll go and do some research of my own," she said.

He rubbed his chest absently, a small smile curving his lips. "Come here."

Skylar had to force herself not to move, but her legs ached with the need to go to him. Was this another of those weird, vampire seduction skills?

When she didn't move, he raised an eyebrow in query. He placed his feet on the floor, pushed himself up, and took a step toward her. She had the distinct impression she was being stalked.

Picking up her hand, he lifted it to his mouth and kissed her fingertips.

Her legs trembled. She opened her mouth to say something, though she wasn't sure what yet. Someone tapped on the door, and they both turned to look. Al's slight figure sidled into the room. He blinked.

"Skylar—?"

"Yes?"

"You said you wanted to see the engine rooms."

She smiled. "I did, didn't I?"

Rico was staring at Al, his lips pursed, but he didn't speak.

"Well," she said. "Seems I have to go. I'll see you around."

She thought he was going to argue, but he still said nothing as she pulled her hand free, turned, and followed Al out of the room. She let out her breath as the door slid shut behind them. Whether from relief or disappointment, Skylar honestly wasn't sure.

She reached out and tousled Al's hair. "Good move, kid."

He grinned, for a moment his expression unguarded, and she looked at him sharply. There was something not quite right about Al, something different, but the details eluded her. She shook her head. Whatever it was it could wait.

Al caught her staring and ducked his head. "Do you really want to see the engine rooms?"

"Nah, I'm going to slip off to my shuttle, catch up on a few things."

"Okay." Al nodded solemnly. "And don't worry—I told you—I won't let the vampire eat you."

"Thanks, kid."

She made her way through the ship, back to the docking bay. She entered her shuttle, locked the doors behind her, and sank into the only chair with a groan of relief.

She needed some time alone. Her head was a mess, and she needed to sort it out. She scowled. Who was she kidding? Her head was the least of her concerns. It was the rest of her body she had to worry about.

Oh, God, she'd wanted him back there. She rubbed her palm over her nipple, still sensitive from his touch, and a shiver ran through her. She squirmed in her seat as she remembered the feel of his big hands caressing her. The taste of him when he kissed her.

It had taken all of her willpower and ingenuity, not to mention a few bribes, to keep out of Rico's clutches for this long. Could she survive another five days?

And if she didn't, would he really be able to tell so much from her blood?

She banged her head against the back of her seat and ground her teeth. She couldn't believe she was even thinking like this. She'd never had a problem keeping her mind on a job before, though this was the first time she'd ever been alone and cut off from the rest of her people. On the whole, she liked it. She hadn't realized how much the intrigue and politics had riddled every facet of their existence. She supposed it was inevitable given their natures, but it was wearing. There were no politics on *El Cazador*.

Just a very sexy, very hungry vampire. Whom she wanted. More than she had ever wanted anything.

But it was more than that—she liked him. Since that first evening, he'd joined them every night after supper and she'd found, once she could relax in his presence, he was amazingly good company. In his deep, rich voice, he would tell them tales of Earth in times before space travel and of how men had finally conquered the skies. He'd taught them poker and was teaching them several other card games, though he hadn't mentioned strip poker again. It was fun, and fun was something that had been missing from her life for as long as she could remember.

She picked up a photograph from the console in front of

her. The man in the picture was as different from Rico as it was possible to get.

Though they did have one thing in common. Daniel was also dead, if not in quite the same way as Rico.

Daniel had been dead for many years now. But that had been his decision. A wave of old bitterness washed over her at the memory. He'd been given the chance to stay with her forever, and he'd rejected that chance. He had made his choice, as she had made hers. She didn't regret it.

Not really. Just sometimes, she wished…

She sighed and pushed the memories away. Reaching across, she switched on one of the holographic screens. Maybe she'd just stay shut in here for the next five days. But at least she could find something useful to do in that time. She tapped, 'how to win at poker' into the search box, then settled back to learn how to beat the vampire at his own game.

CHAPTER NINE

Skylar had the main meeting room to herself. It had been two days, and if she spent any more of her spare time in her shuttle, she was in serious danger of going shuttle-crazy. She'd just have to hope that her team of guards would keep her safe — they'd done a great job so far.

She'd come here after the evening meal, wanting to go over some of the intel. They still hadn't found a source of information on the high security section of the prison, and she was starting to get twitchy. Unless they came up with something soon, they'd be going in blind. And she wasn't sure that they should risk that; it would sorely reduce their chances of success. And of getting out alive. While that wasn't something that concerned her for herself, she found herself becoming increasingly reluctant to risk the crew of *El Cazador*.

She was unsurprised when Rico appeared in the doorway. When he saw her, a satisfied smile curved his lips. He strolled into the room, came to a halt in front of her, and held up the pack of cards in his hand.

"How about I teach you everything I know about strip poker," he said, placing the pack on the table between them.

Skylar looked beyond him, but there was no immediate help coming. He'd obviously snuck past Al, or whichever member of the crew was on 'Rico watch' tonight. She thought about getting up, leaving, but in the end she stayed put. She'd been feeling so flat, her old restlessness nagging at her mind. Or maybe a new restlessness. Whatever—it had vanished as soon as Rico entered the room. This might not be the most sensible course of action, but at least she wouldn't be bored. And the door was still open—if all else failed she could make a run for it.

Rico obviously took her silence as agreement and sank into the chair opposite her. "We'll keep the rules simple. The loser of each round loses an item of clothing. Okay?"

Skylar glanced down at herself—she didn't have many items to lose. Just boots, her weapons belt, and her jumpsuit. But then she had no intention of losing.

"Why not? I'm all for keeping things simple."

Rico dealt them five cards each.

Skylar turned up the corner of her cards and tried to keep her expression blank as excitement filled her. She discarded two cards and couldn't keep the grin from her face as she peeked at the new ones. Rico had his poker face on, and she could tell nothing from his expression. He placed his cards face up in front of him. "Three nines."

Skylar slammed her cards on the table. "Four tens. I win."

"So you do."

Rico didn't appear inordinately disturbed by losing. He

stood up, and some of Skylar's elation left her as his hand went to his waist and flicked open the fastener on his weapons belt. His hand moved to his thigh and he snapped the second, then he laid the belt on the table in front of him.

"I'm unarmed now, and at your mercy."

Somehow, Skylar doubted that. She'd felt his almost inhuman strength when he'd held her. While she was stronger than a normal human, she had an inkling that the vampire was far stronger.

"So, tell me about vampires," she said. "What are you? Where do you come from? Or is it some deep dark secret? Do you take a vow of silence—or maybe a blood oath—when you become a vampire?"

He sat back down, gathered the cards, and dealt another hand while he considered his answer.

"Actually, back on Earth, when I was changed, we did exactly that. They were very into rituals and ceremonies back in the Middle Ages. We took a vow of secrecy—they were very into secrecy as well—and consecrated it in blood. But it wasn't my blood."

"Whose was it?"

"The blood of a priest. Luckily, there were a few around that I didn't mind donating to a good cause."

Skylar picked up her cards, discarded three this time. "What happened to the one who changed you? Is he still around?"

"No," he said and tossed her three cards.

"No?"

"I killed him."

She flashed a glance from her hand to his face. "Seems a

little…ungrateful."

"Well, you see, there's a compulsion between a vampire and his maker, which means Stephano had the power to make me do things I sometimes didn't want to do. He used it one too many times, so I got rid of the problem." He gave her a slow smile. "I'm good at getting rid of problems."

She kept her gaze on her cards. "Any problems you're working on right now?"

"Maybe."

She opened her mouth to ask what, but he tossed his cards on the table. "What have you got?" He smiled as she placed her cards face up in front of her. "Looks like you win again."

She waited while he tugged off one long boot. "Now, I can't even run."

"Are you still bound by this vow of secrecy?"

"Not really. I'm guessing just about everyone who was around back then is long gone. Most vampires don't take well to change and were unwilling to let go of the old ways. A few of us left Earth, but most stayed and chanced their luck. And everyone knows how well that ended."

Skylar had heard the stories, though no one really knew what had happened to Earth. The ships that had left in search of a new home had lost contact with the planet after just twenty years. Everyone presumed the planet had been destroyed.

"So if you're no longer bound by secrecy—where do vampires come from?"

He grinned with a flash of fang. "Straight from hell, sweetheart."

She studied him, head cocked to one side. "Do you really believe that? Do you even believe in heaven and hell?"

"I believe in something, but not the crap spouted by the Church of fucking Everlasting Life. Now play cards—I have a lot of catching up to do."

Half an hour later, and she won her fourth round. Rico was down to his shirt and pants now. And the shirt was just about to go. Maybe she should stop this, but instead she sat glued to her seat, cards clutched in her hand.

"Holy Meridian." Skylar couldn't look away as Rico slowly unbuttoned his shirt. She peeked at his face—a lazy smiled curled his lips as he shrugged out of the shirt and tossed it behind him. She totally failed to drag her eyes from the vast expanse of bare flesh on show. He was lean, each rib clearly visible beneath the glossy skin, his belly ridged with hard muscles. He had dark nipples, with tufts of silky hair, and more dark hair formed an arrow disappearing into the waistband of his pants. She swallowed again.

"One more round," Rico murmured. "If you win again— this will be the last."

"It will?"

Her gaze shot to his face. He was watching her, his expression tinged with faint amusement and something else. Hunger lurked in his dark eyes. "These,"—he gestured to his pants—"are all I have left."

She swallowed, cleared her throat. "Really?"

"Unless you want to bet for something else after that."

"Something else?"

"I'm sure between us we could come up with suitable stakes."

Was he lulling her into a false sense of security? Trying to lose, or at least not trying to win, before he turned the tables on her? She wasn't sure whether she wanted to win or not. An entirely naked Rico might be more temptation than she could take. But she'd just play this last round, and then she'd head off to bed. Alone.

"Deal," she said.

She was unsurprised when she won the next round. This time, her "I win" sounded subdued to her ears.

"Are you cheating?" Rico asked.

"No." She glared at him. "Are you letting me win?"

He grinned. "Why would I do that? Anyone will tell you that I hate to lose."

It did seem a little unlikely. But maybe he believed if he were naked, she'd be quite unable to resist him. And maybe he was right. But she wasn't telling him that. Instead, she sat back in her seat, folded her arms across her chest, and raised an eyebrow.

Rico pushed himself to his feet. Skylar tried to keep her gaze fixed on his face, but it was drawn relentlessly downward. His fingers were toying with the fastener of his pants as though he was teasing her. She could see the bulge of his cock beneath the material, pressing against his fly, and her mouth went dry. Unlike other parts of her body, and she squirmed in her seat as moist heat flooded between her thighs.

He flicked the button open, and she licked her lips.

A movement behind him broke the spell. Al stood in the open doorway—he was out of breath. "Sorry, I didn't…" he stopped and clamped his lips together, his gaze flashing between the two of them, taking in Rico's almost naked form.

Skylar shrugged, feeling almost guilty. "We were playing strip poker."

Al's eyes widened. "You won?"

"I did."

Rico's hand still hovered at his waist. "You want me to finish—you did win after all."

"No." Skylar and Al spoke together.

Al shook himself. "The captain wants everyone on the bridge. She says Janey has found something."

Rico was already pulling his boots on. "Maybe we can finish this later," he said.

"Or not," Skylar muttered under her breath.

They found everyone gathered on the bridge. Tannis's upper lip curled as she took in Rico's state of undress. He still hadn't fastened his shirt—it hung open, framing his chest, and he carried his weapons belt in his hand. He tossed it onto an empty chair and flung himself onto the seat beside it.

"Hope we didn't interrupt anything," Tannis said, the sarcasm clear in her voice.

"You did, actually," Rico replied. "Skylar was beating me at strip poker."

Tannis frowned, and glanced from Rico to Skylar. "She was? How come?"

"I think she's been practicing in secret. She has some nefarious plot involving getting me naked."

Tannis snorted. "Yeah, like that's going to be difficult. About half the pleasure providers in the civilized universe have seen you naked."

Rico ignored the comment. "Anyway, you saved my modesty."

"You don't have any modesty," Tannis said.

Skylar decided it was time to get to business. "Okay, what

have we got?"

Tannis turned to where Janey was sitting at her console, fingers flying over the keyboard. "Janey? You want to explain?"

She swiveled her chair around to face them. "I've been trying to find us a source of internal security at the prison. I've been looking up ex-guards. I found one possibility—a guard turned mercenary, but I haven't been able to locate him."

"So what have you found? Don't tell me Skylar lost the chance to see me naked just so you could tell us you haven't found anything."

Janey shrugged. "I'm sure there will be other opportunities, but no, I didn't. I think I've got a lead."

"Another guard?" Tannis asked.

"No. A reporter. I think."

Rico ran a hand through his hair. "Can we get to the point here?"

"I found a fragment—"

"A fragment of what?"

Janey ground her teeth. "If you all give me a second, I might get the chance to tell you."

Rico settled back, clasped his hands behind his head. "Go ahead."

"It's a fragment of an article. The original comm was deleted, but I found references to it in other pieces."

"And how does this help us? Unless it was an article on how to break into a maximum security prison."

Janey rolled her eyes. "Not quite, but the next best thing. It was an article written by a reporter who went undercover as a guard at the prison on Trakis One. He was doing a piece exposing corruption in the prison service. But apparently, the Collective weren't too happy about that and pulled the piece—deleted all traces—just about."

"So we haven't actually got anything then."

"Captain, will you please give me one second."

Tannis shoved her hands in her pockets and paced the bridge. "Sorry."

"Okay, I can't get the original comm back—it's gone for good. But I've managed to locate the reporter. I'm thinking he can give us the lowdown on what's going on inside the prison."

"Sounds good. But why should he?"

"Well, if it was me and my piece, I'd be pretty pissed off if the Collective pulled it."

"So tell us about this reporter," Rico said.

Janey tapped a few keys and a screen opened up. "Fergal Cain," she read. "He's thirty-eight years old and has worked as a journalist for the *Trakis Times* for the last ten years. He's an investigative reporter, specializes in exposing corruption in high places, showing the world what a bunch of assholes the rich and powerful are."

"Useful job."

A man flashed up on the screen. Tall, with shoulder-length blond hair and pale grey eyes that looked almost silver.

"Nice," Daisy said.

Skylar wasn't sure 'nice' was the right word. He was handsome enough, but there was a reckless quality about his thin face—a slightly mocking smile twisted his lips, the mockery reflected in the icy cold eyes.

"Does he go after anyone in particular?" Tannis asked.

"Doesn't look like it. If you're rich and powerful then

that's enough for him."

"Do we know why?"

Janey shrugged. "No. I haven't been able to find out anything about him prior to when he worked at the *Times*. Which is a little odd. If you give me more time, I might pull something up."

Rico shrugged. "It's probably not important. All we want is some information from him—no reason why he shouldn't be happy to cooperate."

"Unless the Collective have suggested it might not be in his best interests to talk about his time on Trakis One."

"If they'd really wanted to shut him up, he'd be dead. Keep looking for the background stuff, but don't worry too much."

"Okay. So how do we want to do this?" Janey asked.

Rico got to his feet, fastened his shirt, and strapped the weapons belt around his waist. Obviously, playtime was over and he was back to business. "Where's this Cain based?"

"At the Times head office on Trakis Five."

"Well there's no time like the present," Rico said. "Call him up."

"You want to talk to him?" Janey asked.

"No you get him first. Give him a smile."

Skylar moved closer, so she could see over Janey's shoulder. Janey pressed a few keys and a few seconds later, a face showed up on the screen.

"That doesn't look like his picture," Tannis muttered. The man who filled the monitor was older, on the pudgy side, his eyes a sludgy green.

"Is that Fergal Cain's office?"

"Yes."

Janey smiled. "I'd like to speak to Fergal Cain, please."

"He's not here."

"Could you tell us where we can get hold of him?"

"No."

Tannis elbowed Janey out of the way and leaned in close to the screen. "Look Mr. …"

The man sat back in his chair as though he could increase the distance between them. "Spencer Burke," he said.

"And you are?"

"I'm Cain's editor, and I don't give out his whereabouts to anyone."

"We'd just like to talk to him. It's a possible story."

"I cannot give out personal information."

"Asshole," Tannis muttered. She thought for a moment. "I don't suppose we could offer you a bribe?"

"Well, you could, but it wouldn't do any good."

"Shit." Tannis scowled, then swiveled her chair around to face Rico. "Any ideas?"

He shook his head. "Nothing we can do from here."

"No." She turned back to the screen. "Could you pass on a message when you next contact him? Ask him to call." She punched the screen off and sat back. "This is our only lead?" she asked Janey.

"So far."

"At least Trakis Five isn't far off our planned route," Rico said. "I vote we go see this guy in person."

"Anyone got any better ideas?" Tannis glanced around the room at each of them.

Skylar kept her face blank. She wasn't too happy about heading home, but the corps kept pretty much to themselves, and she was unlikely to run into anyone she knew in the business district. And if this was their only hope of getting information about the internal working of the prison, then they didn't have a lot of choice. "I'm for it," she said.

"Me too." Daisy was almost bouncing with excitement. "We can go clubbing."

"You'll be working," Tannis said.

"No, *you'll* be working," Janey added. "You don't need us to talk to one itty-bitty reporter, and we haven't had time off anywhere civilized in months."

"Okay, but just stay out of trouble."

"Of course we will."

CHAPTER TEN

They'd docked in the main port on Trakis Five, just outside the capital city of Maltrex. This was where the Collective had their administrative center. It was also the base of the Corps, their private army. Rico felt just a little twitchy being so close.

As far as Rico was aware, there was no one after them at that moment. Except of course, the unexplained star cruiser that had attacked them the day Sklyar had come on board. And he was beginning to have a few theories about that.

No, for once, they had nothing to hide and no contraband on board. Except for Skylar. If she was really whom she said she was, then she was wanted by both the Collective and the Church. But as long as she kept a low profile, there was no reason for anyone to know she was around. This was going to be a simple in and out job. They just wanted to talk to someone. What could go wrong?

They were waiting now for Tannis to get back. She'd gone off to hire them a speeder. The docking bay doors were open and through them he could see the bustling port. The suns were just setting, casting a rosy glow over the ochre buildings. Trakis Five was one of the more hospitable of the planets, but still, water was scarce and vegetation almost non-existent except in the irrigated agricultural areas outside the city.

"I think I should come along," Skylar said.

"And I don't," he replied.

She was leaning against the curved wall of the docking bay, one hand resting lightly on the laser pistol at her waist. She'd gone back to keeping her distance since their poker game. He still couldn't believe she'd gotten the better of him; she must have been practicing. Not that he minded stripping for Skylar—but all she had to do was ask. And he'd liked the way she'd looked at him, as if she was ready to eat him up. He shifted at the thought, and a smile tugged at his mouth.

"Why?" she asked, her tone bordering on belligerent.

He dragged his mind from happier thoughts. "Why what?"

"Why shouldn't I come?"

He sighed. He really hated having to explain himself, but he supposed she was paying. "We don't want to scare this guy. I think two people should be sufficient. I'll go with Tannis. Hopefully, it will be straightforward. We'll find him where he's supposed to be, get the information we need, and we'll be back here before you can say…" He shrugged. "Anyway, you're not missing anything."

"So why you and Tannis? Why can't I go with one of you?"

"Tannis is going because she's captain, and she gives the orders. I'm going—"

"Then I'll go with Tannis."

Rico ignored the interruption. "*I'm* going, because while

we don't necessarily *want* to scare the guy, we might actually *need* to. I'm presuming he'll have no problem giving us the information. But who knows. If the Collective pulled the original comm, they may have gotten to Fergal Cain as well. We might have to use my unique persuasive abilities."

He grinned, flashing a fang. Skylar scowled but obviously appreciated the sense of what he was saying and clamped her lips tightly closed.

"You can come with us, Skylar," Daisy said from behind them. Skylar glanced past him, her eyes widening, and he turned to see what had caught her attention. Daisy and Janey had just entered the docking bay.

His eyes ran over the green girl, and he winced and fought the urge to reach for a pair of dark glasses. She was dressed in her usual black pants and boots, but she'd replaced her shirt with a tube top in bright orange. Skin tight, it skimmed her breasts and left her midriff bare, showing vast amounts of pale green flesh. Her jade hair was teased into a knot on top of her head, strands dangling down. Beside her, Janey looked elegant and almost subdued, in a black figure-hugging dress and black shoes.

"Where are you two going?" Rico asked.

"Clubbing," Janey said. "Girly night out. And don't worry—we've cleared it with the captain, and we won't get into any trouble."

Rico wasn't about to argue. The crew needed to let off steam occasionally, and it wasn't often they docked somewhere that actually had clubs and bars, at least not the sort you could guarantee coming out of alive. So they made the most of any opportunities that came their way. On the other hand, he wasn't sure he liked the idea of Skylar going with them. Maybe she should come with him and Tannis after all.

Al sidled into the docking bay behind them. "Can I come?" he asked.

"No," Janey said. "You're not a girl. Besides, you're too young—Daisy's looking to get laid tonight, and you'll cramp her style."

Daisy was looking to get laid? Scary thought.

Al's lower lip stuck out, he opened his mouth to argue, then caught Rico watching him. He clamped his lips shut, shoved his hands in his pockets and sulked.

Skylar studied the two women for a few seconds, then her stern features relaxed, and she grinned. "Okay, I'm in."

Janey grinned back. "Great. But lose the weapons belt or you'll cramp Daisy's style even worse than Al."

Rico watched the expressions flit across her face. Initial surprise—he got the impression she didn't go many places without her laser pistol. He supposed that was expected if she'd been with the Rebels as long as she'd said. Although the Rebels' main target was the Church, they had a way of making themselves unpopular and were actually wanted by just about everyone.

He'd had Janey run a background check on Skylar, and her story held up, which meant there was a substantial bounty out for her. Maybe she'd be better off staying on the ship and not heading into Maltrex at all. Yeah, he reckoned it was only common sense that she stay on the ship.

Her brows drew together as she considered the idea. Finally, her expression cleared and she nodded. She unstrapped the weapons belt from her waist and tossed it to Al. "Look after this for me will you, kid?"

Al caught it, his expression still sullen.

The more Rico thought about it, the more he decided it would be sensible for Skylar to stay safely on board *El Cazador*. If she went into the city, she could be spotted by anyone after the reward. "Maybe you'd better stay on board. If you're wanted by the Collective, then this isn't the place to go wandering about unless you have to."

Janey leaned across and whispered something to Skylar, who nodded.

"I'll be back—don't go without me," Sklyar said and hurried away in the direction of her shuttle.

Rico eyed them dubiously. He hated it when he had no clue what was going on. And he hated it even more when his orders were totally ignored.

"Don't worry," Janey murmured. "I'll look after her."

Why didn't that make him feel any better? Maybe because Janey was extraordinarily beautiful and would no doubt attract God knows what lowlife scum to the little group. Perhaps he should order them all to stay on *El Cazador*. Yes, that was the best idea. He'd order them all to stay on board. Only thing was, he suspected he might have a mutiny on his hands if he suggested it. And what could he really say? He didn't want Skylar even considering getting laid by anyone but him. That would no doubt cause immense amusement.

The sound of a speeder drawing up outside pulled him from his less than happy thoughts. He glanced out to see Tannis jumping down from the vehicle. She strode through the docking bay doors and up the ramp to halt in front of them.

"Are we ready to go?"

"We're just waiting for Skylar."

Tannis frowned. "I thought she was staying on the ship."

Skylar appeared at the door of her shuttle at that moment. She was wearing the long blond wig she'd worn when she came on board. It totally changed her appearance. She sauntered down the ramp. "No, I'm going clubbing with Daisy and Janey."

For a moment, Rico hoped that Tannis would order her to stay, but she just shrugged. "Okay, let's go then. This shouldn't take long though, so you've got three hours, then I expect you back here and ready to take off."

"And stay out of trouble," Rico added.

. . .

They dropped the women off in the west end of the city, where most of the nightlife was located. Now, Tannis was driving through the business district. Rico relaxed back in the passenger seat and tried not to think about what Skylar was doing.

Since when had he cared what a woman got up to when he wasn't there?

The avenues were wide, and the whole area had an air of affluence. Darkness had fallen, but the streets were brightly lit, the traffic low—a few speeders—but overall it was quiet. Tannis punched in the new coordinates, set the speeder on automatic, and sat back with arms folded across her chest. Rico got the idea he was in for a lecture and searched his mind for what he could have done to piss her off this time.

"You want to tell me what the fuck's going on with you and Skylar?" Tannis said.

Rico glanced at her sideways. "There's nothing going on."

Hopefully that should be the end of it. It wasn't like Tannis to get curious about his love life; it was a subject she usually avoided.

"Yeah, that's my point. I've known you a few years now, and I would never have put restraint high up on your list of characteristics."

"What would you have put?"

Tannis grinned. "You really don't want to know."

No, she was probably right. He decided to stay quiet and see where she was going with this.

"So?"

He shrugged. "I made a deal with Skylar, and we agreed *after* the job."

"Yeah, and you're a man of honor—never go back on a deal, right?"

"Actually…" Okay, maybe sometimes, but he usually had his reasons.

"I'm guessing you still don't entirely trust her," Tannis continued. "And if that's the case, then I want to know why."

"Does it matter as long as we keep a close watch on her? After all, the money is good. You like the money don't you?" He kept his tone soothing, and she cast him a disgusted look.

"Don't try and work me, Rico, I'm not in the mood. If she's taking my crew into a goddamn trap—though I can't work out what she could get out of that—then no amount of money will be enough. I don't like to be double-crossed."

"Okay, the truth?"

"A somewhat novel concept, but why not spoil ourselves?"

"You're right, I don't trust her. But then there aren't many people I do trust, so no big surprise there. I think she has another agenda, but I can't work out what it could be, and I want to know."

"Why not just torture it out of her? Take what you want."

"I'm not sure she'd talk, plus we'd lose the second payment, and as I said, the money is good. Besides, I like my women willing. Always have."

At that moment, the speeder drew up in front of a large square building. Tannis gave him a long look then leaned forward and switched off the engine. "I'll leave it for now. But you risk my crew, and you'll piss me off."

"Like I've never done that before."

She smiled; it didn't reach her cold yellow eyes. "And you remember what happened last time?"

A shudder ran through him. "Oh, yeah."

"Let's go talk to Fergal Cain."

Rico followed her through the double doors and quickly assessed the area. Apart from two security officers standing at the far side of the room beside a bank of elevators, and a young man at the reception desk, the place was empty. The young man was smooth, perfectly groomed, his pale eyes assessing them as they approached. Rico strolled up doing his best to look unintimidating—at least he'd left his sword behind, though he felt naked without it. From the glances he was receiving from the receptionist, he wasn't succeeding. He decided to let Tannis do the talking. At least to begin with.

"We'd like to see Fergal Cain"—Tannis leaned closer and read the name on the badge attached to the young man's chest—"Rodney."

"He's not here."

"Shit," Tannis muttered. "Will he be around in the morning?"

"I don't know."

Rico thought for a moment. "When was the last time he was here?"

"I'm afraid I'm not allowed to give out information on company employees. Now, if you'd like to leave a message for Mr. Cain…"

Tannis stepped up closer to the desk and shoved her face close to his. "No, I wouldn't like to leave a goddamn message, you pompous little dick."

Alarm flared in Rodney's eyes. Rico sighed, and laid a hand on Tannis's arm—"Play nice," he murmured. "He's only doing his job." He turned to the man and smiled, just enough to show the tips of his fangs. "Aren't you, Rodney?"

Rodney swallowed, and then nodded.

"So what about Mr. Burke? Is he here?"

Rodney nodded again, more vigorously this time. "I'll call up and see if he'll see you."

"Do that."

Rico leaned against the desk, arms folded, and engaged in a staring contest with the taller of the two security guards. Hunger rumbled through him. He could go a long time without feeding, but if he left it too long then it could cause problems. Tannis might not be impressed by the amount of restraint he usually showed, but it was a vast improvement on what he was like if he allowed his appetites free rein. And if he wanted to maintain his distance from Skylar, give her some space, then maybe he should do something about feeding before he got back to the ship. The guard rested his hand on the pistol at his thigh, and Rico sighed and turned away. Time for that later—business first.

Rodney cleared his throat and Rico turned back. "Mr. Burke will see you. Fifth floor. I can get someone to show you."

"We'll find it. Thank you, Rodney." He grinned at Tannis as they crossed to the elevators. "See, you have to work on your people skills."

"Piss off."

The fifth floor was halfway up the building. The elevator doors opened into a large room, which spanned the whole floor. It was quiet, though a few of the desks had people tapping away at their consoles. They glanced up as Rico and Tannis stood just inside the door, looking around.

"Go on, try," he whispered to Tannis. "I know it's hard, but see if you can be nice."

A low growl emerged from her throat, and he grinned. "Okay, I'll do it then."

He approached the nearest occupied desk, but before he could get the question out, a man emerged from one of the side offices. Rico recognized him straightaway.

"He doesn't look happy to see us," Tannis said from beside him.

"Funny, we seem to get that a lot. You know you could try smiling." She stretched her lips into the semblance of a grin. "Or maybe not."

Burke didn't seem too bothered; he nodded in the direction of his office and disappeared back inside.

"Did you know," Rico said as he and Tannis followed the man, "that I used to be a reporter for a while, back on Earth.

On the night shift, of course."

"Are there any jobs you haven't done?"

"You mean apart from a cowboy? Hmm, dentist, doctor, anything really that might involve blood."

"Don't tell me you're squeamish."

"No, I just get a little…twitchy."

"I bet."

Tannis took the seat in front of the desk and Rico leaned against the wall to the side of the door. He had a feeling that Burke wouldn't be easily intimidated; despite the pudgy appearance, the man gave off an aura of no-nonsense confidence.

"So, what can I do for you? Fergal's not here, and I can't get hold of him right now."

"We believe he might help us with a small job we have."

"Can you tell me what this is about? I'm his editor, perhaps I can help."

"We'd rather speak directly with Cain," Rico replied. "If you could contact him, tell him we'd like to talk." He was getting a bad feeling about this. A 'we just wasted a whole load of time we don't have chasing across space after a man who isn't here' sort of feeling. There was no reason for the editor not to put them in touch unless he didn't know where Cain was and had no way of contacting him.

"And as I said, he's not here."

"We want some information from him—nothing illegal—and we're willing to pay."

"That wouldn't make any difference if Fergal didn't want to talk to you. Give me a clue—I might be able to help."

Rico studied the other man and made a snap decision. "A

couple of years ago, Cain did an article on the prison on Trakis One. The article was pulled by the Collective—"

"Yes, it was, and it pissed Fergal off."

"Do you have a copy of that article?" Tannis asked.

"No, the Collective made sure about that."

"Any files, notes?"

"Nothing. Their tech experts went through the place and cleared everything."

Rico turned to Tannis. "You reckon it's worth Janey going through the systems?"

"Nobody is going through my systems," Burke said.

Rico ignored him, but Tannis shook her head anyway. "No, they'll be gone. We need Cain."

Burke sat back, his fingers tapping on the arm of his chair as he considered the two of them. "You really just want to question him about his time on Trakis One?"

"What else could we want him for?"

A brief smile flickered across his face. "Fergal has a habit of pissing people off."

"Sound familiar?" Tannis murmured.

"Anyway," Burke continued, "I thought you might be looking for payback. But I've learned to go with my gut instinct in this job and something tells me you're telling the truth."

"It's my honest face," Rico said. "So where is he?"

"The truth—I don't know."

"So what happened?"

"He's on a job."

"Another undercover job, I'm guessing."

"Yeah, it's the only sort Fergal likes. Anyway, he went ten

weeks ago. We had one comm from him right at the start and then nothing since."

"Where is he?"

"That's just it—I don't know. It's the way he works—total secrecy until the job's done."

"So why are you telling us?"

"Because I think he's in trouble."

"Or dead," Rico said. "*Mierda.*"

"Yeah, or dead. He's gone dark before but never for this long."

"You made any effort to find him?"

"Not yet. Apart from calling him, but there's no answer from his private comm unit."

"And you think we might find him?"

"You seem pretty determined. You find him, and you get your information—presuming you can persuade Fergal to talk—and I get my best reporter back."

"And your friend, I'm guessing."

"Yeah, we're friends. Even if he is a complete fucking asshole."

Rico moved so he could stare out of the window at the passing speeders while he thought it through. There was no guarantee that Cain was anywhere close by even if he was still alive. There was a whole goddamn big universe out there, and they had no time for extensive deviations if they were going to intercept the transport ship. But he was still their only potential source of information.

"Do you have the last comm he sent?"

"Yeah."

He turned to Tannis. "Could Janey pull a location from

the comm?"

"Maybe."

"Okay—let's try. Here or at the ship."

"The ship would be better—she knows the systems."

Rico just hoped the girls weren't enjoying themselves too much, because he was about to spoil their fun. Oh dear. He pressed the comm unit on his wrist. "Janey?"

No answer. He tried Skylar; she picked up straight away, but he could hear her heavy breathing as though she'd been running.

"It's Rico," he said. "We need Janey back at the ship, now."

"Well, there might be a small problem with that."

"And that would be?"

"She's just been arrested."

"Arrested for what?"

"Murder."

CHAPTER ELEVEN

Skylar had stared after the disappearing speeder with a strange mixture of anticipation and regret. Part of her wished she were with them going to interview Cain. That was the mission, and she wanted to be in on it, make sure it didn't go off track. But the rest of her was filled by a sense of freedom. Nobody here knew who she was, or what she was. For a few hours, she could just let go, pretend she was a normal person with normal friends, have fun. It seemed like a totally alien concept.

Tannis had dropped them off in the west end of the city. Skylar had lived on Trakis Five most of her life, but she rarely ventured into this part of Maltrex. The Corps barracks were in the countryside north of Maltrex, so she'd stayed out of the city unless she had specific business there.

She glanced over to her two 'normal' friends. Daisy appeared amazingly green in the bright street lights. She was bouncing on the balls of her feet, craning to look in all directions.

Janey seemed more subdued but she smiled when she caught Skylar's glance. "So where are we going? You want to get laid as well?"

Skylar's mind filled with an image of the vampire, her senses flooded with the memory of the feel of him, the taste of him. "No," she said. "How about you?"

"Me neither," Janey replied. "Frankly, I'm quite happy if I never get laid again."

Skylar frowned. While Janey oozed sexuality, Skylar got the impression she didn't actually like men. Skylar found herself intrigued by the crew of *El Cazador*. How had someone like Janey ended up on a pirate ship? Janey was beautiful and intelligent and could fit in anywhere.

But really, was it any of her business? And maybe she shouldn't get too deep into these peoples' lives. Once the job was over, she didn't know what would happen to them, but she suspected it wouldn't be good. If they did succeed in breaking into the Collective's maximum security prison on Trakis One, then it was unlikely that the colonel would be happy to let them go on their way. No, they would be imprisoned or worse, maybe even end up shipped to the Meridian mines. Skylar doubted whether Daisy's bright optimism, or Janey's cool beauty, would last long on Trakis Seven—the planet was a hellhole.

A wave of guilt washed through her, but she forced it down. She wasn't being disloyal. Rather, she was being loyal to her own people. She must not forget who and what she was.

She'd made a mistake coming out with them tonight, pretending even for a little while that they were her friends.

But she couldn't see how she could back out now without causing suspicion. All she had to do was keep her wits about her, not get in too deep, pretend she was having fun, and they'd be back at *El Cazador* safe and sound in no time at all.

"I love dancing though," Janey said, breaking into her less than happy thoughts.

Skylar couldn't remember whether she liked dancing or not—it had been so long. She tried to remember just how long. She was pretty sure it was before Daniel had died. A long time before he had died.

"Me too," she lied, though maybe it wasn't a lie—she'd no doubt find out soon. "So dancing for us, and an endless supply of gorgeous and available men for Daisy." She stood for a moment glancing down the length of the street. Every second building seemed to house a club of some sort. "Which one?"

Daisy pointed opposite, to where a group of young men were disappearing through a large set of scarlet double doors. "That one."

"Let's go, then."

Inside the club, the music was loud and insistent. The beat throbbed through Skylar's head as they made their way toward the bar. The skin down her back prickled as though she could sense people watching her, and she scanned the room for any suspicious activity. All she saw was people having fun, mainly in groups, but with the occasional lone male on the lookout for some action. Their little party was getting quite a lot of attention; she doubted Daisy would have a problem hooking up.

She was being an idiot. The truth was, she had lost the ability to have fun, to be normal. That was no doubt where her restlessness stemmed from. She needed to relax, take time off away from the job. And she would when this mission was over. She'd take a holiday—maybe visit Trakis Two.

Daisy tapped her on the arm. "Look over there." She nodded at a group at the far side of the bar. "They're Collective—look at their eyes."

They were indeed—their eyes glowing in the dim light, a bright, inhuman violet. Skylar scanned the group quickly, but luckily, she didn't recognize any of them. All the same, she turned her head away as they passed.

At the bar, Daisy ordered them drinks. For a brief moment, as she sipped the sweet soda, Skylar wished she had some of Rico's whiskey to loosen up her rigid control. She eyed the dishes of pinkies—the recreational drugs available in all bars—but couldn't quite bring herself to try them. Daisy and Janey both took a couple.

"Come on, let's go dance." Janey said.

On the dance floor, Skylar couldn't shake the feeling that she was out of place. The other two threw themselves into the music with abandon, clearly enjoying themselves. Why couldn't she let go? Just for a little while. She closed her eyes, tried to feel the music, but all she felt was unsafe, and she opened her eyes again.

Finally, she gave up. She tapped Janey on the arm. "I need a drink. I'll see you back at the bar."

Janey nodded and whirled away.

Skylar found herself an empty stool at the bar and tried not to feel like she was in the wrong place. She kept her internal links firmly locked down, but still the force of so many people, so many emotions hammered at her mind. She couldn't shake the feeling that something was about to happen. And not something good.

"Are you looking for company?" A voice spoke from beside her, and Skylar paused her scanning of the room to look at the guy who had spoken. Blond, blue eyed—he looked… nice. Why didn't 'nice' do anything for her? She was so unused to men approaching her that she could feel a puzzled frown forming on her face.

"Perhaps I could buy you a drink?"

He blocked her view of the room. "No," she snapped. "Thank you," she added when he stepped back in alarm. Yeah—she was definitely out of practice. But he'd gotten the message and melted away into the crowd.

All around her people were hooking up, leaning in close, smiling, laughing, but after that first guy, there seemed to be an exclusion zone around Skylar. No one else came near. She reckoned she must be giving out some scary keep-off vibes.

A tingle ran between her shoulder blades, and she slowly turned. Her eyes focused on a woman across the room. The woman wasn't paying attention to Skylar, but to Daisy and Janey on the dance floor, a curious, intent expression on her face. But when Skylar looked again she was gone. She shook off the feeling; she was in danger of becoming paranoid.

At last, Janey and Daisy appeared, pushing through the crowds. They were both laughing and Janey was pointing to certain men—no doubt suggesting potential targets.

"Abomination."

Skylar heard the whispered word off to the side. Turning her head, she saw a group of men, their eyes fixed on Daisy, their expressions ugly. Skylar's muscles tightened.

There was little evidence of discrimination against GMs on Trakis Five—Skylar had never encountered any. But she was aware it existed, just as she knew the Collective had supported the Church's request to have GMs down-graded to non-human status. She presumed the decision had been a political one, as within the Collective she'd never seen any signs of prejudice. That wasn't going to help them now.

Daisy was almost back at the bar and seemed unaware of the waves of hatred pouring her way. Then a second man spoke, louder this time. "Abomination."

Daisy stopped still in her tracks, the laughter melting from her face, leaving it a cold, green mask. She turned her head and stared at the men. Janey touched her lightly on the shoulder and spoke close to her ear. Daisy listened but then shrugged off the hand, shoved her hands in her back pockets and sauntered toward the group.

Skylar swore under her breath. Should she just back off, slip out, and head back to *El Cazador* alone? She couldn't get involved in this; she couldn't risk getting pulled up by the security forces. But despite the logical thoughts running through her mind, she found herself climbing off the stool and stepping closer to the group. She assessed them quickly. All were armed and she swore again. On the positive side, they didn't look like fighters, maybe businessmen or, more likely, Church officials, from their comments.

Daisy stood in front of the one who had spoken. She looked so tiny, only coming up to his shoulder, so she had to tilt her head to peer into his face.

"You said something?" Her tone sounded almost friendly.

A sneer curled the man's thin lips, making him even uglier.

"I said 'abomination.'"

"And were you referring to me?"

"Hell, yeah, they shouldn't let your type in here."

Skylar stepped a little closer. "Can I suggest we get out of here," she said in a low voice. "Come on Daisy, they're not worth it."

Daisy glanced over her shoulder. "No. I want to have a chat with these nice men."

"Crap," Skylar muttered under her breath. She could only presume that Daisy was high on the pinkies. Otherwise, she was sure she'd never take on five armed men with only two unarmed women as backup.

Should she take the initiative and take the guys down before this went any further—she was sure she could do it, but it would hardly be inconspicuous. Then she caught a flash of silver at Daisy's back. From somewhere she'd drawn a small knife. She depressed the button on the handle and a wicked serrated blade sprang out. Daisy moved fast, almost a blur, and the tip was against the man's belly.

Things were just getting better and better.

Skylar held herself very still; a wrong move now and this could escalate out of all proportions. People immediately around them were starting to take notice, but most were still dancing and talking. They needed to get out of here before that changed.

She'd not taken Daisy for a fighter, but the hand that held the knife was rock steady. She flicked it upwards, slicing through the front of the man's shirt, then hooked the blade in the chain at his throat.

"Look at this," she murmured, holding up the cross so it

glinted in the dim light. "What a surprise." She yanked, the chain broke, and the cross fell to the floor. The knife was back at his throat before he could move, and a bead of crimson welled up from where the tip pierced the skin.

"Have I mentioned that I hate the goddamn Church?" Daisy said, her tone icy. "They killed my family, you know. Right in front of me. Now, here you are."

The man was focused on the knife at his throat, and obviously didn't notice Daisy readying herself. But he noticed when Daisy kicked him viciously in the balls. He grunted and collapsed to his knees.

Daisy stepped back as the other men reached for their weapons. But Janey had already pulled a tiny laser pistol from God knows where—Skylar couldn't see where she could have hidden it in that outfit—and pointed it in their general direction. She waved it around a little. "Anyone else want to say anything? No? Well, I think it's time for us to go."

She backed away, keeping the pistol aimed.

"Why the hell am I the only one unarmed here?" Skylar said as they slipped into the throng and the dancers closed around them.

Janey grinned. "You have to learn to be subtle."

It seemed to take forever to weave their way through the crowd, but finally they reached the door.

"Well that was fun!" Janey said as they tumbled out of the bar.

"Almost better than sex," Daisy replied.

"Does it bother you—people like that?" Skylar nodded back at the bar.

"Nah, it doesn't bother me. They're pig-ignorant bastards."

Then she thought for a moment. "I suppose that's not totally true. If it didn't bother me then I wouldn't have taken any notice."

"Instead, you kicked him in the balls," Janey said cheerfully.

"Hey, he'll live—which is more than you can say about my family."

"What happened to them?" Skylar asked.

"They were scientists. What they were doing was against the law, but they truly believed that plant-human hybrids were the way forward, that they would solve food shortages forever. They were based off-planet on a space station—they thought it would be safe from the Church. But the Church came anyway. They killed them all. All except me. My father managed to get me to one of the escape pods. Anyway— enough of the past. Where next?"

"Back to the ship," Skylar said. *Christ what was she—their mother?*

"Hey, but he night's still—"

"Shit," Janey said, cutting her off.

In the streetlights, Skylar could see Janey's face suddenly leached of color. She was staring at something across the street, and Skylar followed her gaze. A squad speeder had parked up opposite where they stood. Four officers, all in the dark blue uniform of the local force, were standing beside it talking to a woman. Skylar recognized her immediately—the woman who had been watching Daisy and Janey as they danced. She had a real bad feeling about this.

"Who is it?"

"My sister-in-law, or rather, ex-sister-in-law." Janey shook her head as if coming out of a trance. "Look, get Daisy back to the ship and get the hell away from here. This is my problem, my mess."

"No way," Daisy said. "What's going on?"

Janey still held the small laser pistol, now she shoved it into Skylar's hand. "Keep out of this." And she strolled toward the small group.

Daisy made to follow, but Skylar stopped her with a hand on her arm. Daisy tried to shake it off, but she tightened her hold. "Wait," she said. "We have no clue what's happening here."

"Janelle Duncan?" One of the officers spoke.

"That would be me," Janey replied.

"We're arresting you for the murder of Michael Duncan."

Skylar went cold at the words. She had no clue what was going on here. "Who's Michael Duncan?" she whispered to Daisy.

"Janey's husband?"

"She has a husband?"

"Well, obviously not anymore if she murdered him."

"Christ."

The officers were taking no notice of her and Daisy. At the moment. She was sure that wouldn't last. A second squad car had pulled up behind the first; soon the place would be swarming with uniforms.

They were reading Janey her rights, now. Janey stood straight, a small smile playing across her lips as though she had no cares in the world. Then her gaze hit Skylar's and her brows drew together. She glanced between her and Daisy. "Go," she mouthed the word.

Skylar nodded once, and tugged at Daisy's arm. Daisy

resisted. "We've got to help her."

"No. What we have to do is get the fuck away from here before they decide to arrest us as well. Come on Daisy, get a grip. If they take us then we've no chance of helping Janey."

"You're going to help her?"

"Jesus," Skylar muttered.

She knew she should take Daisy and get the hell back to the ship. This wasn't her problem. Christ, even Janey had said that. She could risk the whole mission. But right now, she needed Daisy to cooperate. Although she could just leave Daisy as well. Let her take her chances with the squaddies. What were these people to her anyway? Just a means to an end.

But she couldn't do it.

She took a deep breath. "Yes I'm going to help. Fuck knows how, but we'll think of something. Just for now, let's get the hell away from here."

The tension went out of Daisy and she allowed herself to be pulled along. They were running when Skylar's comm unit beeped. It was Rico.

She swore—what had he said? Ah, that was it—stay out of trouble.

Shit, he was going to be pissed.

CHAPTER TWELVE

"Murder? Janey?" Even over the comm unit, Skylar could sense the waves of disbelief. *"Dios,* who the fuck did she murder?"

Skylar shrugged despite the fact that he couldn't see it. "No one I know."

"You mean she just went up to some complete stranger and killed them. Hell, even I've got more restraint than that."

Skylar rolled her eyes. "She didn't murder anyone tonight. I'm guessing it was a while ago and someone recognized her."

She could hear a muttered conversation in the background—obviously, Tannis had joined in.

"Skylar, what the hell have you done with my crew?"

Skylar ground her teeth. "Fuck-all, captain. They managed to do it all on their own."

"What about Daisy?"

"Well she never got laid, but apart from that…"

Rico came back on the line. "Where are you?"

Skylar gave her coordinates. "But I don't think you should come here. I think you should get back to *El Cazador*. Get her off planet and into orbit, then send the shuttle back for us."

"You have a plan."

"No, I'm still trying to come up with the plan part. But I have a suspicion it's going to include a fast getaway."

"Sounds like fun." His earlier irritation had vanished. "We'll wait to hear from you then. Don't be long."

Skylar went to switch off the comm then hesitated. "Did you get the information we need from Cain?"

"Hell, we didn't even get Cain."

"So, a great night all round then." She didn't wait for an answer, just stabbed the off button.

"So what's the plan?" Daisy asked. She'd been subdued, but seemed to have perked up a little. It was obvious she had a huge crush on the vampire.

Skylar hadn't completely lost sight of her mission. If she could pull this off without getting back up, then she would. She'd only call in help as a last resort. She was trying to convince herself she was doing this purely because they needed Janey. While Rico hadn't found the reporter, he must have gotten something, because he'd said they needed Janey back at the ship. So they must have a lead.

And they had no time to waste if they were going to free Janey. Once the police got her to the station there would be no hope; Skylar had been there—the place was like a fortress. So they had to intercept en route.

She had to pull this off—somehow get a prisoner out of a guarded squad speeder and off-planet. She wished she had her platoon, but it would be hard to stay undercover with a platoon of Corps at her back. No, she'd have to make do with Daisy, part-human part…?

"What sort of plant are you?" she asked.

Daisy grinned. "What do you think?"

Great, all she had to help her was a part-human, part-flower. "I suppose you were lucky—you could have ended up being called Cabbage." She headed off back the way they had come, Daisy at her side. "First, we need transport."

"What sort of transport?"

"I'm thinking a speeder for me and a flyer for you." She glanced at Daisy. "So do you know the deal with Janey?"

"Not really." Daisy shrugged. "Maybe a bit of it. I think she killed her husband, that's why she's been hiding out on *El Cazador*. But I'm guessing that just from little things she let slip, and I don't know why she killed him."

Skylar held up a hand and Daisy stopped. "There," Skylar said.

It was one of the local police flyer-bikes. A single-seater and the fastest thing on the streets.

"We're going to steal a police flyer?"

"Any better ideas?"

Daisy shook her head, her eyes gleaming with excitement.

"You reckon you can fly that thing?" Skylar asked.

"Oh yeah."

They were just outside the social district in one of the industrial areas. The streets were quiet. Skylar set Janey's laser pistol to stun and held it loosely down by her right thigh.

The officer was standing to the side. A speeder flew past, and Skylar waited until the lights had vanished then approached him from the front.

"Officer, there's been an accident."

He looked up, his gaze taking in Skylar. Without hesitating, she took the last steps, placed the pistol to his belly, and pulled the trigger. He went down straight away, and she dragged him into the cover of a doorway. She glanced back at Daisy, still in her neon orange tube top. Crouching down beside the fallen man, she tugged him free of his jacket and tossed it to Daisy. Then she pressed the laser to his neck and gave him a second blast. She didn't want him coming around and sending out a warning. This would only work with surprise on their side.

Daisy had already climbed onto the flyer and was inspecting the control panel.

"Okay, that's you sorted, now me," Skylar said. "I want something big, solid. Nothing flashy. And make it fast—we're on a schedule here."

She swung a leg over the back and perched behind Daisy—these things weren't meant to carry two, but she reckoned their combined weight was not much more than the downed officer. Plus, it wouldn't be for long—hopefully.

"Head west," she said to Daisy, "we need to intercept them before they hit the station."

The flyer lurched off the ground. For a second she thought they were going to crash, and she readied herself to leap from the vehicle. But Daisy got the feel for the controls and soon they were flying smoothly a few feet above the ground. Skylar scanned the streets; she wanted to find a vehicle before they got into the busier section of the city.

"There." She nudged Daisy on the shoulder and pointed to the ground. A man had just parked his speeder and was climbing out.

Daisy reacted quickly, swooping down. Skylar stunned the man before they had even stopped. She swung her leg over the flyer and dropped to the ground. The man was out cold. Skylar checked under his jacket and found a laser pistol—she stuffed it down her boot.

The speeder was an old-fashioned model, built for functionality rather than beauty, open topped but with a roll cage around—perfect for Skylar's needs. She strapped herself in, then leaned over and spoke to Daisy, who was hovering the flyer close by.

"Stay close for now."

She went over the route in her mind as she drove, working out the best place to intercept the speeder carrying Janey. She couldn't afford to get too close to the station and she could only hope that the second speeder wasn't still with them. But why would it be? Janey was only one unarmed woman and it sounded like she was wanted for a domestic crime. There was no reason to give her an armed guard.

She spotted them cruising along the main street and increased her speed to get ahead, finally slowing down to speak to Daisy.

"They're two streets back," she said. "I want you to come around in front of them and get them to stop as close to this side street entrance as you can. Whatever you need to do, but don't let them shoot you. Tannis will kill me if you turn up dead."

Daisy grinned, and the flyer peeled away. Skylar stationed herself just down the entrance of the side street where she could see the speeder approaching with Janey in the back. "Come on, Daisy," she muttered. The flyer was nowhere to be seen.

Daisy swooped down from high above, hitting the brakes as she came level with the squad speeder. The driver had no choice but to pull to a halt or smash into the flyer. Skylar slammed her hand onto the accelerator. She hit them side-on with a crunch of metal. The other vehicle smacked against the wall of the building opposite and then crashed the few feet to the ground.

Skylar leapt out and pulled a laser pistol from each boot, shooting into the front of the speeder before even touching the ground. Two officers went down immediately. Skylar took down the third and fourth as they climbed out. She reached inside and dragged out the unconscious bodies.

Janey was cuffed to the vehicle. With no time to free her, it looked like they were taking the police speeder. They were drawing attention despite the late hour, and police backup would be arriving soon. They had to move fast.

"Daisy, come on."

Daisy looked stunned. "Wow," she said. "Remind me never to piss you off." She parked the flyer and jumped in beside Janey, giving her a quick hug. "Did you know your lipstick's smudged?" she said.

"Thanks!"

Janey had a glazed expression, as though it had all happened too fast for her to make sense. Skylar didn't have time for explanations. She leapt into the driver's seat, saying a quick plea that the vehicle hadn't been too badly damaged in the crash. But it started easily enough.

She drove the speeder high up above the normal traffic lanes and headed north before pressing her comm unit.

"Rico?"

"Yeah. You got her?"

"We have. But you know that fast getaway I mentioned…"

"I'm on my way, just give me coordinates. Or better yet, switch on the tracker on your comm unit—I'll find you."

"Okay, I'm heading north out of the city."

"What are you in?"

"A police speeder."

"Ballsy. I like it."

He switched off, and Skylar concentrated on driving and keeping an eye out behind for anything following. She tossed one of the laser pistols to Daisy. "You're going to have to cut through those cuffs," she said.

Her nostrils filled with the scent of scorched megaplastic, but she kept her gaze ahead, searching the skies for Rico. She caught sight of the shuttle just as Daisy shouted that they had incoming behind them.

She tossed the second pistol to Janey. "Keep them occupied. We're almost there."

A shot deflected off the cage of the speeder, and she felt the heat of the blast against her skin. Behind her both Daisy and Janey were continually shooting. She pressed her comm unit. "Rico, I have visual."

"Whenever you're ready."

"Now would be good. And we have company."

They were out of the city and speeding through the rocky open country. Up ahead the shuttle hovered just above the ground. Skylar glanced over her shoulder. They would have seconds at the most.

"Are you two ready? We're going to have to move fast."

"Well I'm not staying here," Janey said. "I've had enough clubbing for one night."

Daisy laughed.

"Okay—go!"

Daisy and Janey were out and racing to the shuttle as Skylar halted the speeder. She leapt after them, hurling herself inside as the shots whizzed around her head. She crashed to the floor and the doors slid shut behind her, then they were off. Skylar rolled onto her back and stared upward. Rico was in the pilot's seat, one eyebrow raised and an amused expression on his face. She wasn't about to tell him, but she was real pleased to see him.

"Are we clear?" she asked.

"Well, they're still shooting. But we soon will be."

A blast hit the shuttle and they veered off course. Rico turned away, took the stick, and controlled her with ease.

Skylar lay for a minute longer, getting her breath back, coming down from the adrenalin high. "Remind me never to go clubbing with you guys again," she said to the room in general.

Rico grinned. "Hey, it was a good night—nobody died."

"Well, not recently anyway." She cast a glance at Janey, who was for once looking less than perfect. She'd kicked off her shoes and was slumped on the floor of the shuttle, her back leaning against the curved wall, arms around her chest.

Janey caught Skylar's glance and shrugged. "Sorry."

"Hey, don't be. It wasn't your fault." She thought for a moment. "Well, the dead husband might have been your fault. You'll have to tell me about that sometime."

Janey gave her a weak smile. "Yeah, maybe next time

we go out clubbing." She closed her eyes as if to end the conversation.

"Daisy, take over." Rico eased himself out of the pilot's chair and crossed to where Skylar lay. He stood, legs braced, looking down at her, a lazy half-smile curling his lips. "You all have fun without me tonight?"

"Oh, yeah. Daisy nearly knifed a guy for calling her names—"

"She did? Good for her. I hate name-calling."

"Janey got arrested, and I stole a vehicle—two vehicles, actually—and crashed into a police speeder. Great fun."

He held out a hand and she slipped hers into it and allowed him to pull her to her feet. For once, she didn't put up her guards with him. They were in a crowded shuttle, nothing was going to happen here, and she liked the feel of his cool palm in hers. She shouldn't, but she did. The thought worried her a little.

Rico reached up, wound a strand of long blond hair around his finger, and then tugged the wig from her head and tossed it to the floor. "I like you better without it," he said. "Less to hide behind."

"I've nothing to hide," she said.

"Of course you haven't." He studied her, a slightly perplexed expression on his face. "I missed you tonight."

Nobody had missed her in a long time. She was sure it was just another line. All the same, the words made her feel a little warm and fuzzy inside, and she didn't resist when he wrapped a hand around the back of her neck and pulled her toward him. She blinked into his dark eyes as his face lowered to hers. Then she held herself very still as he kissed her. The kiss was light, quick, different, missing the overt sexuality she expected from him. Still, warmth flickered through her veins, and she closed her eyes and rested her forehead against his chest.

"We're home," Daisy said.

Skylar peered over Rico's shoulder and saw the hull of *El Cazador* filling the monitor. The docking bay doors opened, and Daisy took the shuttle inside.

It did feel like coming home. Skylar knew she was in trouble.

She'd crossed a line tonight. However much she tried to tell herself that she had done what was best for the mission, she knew it was a lie. She should have just walked away. Now she needed to find a way to distance herself from these people. An ironic thought when she was plastered against the long hard length of Rico's body. And she didn't want to move.

In the end, it was Rico who pulled away, but she didn't try and hold him.

The shuttle doors opened, and Tannis strode up the ramp. She glanced around, taking in Daisy and Janey. Then her gaze returned to Skylar.

"Thanks," she muttered.

Beside her, Rico let out a short laugh. "Make the most of that, you probably won't ever hear it again."

Skylar felt some strange emotion twist through her. She analyzed the sensation and came up with the only possible answer. She was feeling guilty. Tannis had thanked her, and she was feeling guilty. Because one day soon she was going to betray them all, and there was a good chance that none of them would survive that betrayal—or if they did, they'd wish they hadn't.

She so didn't need this right now.

"Let's go find Fergal Cain," she said.

CHAPTER THIRTEEN

"Okay, so what do we have?" Skylar asked.

Rico relaxed back in his chair and let Tannis do the talking. Instead, he watched Skylar through half-closed lids. Something had changed in her tonight. He wasn't sure what, and he wasn't sure how she felt about it. In fact, he wasn't sure about anything anymore.

Except he was still hungry.

And that there was far more to Skylar than met the eyes. She had gone back for Janey tonight when she didn't need to. Yeah, Tannis would have been pissed if she'd left Janey behind. But Skylar wasn't crew—she was a client—and it wasn't her responsibility to keep the crew from harm.

No, she could have quite easily just walked away and left Janey to her fate. Instead, she had gone in there and rescued her. And he was guessing, from her reactions, that she'd surprised herself by it.

"Cain hasn't been in touch with his employer in ten

weeks," Tannis said.

"Is that normal?"

"No. Apparently, he's a secretive bastard, but he usually calls in regularly. They have some sort of code set up, so he can let them know if he's in danger."

"But he didn't use it?"

"No, they got a single comm, shortly after he left, then nothing. We do have the comm though. It's scrambled, but we're hoping that Janey can get us its origin. Though Burke—Cain's boss—wasn't able to get anything from it."

"That's what you needed Janey for?"

"Yup."

"It's not much."

"Well, it's all we've got."

Janey appeared at the doorway then. She was once more back to her immaculate self, though she had a bandage around one wrist. Skylar had given him a rundown on what had gone on, but if Janey was in any way bothered, she was hiding it well. She was a cool one. As long as it didn't interfere with the flying of his ship, he didn't give a toss how many husbands she'd murdered.

She sauntered across the bridge and seated herself at her console. "Okay, what do you want me to do?"

"Cain's boss should have sent you a file."

Her fingers flew over the keys. "Here it is. What do you need?"

"The location of where that comm originated."

"Shouldn't be too hard." She tapped some more keys. "On the other hand…" Her eyes narrowed on the screen and her brows drew together. Looked as if it wasn't going to be easy after all.

"Problem?" Tannis asked, and Rico almost smiled. Tannis was the most impatient person he knew.

"Maybe. I think I can locate it, but it's going to take some time."

"How much time?"

Janey frowned. "As much time as it takes. I'll go as fast as I can—honest—just keep out of my face."

Obviously, however well she was hiding it, Janey was rattled by the night's events—he'd never heard her be impolite to anyone before.

Tannis must have realized it as well and she backed off. She paced for a few minutes, then sank into a chair and sat tapping her booted foot on the metal floor. Janey swiveled in her seat and glared.

"I'll just go to bed and get out of the way then shall I?" Tannis pushed herself to her feet and stalked from the bridge, halting in the doorway. "Let me know when you find something. The minute you find something."

"I will." Janey was already back at work.

Tannis turned to Skylar. "You did good tonight."

"No problem—it was…fun." Skylar stood up. "I think I'm going to get some sleep as well."

For a moment, Rico considered offering to go with her. But she looked tired, probably needing sleep after their exciting night. Instead, he turned to Daisy, who was in the pilot's chair. They were currently orbiting Trakis Five, and until they decided where they were headed next, there wasn't a lot to do. "Go to bed as well," he said. "I'll keep watch."

She nodded and followed Skylar out. Rico closed his eyes;

he didn't need to sleep, but he allowed himself to doze to the relaxing sound of Janey's fingers clicking on the keyboard.

"Rico."

He heard the voice from a distance, but he was deep in this really good daydream involving Skylar, a set of handcuffs and a police speeder, so he ignored it. Someone touched his arm and he came fully awake. The scent of fresh blood was so close, a growl rose up in his throat.

Janey quickly backed away, alarm flaring in her eyes

Shit. He was going to have to feed soon; he was getting twitchy. He blamed it on Skylar and unrequited lust.

"Sorry," he muttered and ran a hand through his hair.

Janey eyed him warily. "You okay?"

He growled again, and she backed away a few more feet. He resisted the urge to tell her that wouldn't help. "I'm not about to eat you if that's what you mean."

"No need to be grouchy."

"Hungry, Rico?" Tannis asked as she strolled onto the bridge.

He thought about denying it but what was the point? "Yeah. Starving," he added for good measure, because he hated it when they looked at him as if he was some sort of monster who couldn't control his bodily urges. Had he eaten any of them yet?

"Well, you'll just have to hold on a little longer, because I'm not volunteering."

"Me neither," Janey said quickly.

"Who's asking? Pair of bad-tempered bitches like you two would probably taste like crap anyway," he muttered.

"My, we are in a grumpy mood."

Rico curled the corner of his lip, showing one fang.

Tannis just laughed. "So what have you found?" she asked Janey.

"I'll show you, it will be easier. Maybe someone should go get Skylar so I only have to go through this once."

"Can't you comm her?"

"She's not answering."

"I'll go," Rico said.

"No you won't. I don't trust you the way you look right now. I'm not waiting while you have a snack and a shag." She looked around, her gaze locking on someone over his shoulder. "Al?"

Al was curled up in a seat in the corner of the room, head resting on his knees, watching them. He was always watching them. The boy had a way of sneaking around and disappearing into the background. It was spooky.

"Yes," he said.

"Go wake up Skylar. Get her down here. And fast."

Al scampered out of the room.

• • •

Skylar was dreaming. She was being chased by something big and dark with huge teeth. She was keeping just in front, and however hard she tried, she couldn't seem to slow her speed so she was always just a few paces ahead. And she wanted to be caught. She could feel his hot breath feathering against her skin. He was so close…

The buzzer woke her. She rolled over and peeked into the viewer, half-hoping it was Rico. Her body felt achy, her skin sensitive. But it was Al outside the door, one skinny shoulder leaning against the wall. She hoped he was here to tell her Janey had found something—she needed to get this mission back on course.

She hadn't bothered undressing, and now she got to her feet and pressed her palm to the panel, rubbing her hand across her face, trying to dispel the dream. Al straightened when he saw her and grinned. He held out the weapons belt Skylar had given him to look after before the trip to Maltrex, and she took it and strapped it on, feeling immediately better. There was something comforting about a laser pistol.

"Janey's found something," Al said.

"Good. Just give me a second. She stepped back into the room and found her boots where she'd kicked them off. After pulling them on, she peered into the mirror. The reflection was no longer a stranger—she looked…normal. She ran her hands through her hair, then bit her lip, and realized she was primping.

What the hell was wrong with her?

"Come on," she said to Al. "Let's go."

"You should have taken me with you tonight," Al said.

Skylar kept moving, but glanced down at him. "Why?"

"I could have kept watch or something. I'm good at that."

"You are. But you've got to know what you're watching for, and we weren't exactly expecting Janey to be arrested."

"Well, I could have helped you rescue her. Next time you should take me."

Yeah, like there was going to be a next time. "Course I will, kid."

Rico was perched on the edge of the console, arms folded across his chest, legs crossed at the ankle. His midnight hair was loose, and he eyed her hungrily as she came in. Al scuttled off into the corner as Rico pushed himself up and stalked toward her. Skylar held her ground. He halted just in front of her, leaned down, and kissed her neck. She felt it all the way down to her toes, but still managed not to move.

Then he stepped back and turned to Janey. "Okay, what have we got?"

She released her breath and stepped up closer to where Janey was bringing up information on the console.

"The reason why I couldn't get a lock on the position was, it's moving."

"Shit," Tannis said. "He's on a space ship? That's a pain-in-the—"

"Will you let me finish?" Janey threw a dark look over her shoulder. "I don't think the comm originated on a space ship. I think it came from a space station."

She flicked a key, and an image of a huge space station came up on the screen. Silver, it looked about the size of a small moon. "It's orbiting Trakis Five," Janey said.

"Well that's good. Is it government?" Tannis asked.

Skylar waited for the answer. But she was pretty sure it wasn't—she would have heard if the Collective owned it.

"No, it's a private company," Janey said.

"They must be huge. That thing would have cost a fortune to launch."

"I'm still getting information together. It's owned by a group called Tyrone Holdings, but that looks like a shell company.

"Where is it now?"

"It's on a parallel orbit with us, a bit closer to the planet.

If we take the closest orbit ring and slow down to minimum speed, it would reach us in approximately six hours. But we could reverse orbit, and we'd intercept in less than two."

"Isn't that illegal?" Skylar said. The direction and speed of orbit was strictly controlled around Trakis Five.

"Something being illegal has never stopped us before," Tannis replied.

"Maybe not. But traffic is closely monitored in the orbits—we'd be picked up straightaway if we turn around, and no doubt pulled in for violation of traffic laws. And those traffic cops are bigger badasses than the Corps."

"Good point." Tannis thought for a moment. "How are we doing for time? When is the transport ship due to take off?"

"Right about now."

"Shit."

"It's not so bad," Rico said. "We're faster than they are, and we don't want to be trailing in their wake—more chance they'll pick us up."

"It's going to make it pretty close though. Janey?"

"Give me a second, I'm working it out." Janey definitely sounded irritated, but then she hadn't had a chance to sleep like the rest of them, and the night's events were bound to be playing in her mind. "We can do it—it will be tight, but we should make the planned interception point."

"Good. Rico, slow her down and shift the orbit."

Rico sat himself in the pilot's seat and adjusted the controls. Skylar sensed the ship slowing, until *El Cazador* seemed to be almost drifting in space. He turned his chair to face them. "So, what do we know about this company? What's got Fergal Cain so interested he's gone in there and hasn't come out in ten weeks?"

Janey opened up a floor to ceiling screen and a visual came up. Skylar stepped closer to examine it, trying to make sense of what she was seeing.

"Looks like a spider's web," Rico said.

"Huh?"

He smiled. "An organism from Earth, they made complicated webs to catch their prey."

"Well, I don't think this is to catch anything. I do think it's to hide something though."

"And that is?" Tannis was peering at the image, a scowl on her face.

"Whoever is at the center."

Janey went back to the board and tapped a few keys. Some of the lines faded away. "False trails," she murmured. She studied it again, her head cocked to one side, then tapped some more. This time when the lines faded only two entities were left—one on the outside and the one at the middle of the original ring. "They're the only 'real' companies," Janey said.

"What makes them real?" Tannis asked.

"They're the only ones with any actual activity. The rest are decoys."

"Tyrone Cybercom and Tyrone Cyberlife."

"I've heard of Cybercom," Rico said. "Aren't they the company that makes artificial limbs and other body parts for people careless enough to lose them?"

"That's right," Janey said. "They're the company out in the open, nothing hidden about them. They get a lot of government grants—the reports are all aboveboard, nothing dodgy I can see."

She studied the data for a while. "Which isn't the case with Cyberlife. That's the one in the center of Rico's web. There's nothing, no reports submitted, no accounts, no company statement of intent."

"Don't they have to do that for the legal requirements?"

"Oh, I don't think this company is legal."

"Then why set up the company at all?" Tannis asked. "Surely that's just alerting the world that something is going on."

"I'm guessing they have to be accountable. They must have people investing huge amounts of money in this. That space station is too big to be funded by any one person. And those investors will want to see what they're getting for their credits. Besides, unless you really went digging, then you're not going to find them."

"Can you get a list of investors?"

"I'm trying."

Skylar paced the bridge. What did it matter what the company did? The only thing that was important was they find Cain and get the information they needed from him. Skylar clamped down her impatience. There was little else they could do for the next few hours anyway. She wandered away from the screen and forced herself to sit down, close her eyes, and try to relax.

Fingers stroked down the back of her neck, sending frissons of pleasure skittering down her spine. She opened her eyes and looked up into Rico's face.

"You alright?" he asked.

"Just worried about Jonny. If we don't get some intel on the prison, this whole thing is a waste of time."

"We'll get it."

"How can you be so sure?" She was whining, but she couldn't seem to help it. Guilt, she supposed. She'd jeopardized the mission tonight—her actions totally irrational. On the other hand, if she hadn't gotten Janey back, then they would never have cracked the comm, and would have no clue where to find Cain. She was going around in circles.

"Gut instinct," Rico said. "He's there." He nodded at the picture of the huge space station that filled the monitor. "We just have to find him."

"The place looks as big as a small planet."

"Well, thanks to you, we have Janey. She can hack into the systems—we'll find him. After all—we're the best."

"I hope so."

CHAPTER FOURTEEN

The shuttle locked onto the docking port.

"You ready?" Tannis asked.

"Don't I look ready?" Rico replied.

Skylar gave him a quick inspection. He looked more than ready; he looked stunning. He was dressed in a black suit, which appeared to be made of real silk and which showed off his broad shoulders and long lean figure. Beneath it was a black shirt. His hair was pulled back into a neat ponytail, revealing his perfect bone structure.

His weapons were conspicuously absent, though she knew he had a laser pistol stuffed down the back of his pants and another strapped to his ankle. He caught her staring and a small smile curved his lips. "Like what you see?"

She did. But no way was she going to give him the satisfaction. He was already entirely aware of how good he looked. So instead, she rested her hand on the laser pistol at her waist. "Let's go."

The plan was that they would get onto the space station under the guise of being potential investors, ask for a tour of the place, and after that…

Well, after that, there wasn't really a plan. They would have to play it by ear, but Rico had assured her that they always played it by ear and so far, they were still alive. Skylar would have preferred more of a plan. Maybe she was just still feeling a little edgy.

Janey had managed to hack into the list of investors and they had 'introductions' from two of them. Rico was a rich businessman looking to invest some of his credits, Janey was his assistant, and Skylar and Tannis were his two bodyguards. They had dressed the part in identical black jumpsuits, boots, and lots of guns.

Janey switched off the monitor and stood up. "Well, there's a reception committee. Let's go see what they have to say."

The shuttle doors slid open and they made their way down the ramp. A group of three men waited at the bottom. The man in the center was clearly the boss, the two others wore the uniform of security guards. Skylar quickly glanced around, taking in the place in case they needed to make a hasty retreat. They were in a huge docking bay, empty except for their shuttle. Probably only used for visitors. The place was big enough to fly around; if worse came to worse they could take off and blast their way out. And apart from the two guards here to greet them, she couldn't see any other overt signs of security. This was obviously a research facility. They kept a low profile and probably relied upon secrecy rather than force.

Skylar turned her attention back to the group, concentrating on the tall man. He looked somewhere in his middle years, which would make him around seventy or so unless he'd been enhanced in some way. He was handsome and smooth, bland, his face giving nothing away. He smiled politely at Rico, ignoring the rest of them, though the smile didn't reach his cool blue eyes.

"Mr. Sanchez?"

Rico stepped forward and held out his hand, an equally cold smile on his lips. "Yes, and you are…?"

"I'm Harris Walker, the facilitator here." He took Rico's hand briefly, and then glanced at the palm screen open on his other hand. "I believe you know Francis Taylor and James Mellow."

"We've done business together."

"And they recommended our company to you?"

"They suggested I might be interested in what you're doing here. And seeing this place — so far — I'm impressed."

"And what sort of funds do you have to invest?"

Rico waved toward Janey, who stepped up and flashed a palm screen in Walker's face. His eyes widened slightly, and then he nodded. "I was told you would like a tour of the facility."

"I would."

"Your guards will have to stay with your shuttle."

"I don't go anywhere without my bodyguards," Rico replied. "I'm sure you understand. I'm afraid I don't know you, and my security must come first."

Walker pursed his lips, his eyes straying to the screen still open on Janey's palm. "Very well, but they must leave their weapons with security."

"No problem. They don't need their weapons."

Skylar and Tannis handed over their guns and they all followed Walker out of the docking bay and into a wide corridor where a speeder awaited them. Rico got into the front next to the facilitator, the rest of them climbed into the back. The two security guards stayed behind with the shuttle.

Skylar could hear murmured conversation from the front—Rico was making small-talk. She was impressed by how well he'd slipped into his role, but then she guessed he'd played a lot of roles in his long life. Sitting back, she concentrated on the route and getting a fix on their surroundings. Glancing sideways at Tannis, she saw she was doing the same.

The place was like a city. They were driving at first through what looked like a residential area, houses and shops, a whole society existing within a man-made structure. Even the high ceilings were designed to look like sky—pale blue with the occasional fluffy white cloud. Almost better than the real thing. Eventually, the houses gave way to what looked like offices. There was a quiet, organized bustle about the place, and they passed many people going about their business— whatever that was.

Finally, the speeder pulled up outside a row of doors and they all climbed out. Walker led them into a large office, with a huge picture window on the far wall, depicting more blue sky. He gestured to the chair in front of the desk.

Rico turned to Skylar and Tannis. "You two stand guard." He waved a hand at either side of the door. "I'm just going to have a drink with Harris,"

Wow—they were on first name terms already; Rico was a fast mover. Skylar's eyes narrowed as she looked past him to see Walker leering at her, his gaze running down over her body, lingering on her breasts. She had to fight the urge to snarl. *Creep.*

"Female bodyguards—nice idea," he said. "They any good?"

"Very effective," Rico murmured. "There are certain perks attached...they stay with me twenty-four-seven."

"Interesting." Walker's gaze ran over her again. Skylar kept her expression blank and hoped she'd get a chance to pay him back.

"Very," Rico said, sinking into the chair and casually crossing his legs at the ankle—looking every inch the billionaire. Janey took up position behind him. "Now, back to business."

Walker sat opposite and almost rubbed his hands together. "We'll have a drink and go through a few figures first—there are a couple of files I'd like to show you and then we can do a tour of the facility." Leaning across the desk, he switched on the console and pressed his thumb to the panel.

"Will the tour include the research center? I heard that was where the interesting stuff goes on."

Walker's eyes sharpened. "You did? Where did you hear that?"

Rico shrugged.

Walker gave a conciliatory smile. "I'm afraid no one gets to view the research center—it's off limits to everyone but the scientific staff."

"But you have access?"

"I do, but I'm afraid it's outside company protocol to take anyone in there. But don't worry, there's plenty to see elsewhere."

Rico turned his head slightly and caught Skylar's eye. He gave a slight nod, and Skylar readied herself. When he moved, it was so fast he almost appeared a blur. He reached across, grabbed hold of Walker around the throat, and dragged him across the desk.

"I don't like you," he said. "And I don't like the way you looked at my bodyguard—and neither did she. In fact, I would so like an excuse to hurt you right now. Are you going to give me one?"

"Ever get the impression you're surplus to requirements?" Tannis said from beside her.

One thing was for sure, Rico wasn't in need of any bodyguarding. Skylar had never seen anyone move so fast. He was standing now, subduing Walker with ease, despite the other man wriggling frantically. He was also shaking his head, or at least that's what it looked like he was trying to do, it was hard to tell with Rico's fingers wrapped around his neck. Rico must have realized the problem, and he loosened his grip. "Well?"

"No," Walker wheezed.

"Okay, let's try again. We would really like a tour around the research station."

"No one—"

Rico squeezed and the words were cut off. "Look, we're on a deadline here. And I'm hungry. So do you want to rethink your answer?"

Walker nodded.

"Good." Rico released his hold, and Walker crumpled to the floor. He let out a small whimper.

Rico rolled his eyes. "I hardly touched you." He turned to

Janey. "See what you can get."

Janey nodded and strolled around the desk to sit in the chair Walker had vacated. Her fingers flew over the keyboard. Tannis moved to stand behind her. "What are you looking for?"

Janey frowned, but then answered as she worked. "We know approximately when Cain should have turned up here. I'm looking through the incoming records to see if anything matches up."

"Are they the Cyberlife records?"

"No, this is Cybercom—we'll get to Cyberlife in a moment."

"Why? Why not go straight into Cyberlife—that's what we think Cain is investigating."

Janey heaved an exaggerated sigh. "Because, the Cybercom records are more complete. And more transparent."

"Who are you?" Walker seemed to be regaining some of his composure.

At his question, Rico crouched down beside him. "Maybe you shouldn't be asking who I am, but what I am." He smiled then, with a flash of fangs, and the little color that had returned to Walker's face leached away.

"Rico!" Tannis snapped.

"What?"

"We need him conscious—if he faints or drops dead with fright, he's not going to be much use to us. Ask him something useful, like where the hell Cain is."

Rico shrugged, straightened. He reached down for Walker, grabbed him by the arms, and deposited him in the chair in front of the desk, then brushed him down solicitously.

Skylar leaned back against the wall feeling a little superfluous and watched, fascinated, as a change seemed to come over the vampire. The darkness smoothed from his face and he smiled. "Look, we're honestly not here to cause trouble—we don't give a shit what you're doing here or what nasty little secrets you're hiding in the research center. Just cooperate, and we'll be out of here and no harm done."

Walker licked his lips. "What do you want to know?"

"We're looking for a friend of ours. A Fergal Cain. We reckon he turned up here about ten weeks ago."

Walker frowned. "Why? Why did he come here?"

"Well, you see we're not actually sure about that. Could have been an employee, could have been—" He shrugged. "And it's doubtful he would have been under that name."

"Then I don't know how I can help you."

"Oh, I'm sure you'll find a way." It was amazing how he could imbue his words with so much threat.

"I think I've found him," Janey said. "Francis Copeland. Admitted to Cybercom…the dates match." Her brows drew together. "But this doesn't make sense."

"What is it?" Tannis asked.

"He was admitted for a fitting of a cyberlimb—left arm. Anyone heard that he only had one arm? That wasn't in the records."

"His boss didn't mention he'd been in an accident. You'd think he would have said something."

"Unless he didn't know."

Skylar moved around so she could see the screen. She studied the data for a moment. "What's the red flag by his name mean?"

"Give me a second." Janey typed something into the keyboard and a message flashed up on the screen. "Transferred to Cyberlife—status: volunteer."

Walker made a small sound, and everyone swung around to stare at him.

"What?" Tannis asked.

"Your friend—he's gone."

"Gone where?"

The man swallowed, but then continued. "If he's been transferred to Cyberlife, then he's beyond your help. You'd better just forget him."

"Not possible, I'm afraid," Rico said. "You see, we need to talk to him and you're going to take us there."

"I…I…"

Rico shook his head. "You got his location?" he asked Janey.

"Yes and guess what—he's in the research center."

"The place no one goes. What a surprise. Let's go find him."

They hustled Walker out of the room and into the front of the speeder. Tannis and Janey climbed in beside him and Skylar jumped into the back.

"You ever want a job guarding my body," Rico said as he took the seat beside her, "the position is yours. Hell, doing just about anything with my body—I might even pay you." He pulled the laser pistol from the small of his back and handed it to her.

"Thanks. I'll think about it."

"What about me?" Tannis asked, glancing over her shoulder.

"You want a job as well?"

Tannis rolled her eyes. "No, I want a gun."

Rico grinned, bent down, and pulled up his pants leg. He gave the second pistol to Tannis. "Janey, can you get us there?"

"Easy." She reached across the screen at the front of the speeder and pressed a few keys. "There, I programmed it for the research center."

They passed other speeders and a few people on foot. Some nodded at Walker as they passed, but he didn't say a word. Probably something to do with the pistol Tannis had jabbed into his side. Soon they'd left the busy area behind and were driving through a wide, blank corridor, no blue skies here. She guessed this was where the real business of the space station took place.

"So what is it you do at Cyberlife?" Rico asked. "I'm guessing it's illegal and that volunteer status isn't exactly volunteering as we know it."

Walker didn't answer and Rico prodded him in the shoulder.

"We work on Cybernetics."

"Why the secrecy?"

He was silent and Rico prodded him again.

"We're here," Walker said, relief clear in his voice.

The speeder came to a halt outside a set of large clear glass doors. CYBERLIFE was written in gold script across them. They all spilled out of the speeder.

"Why no security?" Skylar asked.

"We have no need for it, except on a minimal basis."

He placed his palm on the panel, stared into the retinal scanner, and the doors swung open.

Inside, all was quiet. They were in a large reception area with corridors leading off in all directions.

"We want G34," Janey said, checking her palm screen. "This way."

They followed Walker down the white corridor. The light was bright here, almost blindingly so. The walls were white, the floor and ceiling white. A faint scent of antiseptic hung in the air. It was like being in the hospital. Skylar hadn't been in a hospital for a long, long time, but she could still remember the smell from a childhood stay, and she shivered. They saw no one, and she was starting to believe the area was deserted.

"I don't like this place," Tannis said.

"Remind you of somewhere?" Rico asked.

Skylar saw a look pass between the two of them.

"Hell, yes," Tannis said. "Let's find Cain and get the hell out of here. This is giving me the creeps."

They were passing doors now. Each had a clear panel and a number. Skylar paused to peer inside. A girl lay on the bed, staring vacantly at the ceiling. When Skylar looked closer, she saw the girl was cuffed to the bed. "I guess not everyone's a volunteer," she said.

"Some of them try to harm themselves. It's a response to the drugs. They usually come through it okay."

"Usually?"

"We lose some. It's considered—"

"We're here," Janey said. She had come to a halt outside a door identical to the others, except for the number G34 in the center. She glanced through the panel. "Well, he's alive, I think, though he's unconscious—we might have to carry him out of here."

Tannis peered over her shoulder. "He's cut his hair and it looks like he's got two arms."

"Maybe one's not real."

"I don't care how many arms he's got as long as he's got a mouth. Let's get him out of here." Rico turned to Walker. "Open the door."

"I can't."

"Try."

"I'm not cleared."

"Shit."

"Want me to shoot out the lock?" Tannis asked.

"No, it will set off the alarms. Janey, can you try?"

"Sure."

It took her five minutes. Rico peered through the open door. "Hey, this is a nice room."

Skylar followed him as he stepped inside. It *was* a nice room, if you could get past the idea that the door locked from the outside and there were no windows. It was big and light, not like a cell at all—more like a bedroom. The walls were blue and matched the cover on the bed. A food dispenser stood in one corner and a comfortable chair in the other, in front of a monitor.

A man stretched out on the bed, naked except for a pair of loose drawstring black pants. He was big, with broad shoulders and narrow hips, and he was unconscious or asleep. Skylar reckoned the latter. She recognized him from the information Janey had pulled up. They'd found Fergal Cain. Now they just had to get him out of there and get him to talk.

Tannis cleared her throat. When nothing happened, she stepped forward and nudged Cain in the shoulder. For a moment, there was no response, then he blinked and came up on one elbow. His gaze fixed on Tannis, who was closest.

"Who the hell are you?" His voice was low, gravelly.

"We're here to get you out."

He frowned. "Well fuck off. I don't want to get out." And he rolled over, buried his head under the pillow and presumably went back to sleep.

CHAPTER FIFTEEN

Rico stared at the man on the bed—if there was one thing he hated, it was being ignored.

"Is he ignoring us?" Tannis asked. "I hate that—it's rude."

Cain didn't move and Tannis glanced at Rico as if to ask what now? Rico shrugged.

Tannis sighed and turned to Walker. "Do something useful and order him to come with us," Tannis said.

"I can't," Walker replied. "I can't tell him to go with you. It's more than my job's worth."

"You know," Rico said to Tannis, "as much as I'd love to question my friend Harris some more, he's beginning to annoy me. Is he annoying you?"

"Yeah." Tannis aimed her pistol and lasered Walker in the chest. He fell to the floor, but at least the crash got Cain's attention. He went rigid then pushed the pillow off the bed and sat up. He looked between them and down to where Walker lay in a crumpled heap on the blue and white tiled floor.

"He dead?"

"Stunned."

Cain didn't seem particularly bothered either way. He did look annoyed though—maybe they'd interrupted his beauty sleep. They needed to get out of there; it was only a matter of time before someone missed Walker and sent out a search party.

"Okay, let's go," Rico said.

"I told you—I'm not going with you."

Rico sighed. "I don't remember asking."

"Look, I'm staying so you may as well piss off."

Rico snarled. "Just get on your feet."

"Make me."

"What the hell." Rico could do with a good fight. Well, what he could really do with was a night of sex and slaking his bloodlust with Skylar, but a fight was the next best thing. He'd never managed to get a good fight from a human yet—too puny—but Cain was the best he was going to get right now. And at least the guy was big. Rico shrugged out of his jacket and handed it to Tannis. "Look after that."

"What am I? Your goddamn valet?" Tannis frowned. "And Rico, we really don't have time to play right now."

"There's always time to play. And I'll make it quick."

Rolling up his sleeves, he took a step toward Cain. He wrapped his hand around Cain's arm, meaning to pull him to his feet. Instead, Cain placed a palm flat on Rico's chest and shoved hard. Rico somehow found himself flat against the far wall.

For a second, shock held him immobile. *Christos,* the man was strong. Way beyond normal.

Cain was on his feet now, stalking toward him. Rico didn't wait for him to get there—he dived for Cain. The momentum sent them both crashing to the floor, and he heard Tannis swear loudly.

He rolled so he was on his back, Cain above him. Sweat gleamed on Cain's forehead, but his breathing was calm and even. He grinned and crashed his forehead toward Rico. Rico twisted out from under him, and heard the thud as Cain connected hard with the floor.

Rico's vision narrowed to the man in front of him, the others faded.

And he realized he was enjoying himself.

He raised his fist and smashed it into Cain's mouth. "Fuck, that hurt."

Blood spurted from the wound, but Cain hardly flinched. He ginned at Rico. "Is that the best you've got?"

Rico stepped back and surveyed him through narrowed eyes. Cain's blood was on his knuckles. He lifted his hand to his mouth and licked the blood then immediately spat it out. "Ugh."

It tasted foul, with a sharp metallic twang. And it occurred to him then that whatever Fergal Cain was—human didn't cover it. Cain raised his left hand. For a second, it appeared normal, then a layer of silver flowed from his shoulder encasing the arm right down to the fingertips.

Cain leapt toward him, punching with his closed left fist. It caught Rico in the belly and felt like he'd taken a direct hit from a blaster. The force sent him crashing to the floor with Cain on top. Rico was vaguely aware of the women scrambling out of the way, but he ignored them, all his concentration on the man on top of him.

Then they were rolling, each trying to get a grip. Which was hard when your opponent was nearly naked. Rico's hands failed to find a hold on Cain's sweat-slick body. Cain had better luck, his fingers clenching in the material of Rico's shirt, and he heard it rip.

He was pissed now.

He scrambled away and pushed himself to his feet, took stock of his surroundings. Janey was nowhere to be seen. Tannis and Skylar had taken refuge on the bed and were leaning against the wall watching, seemingly unconcerned, his laser pistols held loosely on their laps. Why the fuck had he given his guns away? Tannis caught his gaze and mouthed the word: *Quick?*

Hey, he was trying.

Then Cain was on him again. This time as they both went sprawling to the floor, and he swore loudly. He finally got his hands around the other man's throat. He was tempted to break the bastard's neck, but that would hardly get them the information they needed.

Unfortunately, Cain didn't have the same level of restraint. His huge hands came around Rico's throat, and he squeezed.

Rico had never encountered strength like it. And he'd fought with a few people and a few other things in his time. It was inhuman, and Cain wasn't even breathing hard.

Black spots danced in front of his eyes, but through them, he spotted Tannis—she'd actually got her lazy ass off the bed and was standing above them.

He tried to speak. Failed to get the words out. Gathered the last of his strength and tried again. "Fucking zap the bastard," he wheezed.

Tannis raised an eyebrow, but the laser fired. For a second, it looked like it was going to have absolutely no effect, then Cain's eyes widened and his body went slack. The hold on Rico's throat loosened, and he shoved Cain's unconscious body off him and lay back, breathing heavily.

"You took your goddamned time."

"Hey, I thought you wanted to play, and it seemed a shame to spoil your fun," Tannis said with a grin. "So what happened there?"

"I have no clue. The guy's not for real. I'm guessing he's had some sort of enhancement, but I've never encountered anything like it." He got to his feet and brushed himself down. "Bastard tore my shirt."

"Aw, poor baby. You'll live—or do whatever it is vampires do."

"Let's get out of here. Leave Walker, he'll be out for a while."

"I was planning to," she said, tossing him his jacket. "You'll have to carry our friend there to the speeder, though." She waved a hand to where Cain lay sprawled facedown on the floor.

"Remind me," he said, "when I employ my next captain, to choose a nice strong man, who can do his share of the work." But he reached down and hauled Cain over his shoulder.

• • •

They made it back to the docking bay with no incidents and no alarms going off. They stunned the two security guards, who were still in position outside the shuttle, and then drove the speeder directly up the ramp and inside. Rico leapt over the side and into the pilot's seat and the engines fired immediately, the doors shutting behind them. There was no room in the shuttle for people and a speeder, so Skylar stayed where she was in the backseat next to Cain. He was still out, and they cuffed him to one of the roll bars on the vehicle, but all the same, she kept a close watch on him. After seeing him fight with Rico, she wasn't sure he wouldn't just snap the bracelet off.

Rico monitored for anything coming after them, but the space remained clear as they drew farther from the space station. Skylar reckoned from what they had seen that they weren't really expecting any break-ins or breakouts. Which meant the whole set-up must be to maintain secrecy. Cyberlife was obviously flouting a law, probably several laws. But which ones? She studied the unconscious man. He was clearly no longer entirely human. So what was he?

Once they docked on *El Cazador,* Rico uncuffed Cain and dragged him out of the speeder, then tossed him over his shoulder and followed Tannis through the ship to the meeting room.

"Put him down over there," Tannis said. She stepped back and drew her weapon—she obviously wasn't taking any chances.

Rico dropped him onto the chair and stretched. "What the fuck is that guy made of? He weighs a ton."

Daisy hurried in behind them and came to stand over the unconscious Cain.

"Aren't you supposed to be flying the ship?" Rico growled.

Daisy ignored the question. "You've hurt him," she said

throwing him a look of reproach.

"It wasn't me. Why does everyone think it's always me? And he tore my shirt—where's my sympathy? Why does no one give me any sympathy? Anyway, he's only stunned. I hope."

Daisy disappeared and came back a minute later with a dampened cloth and proceeded to wipe Fergal Cain's pale face.

Rico shook his head. "Who the fuck are you—Florence fucking Nightingale?"

"Who?" Tannis and Skylar asked in unison.

"Never mind. I'm guessing this is some sort of female hormonal thing, so I'll say no more. Just get him awake."

As he spoke the words, Cain's lids flickered open. He shook his head as if clearing it, then pulled himself upright in the chair. He looked past Daisy, who hovered with her cloth, to Tannis, who still had her laser pistol aimed at his head. His lips drew down in a frown. "Hey, you shot me. That was hardly fair."

Tannis rolled her eyes. "And who said I was supposed to be fair?"

"It hurt." He rubbed the back of his neck. "You can put the gun down. I'm not going to do anything crazy with you lot all around me."

Tannis looked dubious. She pushed Daisy out of the way and came to stand in front of him. "Before I do that, let me ask you a question, because I'm interested in just how 'crazy' we're dealing with here."

"What?"

"I've been going over this in my mind, and what I want to

know is—did you really amputate your own arm just so you'd have a cover story to get into Cybercom?"

He pursed his lips, then nodded.

"I think I'll keep hold of the gun—we're dealing with way past 'crazy.' Who knows what you'll do."

"I didn't actually do it myself. I have a medic friend."

"Well, that's okay then."

"Besides, I'd done my research—I knew I could get another." He raised his arm and turned it. Skylar looked closely. It appeared to be a normal arm, but she had seen it during the fight with Rico and it had been anything but normal then.

"See, good as new. Better, actually." He glanced around at them. "So who are you guys, what do you want and how long do you plan to keep me here?"

"I'm Tannis, Rico, Skylar and Daisy." Tannis waved at them all in turn. Daisy grinned.

"And I'm Fergal. Now isn't that nice and friendly. And the rest?"

"We want some information, and you'll stay until we get it."

"I don't suppose there's a chance of some food, first? My metabolism has been a little off since…" He waved his left arm in the air.

Rico sighed. "Why not, we wouldn't want you fainting or anything."

He led the way out of the conference room, down the narrow corridor to the galley. "Help yourself." He nodded to the dispenser, which stood against one wall.

Fergal got a tray of stew from the dispenser and ate it

quickly while standing by the machine. He refilled it and took it over to the table, kicked out a chair and sat down. Picking up his spoon, he hesitated, then looked across at them still standing in the doorway. "You've got to get me back there."

"We just rescued you," Rico said. He took one of the chairs opposite Fergal, turned it around, and straddled it.

"I didn't want rescuing." Fergal ran a hand through his short hair. "Why the hell did you come for me anyway?"

"You mean we can't rescue you from the goodness of our hearts?"

He looked from one to the other of them, and a look of incredulity settled on his face. "Piss off."

Rico turned to where Skylar was leaning against the wall just inside the room. "A real charmer, isn't he?"

"He is," Skylar replied. But she didn't care how charming he was—she just wanted the information he had in his head. Her stomach rumbled, and she realized she hadn't eaten in… forever. Fixing herself a tray of stew, she sat down at the end of the table where she could watch the proceedings. It was obvious Tannis and Rico had worked together for a long time, they seemed to know when each should take a part and when they should back down, and Skylar didn't want to disturb the dynamics.

"How about your boss sent us?" Rico said to Fergal.

He glanced at Rico sharply. "You've seen Spence?"

"We talked," Rico replied. "He's worried about you."

"Aw, and you want to put his mind at rest." Fergal's eyes narrowed. "I'm not buying it."

Tannis sighed. "How about you have something we need."

"Something?" He shook his head and took another

mouthful of food. He chewed slowly, then swallowed. "Look, under normal circumstances I'd love to help you—I'm a nice guy—honest. But right now, you have got to get me back. If I don't go back, I die."

Rico grinned. "That's useful to know. It gives us something of a bargaining chip."

Fergal released an exaggerated sigh. "Just get to the point. What do you want?"

"We want information."

Fergal put down his spoon and pushed away the bowl. "And what is it you want to know so badly?"

Tannis took the seat opposite. "A couple of years ago, you did a piece on the maximum security prison on Trakis One."

Fergal's expression became wary. "How did you know that? The article was wiped."

"Janey found traces of it."

"Clever. They did a good job of deleting it—the bastards. Do you know how long it took me to set up that story?"

"Strangely enough, no we don't know. And honestly—we don't give a fuck—we just want some intel on the prison."

"It was a long time and a whole load of credits. And then those bastards came along and pulled it."

"Well, now you can get your own back."

Fergal sat back in his chair and stretched, then tugged at his lower lip. "You know, at the time, I got the impression I was lucky to get away with my life."

"Why was that?" Tannis asked. "Why not just shut you up? You must have broken a few rules to get in there. I'm surprised you didn't end up in the mines."

"When I knew they were coming after me, I contacted

Callum Meridian—"

"You know Callum Meridian?" Tannis's voice was full of awe. Callum Meridian was the leader of the Collective. He was the man who had discovered Meridian five hundred years ago, when his ship had crashed landed on Trakis Seven.

"I did an interview with him a few years back."

"Wow—I'd heard he's almost a recluse."

"Just a very private man, and he's a…good guy. Well, at least he's not the total monster many people make him out to be. He had a word with someone—must have told them to leave me alone."

"Or maybe they just don't go around killing innocent people," Skylar put in. She shouldn't have defended the Collective—but honestly, people were always making them out to be the real bad guys when in truth they were a relatively benign government. Granted, they didn't need much of a reason to kill people, but there was usually something.

"You could be right." Fergal cast her a lazy look, his eyes studying her as though he could see into her mind. She forced herself to hold his gaze. She had to be careful—there was a reason he was the most successful investigative journalist around.

He broke the contact. "Okay, so why do you need the information?"

"Why do you care?" Rico countered. "Just tell us what you know."

"Promise to take me back and I'll think about it. Look, if you were going to torture me, I reckon you would have done it by now, so that's the deal."

Rico pushed himself out of his chair and stalked around

the table. The temperature seemed to drop to near freezing. Most of the time Rico came across as charming and urbane, at least to her, but this wasn't one of those times. He rested a hand on the table beside Fergal and leaned in close, a slight snarl curling the corner of his lip.

Fergal sucked in his breath but apart from that he made no outward sign of fear, and he went up in Skylar's estimations.

"Make no mistake," Rico spoke low so Skylar had to strain to hear. "If we think it's our best bet of getting the information, I will happily torture you and toss your useless carcass out of the airlock." Then he grinned. "But hopefully, it needn't come to that. Daisy has taken a shine to you." He nodded to where Daisy was perched on a chair. She scowled at Rico's words, but Fergal eyes shifted to her, speculation in his face. "And if I kill you off with no good reason then she'll sulk, and then I'd have to kill her as well because I can't abide a sulky crew, and then Tannis would be pissed—"

"Okay, okay—enough—I get the picture." Fergal held up a hand. "But tell me vaguely what you want, then I'll know what to give you."

A look passed between Rico and Tannis, and she gave an almost imperceptible nod. "We want to pay the prison a visit and we'd prefer to get out of there afterward, preferably alive and not en route to the Meridian mines."

Fergal thought for a minute. "I'll tell you what I know, and you'll send me back. And quick."

"If we let you go, what's to stop you contacting the Collective—telling them what we're up to?"

"Why would I?"

"Good point." Rico grinned, all signs of menace gone.

"And we don't want to keep you. Well, maybe Daisy does. But she can't. So yes, we'll get you back."

"Have you a screen and image-maker I can use? It will be easier."

"Janey?" Tannis asked.

"No problem."

Al hurried around, clearing the disposable trays from the table and sending them down the recycler. Janey pressed a few keys on her palm screen and a 3D screen materialized above the table.

Rico straightened up and moved away. "Daisy," he said. "The ship's on automatic, why don't you go change the setting so we head back the way we came, and then see if the Trog's got some liquor ready? I think we could all do with a drink. And ask him to join us—we might need him. Actually, tell him it's not an invite it's an order."

Daisy opened her mouth, no doubt to argue, but Rico raised an eyebrow. She closed it again. "Okay, boss."

A smile twitched across his lips as she hurried away. Rico crossed over to where Skylar sat. He rested a hand on her shoulder and leaned down close. "Happy now?" he asked. The words feathered across her ear, and a shiver ran through her. It took her a moment to realize what he meant—that it looked like they were going to get the intel they needed. The mission had a chance of success now.

Not for the first time, she wondered what was the purpose behind the mission. She had no doubt there was one, but she just couldn't see it. Why did her bosses want Aiden's killer freed from prison? She'd searched her brain and come up blank. But she was a soldier, and a soldier followed orders.

Most of the Corps' work was straightforward, putting down minor rebellions, rescuing people. There were many groups, especially on the outer planets, who believed force was the best way to obtain what they wanted—whether that was supplies, technology, or even men, women, and children. The Corps would often send in a team to clean up, and Skylar had headed up many such missions. Also, over the years, there had been a couple of larger-scale attempts to wrest 'power from the Collective. The Corps had put them down with ease.

But with her move to the Intelligence division, the types of assignments they sent her on shifted. They no longer told her the reasons behind the job or their ultimate aim. She guessed that if she didn't like that, then she could leave. And it was slowly dawning on her that perhaps she didn't like it. Perhaps she wasn't happy carrying out jobs with no clue of the reason behind them.

She really wasn't sure.

"You know, you don't look particularly happy."

Rico's words dragged her from her thoughts. "Sorry?" she said. "I was thinking of something else."

"Want to share?"

"No."

He released her shoulder and sighed. "One day soon, you and I will have a talk."

No we won't.

Instead, she just turned in her chair to say *sure*, but found his face close to hers.

He kissed her. The caress was light, but warmed her insides and banished her worries. Well, at least the kiss replaced those particular worries with different ones. She couldn't allow herself to become attached to someone she might have to sacrifice. She was beginning to hope that once they had gotten 'Jonny' out, she could just take off in her shuttle and leave *El Cazador* and her crew as she had found them.

Then Rico pushed his tongue slowly between her lips and the warm bits deep inside her burst into flame. For a moment, she closed her eyes and forgot everything but the languid thrust of his tongue, the long fingers massaging her shoulder. When she finally dragged her lids up, it was to find Fergal watching them from across the table, a speculative look in his eyes, and she pulled back.

"Why do I get the feeling he's studying us all and coming up with his own conclusions?" she said in a low tone.

"Probably because he is. They're nosy bastards— reporters—and the good ones are incapable of turning it off."

She shuddered, but Daisy appeared at the door before she could say anything else. The Trog was behind her, and they each had a bottle of amber liquid in their hands. Skylar was suddenly desperate for a drink. She pushed herself up and went to get glasses, placing them on the table. She was in front of Fergal when he caught sight of the Trog. He gave him a quick glance, but then looked again. "Don't I know you from somewhere?"

"No." The Trog dipped his head so his shaggy hair covered his face.

"I'm sure I do. Give me a moment."

Skylar could almost see his mind ticking, flicking through memories, possibilities.

"You don't know him from anywhere," Rico said.

Fergal turned to look at him. "I do. I never forget a face…

it's right there."

Rico drew his brows together. "Believe me, you do not know him." He enunciated each word slowly. "Not from anywhere."

Understanding dawned on Fergal's face and he nodded. "Never seen him in my life before." There was an amused quirk to his lips. "You know, I really would like to do a piece on pirates one day."

"You can interview Daisy. When we've finished."

The Trog put the bottle on the table and turned. Skylar was sure he was going to leave, but he took the chair at the end and sat down. Rico poured drinks for everyone and pushed a glass toward her. She sipped it and allowed the warmth to seep through her.

"Jesus, what is this stuff?" Fergal asked.

"Whiskey. Now can we get on?"

"Okay. You know the place is basically in two sections, the regular prison and the maximum security section?" Without waiting for an answer, he raised his hand to the screen and used a finger to draw a circle. "This is the maximum security section and it lies right at the center of the facility." He drew a second circle around the first. "It's entirely surrounded by the regular prison—and that's a big place—up to ten thousand inmates at any one time."

"How many incoming and outgoing prisoners are there in a normal changeover?" Tannis asked.

"It varies, sometimes none, sometimes as many as twenty. I never saw more than that."

"I've already logged on to the transports manifest," Janey said. "There are no incoming this trip."

"Good."

"The prisoners in the maximum security section tend to be short term," Fergal continued. "They're mostly awaiting appeals before heading off to the Meridian mines."

Tannis turned to Skylar. "Your brother—was he on appeal?"

Skylar frowned. "Not that I know of. They denied him the right."

"Not surprising—he killed one of theirs—I'm betting they're pissed. So why was he there at all? Why didn't they ship him direct to the mines?"

Skylar shook her head—she had no clue. Presumably, it had something to do with why they also wanted him out of there. Had Aiden's killer been working for someone inside the Collective? She couldn't believe that one of their own would have condoned Aiden's assassination.

"Your brother?" Fergal took a sip of his drink and grimaced. "What's he in for?"

"You haven't heard?" Tannis asked.

"I've been pretty much cut off for the last ten weeks."

"Skylar's brother assassinated Collective founder Aiden Ross."

Shock flared on his face. "How? Why?"

"Don't know to both questions."

"And you're getting him out?"

"Who's interrogating who here?" Rico asked. He placed his empty glass on the table, topped it up, and then did the same for Skylar's before pushing the bottle across the table. "Do you think we could move on?"

Fergal grinned. "Sorry, occupational hazard. So they bring

the prisoners in on the transport ship, and the timing of that is limited to when they can get past the black hole. You know about the black hole, right?"

"Yeah," Tannis said. "We know."

"Well, the black hole is the best security that place has. We even lost one of the transports while I was there—the pilot got careless and his transport was sucked right in. There was talk afterward about closing the place down, but there's no denying it's effective—there's never been an escape or a successful rescue attempt—though there have been a few attempts."

"I hadn't heard of those," Tannis said. "What happened?"

"The ones I know of—two went into the hole, one was fried on entry into the planet's atmosphere. Have I mentioned the radiation is off the scale?"

"Nice place."

"It's the worst shit-hole in the universe. Well, except maybe for the mines on Trakis Seven, but I've heard it's a close call." He drew a couple of lines on the diagram joining the two circles. "These are the exits from the center to the outer prison."

"So what's the security like?"

"It's actually very low. It's not as though the prisoners are trying to get out—there's nowhere to go—the planet will kill them if they get outside the facility. In the regular prison there was a force of around one hundred guards, about one to every hundred prisoners. Much less than that in maximum security. But then there's not much need in there."

"Why's that?"

"Partly volume of prisoners, but mainly because they're

kept in cryo."

"The whole time?"

"Yup. At least they don't have to dwell on what's to come."

"No, they'll just wake up one day and find themselves in the mines. Lovely." Tannis swallowed her drink and poured another. "What about the rest of the security? How do we get between sections?"

"The rest is top of the line. Biometrics, backed up by randomly generated codes."

"Janey will get us the codes."

Fergal glanced across to where Janey was inputting information into her palm screen. "As I said—clever." Fergal flashed her a smile, and she stared stonily back.

"Biometrics, we'll have to sort out." Tannis stared into space for a moment, thinking of her next question. "Can the transport shuttle crew enter the maximum security section?"

"No, they'll take the cryo tubes into the main prison then hand them over. Usually to the head guard—that's a man called Peters and he's as mean as a snake…" He glanced at Tannis, realizing he might have been less than diplomatic.

Tannis merely stared back, her yellow eyes with their black reptilian slits void of expression.

Fergal grinned. "No disrespect."

"None taken," Tannis said. "But if you try and tell me that some of your best friends are snakes, I might just have to shoot you."

"My point was—the man's a bastard. If you need to get body parts from anyone there's no one will grieve Peters."

"That's good to know."

They started going into details then, and Skylar let the

voices wash over her. Janey was recording the meeting and Skylar would go over the finer points later. Beneath the table, Rico's long fingers stroked her thigh, his touch both soothing and thrilling. She should move but it felt too good.

Finally, Fergal had given them all he could, which was pretty comprehensive.

"You think they would have changed things when they found out who you were?" Tannis asked.

"Probably the codes, but they're changed regularly anyway." He pushed his chair out and stood up. "That's it. That's all I have. Now, can I go please?"

Rico shrugged and glanced around the table. "We got everything we need?" Both Skylar and Tannis nodded.

"Why not, then. As soon as we're within range, you can take the pod. I don't think it would be a good idea if we took you back—we're probably not too popular right now—but we can manage without the pod. You okay with that?" he asked Tannis.

"Yeah, if this works we can buy a new one. If it doesn't…"

"We'll have bigger worries than no pod."

Rico led the way out of the galley and through the ship back to the docking bay. "I've been thinking about this," he said. "Nobody cuts off their own arm just for a story. So what did you really want with Cyberlife? And why will you die if you don't go back?"

Fergal glanced at him but kept walking.

"Go on, you can tell me," Rico urged. "You know we're unlikely to blab about it."

Fergal stopped walking and turned to face him. "Hell, you're as nosy as I am."

Rico grinned. "Sometimes. About some things. And you've got me interested."

Fergal took a deep breath, and Skylar moved a little closer so she could hear. "The truth is, I was never going to earn enough to pay for the Meridian treatment, and I'm not too keen on dying."

"Makes sense so far."

"I'd been hearing rumors for a while, probably a decade, or so. Then one—"

"What sort of rumors?" Skylar asked.

"A private company that's researching how to extend life spans and possibly even attain immortality."

"Meridian?"

"No. Something completely different, tied in with the cybernetics. And my source reckoned they were getting results."

Tannis frowned. "Isn't that against the law?"

"Yeah, selfish bastards don't want anyone else living forever."

"Actually, I heard it was the Church who insisted," Skylar said.

"Does it matter? They're all bastards. But that's why Cyberlife isn't going about advertising what it does. Anyway, no way were they going to let a reporter in there, but I've been undercover a few times, I know how to set it up. And I'm not completely crazy—I got the booking into Cybercom before I got my mate to chop off my arm."

"Very sensible."

Skylar could clearly hear the sarcasm in Tannis's tone and she agreed. What sort of dedication would it take to do that?

Though she was sure people did worse things in their desire to cheat death. Maybe the loss of an arm was nothing when weighed against the chance to live forever. After all, she'd lost more than an arm. She'd lost her husband. Oh, they'd stayed together to the bitter end, but from the point she had taken the Meridian treatment, there had been a distance between them.

Fergal grinned. "Didn't hurt a bit."

"Do you regret it?" Tannis asked.

Fergal cast her a look of disbelief. "Of course I fucking regretted it—I saw what happened to some of the people in there. They went crazy. But I'm through the worst now—I'll make it—if I get back and keep taking the anti-rejection drugs."

They arrived at the docking bay, coming to a halt in front of the small one-man pod in the far corner. Daisy rushed forward and put her palm to the panel to open the door.

"We'll be within the pod's range in thirty minutes," Rico said.

"I'll show him out it works." Daisy ushered Fergal up the ramp. He appeared vaguely bemused but not totally unwilling. He glanced back from the door. "I'll be back to do that pirate piece as soon as I'm done."

"We'll be waiting."

He turned and entered. Daisy slipped in after him and the door closed behind them.

"It's going to be a close fit in there," Skylar said. "I guess Daisy's still trying to get laid."

"She's not the only one."

CHAPTER SIXTEEN

Rico switched the ship to automatic pilot and sat back in his chair, booted feet on the console, arms behind his head. His favorite position. They were on course to intercept the transport ship, and there wasn't a lot they could do now but wait.

Dios, he hated waiting.

Daisy sat in the copilot's chair, but her eyes were shut. She dozed—too many late nights playing poker and too much daydreaming since that reporter had left last night. She was hanging around Rico even more than usual, but he found he didn't mind, and at least she was safe from him. He'd never liked his food green—even when he was human.

Across the room, Skylar and Al huddled on the floor, cross-legged, faces close together. They'd pinched a pack of his cards and were playing some sort of game. These days, he never saw the two of them apart. The boy stuck to Skylar like an unwanted burr.

Al whispered something in her ear, and Skylar threw back her head and laughed. Rico's irritation flared. With a jolt of shock, he realized he was jealous of a scrawny boy. He couldn't ever remember being jealous before, not even when he'd been human.

For a moment, his mind flailed in panic. What the hell was happening to him? What was it about Skylar that made him feel this way? She was beautiful, but there were beautiful women everywhere. What made her different? He had his suspicions. Perhaps it was time to share them with her.

Skylar chanced a peek at him, as if she could feel the intensity of his gaze. She raised an eyebrow when she saw him watching her, and then turned, dismissing him.

He rose to his feet. Definitely time to have that chat.

As he stepped toward them, the door slid open. Janey hovered in the doorway, peering into the room. As usual, her clothes were tasteful, her hair and makeup perfect, four-inch heels supporting endless legs. Now, there was a beautiful woman—who did absolutely nothing for him.

Janey caught sight of him and sidled into the room, taking a circuitous route so she wouldn't pass Skylar and Al.

She came to a halt at his side, almost touching, and tiptoed to whisper in his ear. "I need to talk to you."

"Well, talk." Rico returned his attention to Skylar, who was doing her best to pretend she wasn't watching him with Janey.

"It's about that thing you asked me to do."

Reluctantly, he focused on Janey. "That thing?"

Her brows furrowed, and she glanced around before starting, "You know…"

When he didn't answer, she glared at him. "You asked me to check if that space cruiser was still hanging around, and you told me to be discreet."

The words were spoken loud enough to waken Daisy, and she jumped up. "Space cruiser? Where?"

"Now look what you've done," Janey snapped.

"There's no space cruiser. Go back to sleep," Rico said soothingly to Daisy. He turned back to Janey. "You, come with me." He put a hand on the small of her back, mainly because he knew Skylar was still watching, and steered her from the bridge. Once the door closed behind them, he faced her. "Well?"

"Actually, there is a space cruiser."

He looked at her sharply. "You found it?"

She gave him a smug smile. "Of course. It was easy once I knew where to look. You were right—it was following us, just beyond our normal sensor range."

Rico shoved his hands in his pockets and tried to fathom the implications. This was one of those rare times he'd actually hoped he was wrong. But even knowing, he still couldn't work out what was going on. He paced the narrow corridor while he tried to decide his next move. Whether he should even have a next move, or whether he should just wait it out and see what happened next.

But he was fed up with waiting.

Patience had never been his strong suit.

Tannis would be furious if he got them all blown to hell, or even if he got them blown up just a little bit and they missed the deadline to intercept the transport ship. He briefly considered discussing his suspicions with her, but dismissed the idea—however mercenary Tannis was, she wouldn't risk her crew, and he wasn't ready to give up on this yet. Besides, he didn't think the risk was that big. It all depended on…

The door to the bridge opened, interrupting his thoughts.

Skylar stood there, arms folded across her chest, her gaze narrowing on him and Janey. "Daisy keeps rambling about a space cruiser. Is something happening?"

Suddenly, he knew what he was going to do. He would take the fight to the enemy—if they actually were the enemy. He really didn't know, and that irritated the hell out of him. He gave Skylar what he hoped was an enigmatic smile. "It might be."

"And are you going to tell us what?"

"Why spoil the surprise?" Pushing past her, he strode onto the bridge and sat in his chair. Next to him, Daisy watched, wide-eyed, while the others came to stand behind him. "You might want to sit down and fasten yourselves in. The ride might get a little bumpy."

They didn't move. "Actually, before you go, Janey, can you give me the last coordinates?"

"Last coordinates of what?" Skylar asked.

He ignored the question and waited while Janey reached across and punched in the numbers. She was right; the ship was behind them, just out of range.

He pressed his comm unit. "Tannis?"

"What?" Her tone was grumpy, and he suspected what he was about to say wouldn't cheer her up any.

"If you're not already strapped into anything right now, you might want to consider it."

"What the…"

He closed off the connection and settled back in his seat, locking his safety harness in place. Everyone was still standing. Was no one capable of taking orders anymore?

"Sit," he roared.

Rico gave them ten seconds to comply, then hit the new coordinates. *El Cazador* slowed, shuddered, but before the ship had time to come to a complete stop, he hit the boosters and sent her into overdrive. The engines shrieked as she spun and shot off in the opposite direction, the force of her speed pushing him back into his chair.

Behind him, someone crashed to the floor. They really should have listened.

It was only seconds until he saw the speck of the space cruiser on the screen. They were hurtling toward it, but he didn't slow down. They had to do this quickly, before the other ship realized what was happening.

The ship grew bigger, definitely the same one from the attack the other day. If attack was the right word. He locked on the lasers and fired. *El Cazador* wasn't powerful enough to do any real damage, but he was betting he could still wind them up.

Now was the moment the space cruiser should retaliate. But he didn't think it would. Of course, if he was wrong they would all be space dust in about two seconds, and while he liked to think he was never wrong, there was always a first time.

The other ship wouldn't even have to shoot. They could just keep going, slam into *El Cazador*, and smash her into tiny little pieces. The bigger ship probably wouldn't sustain more than a scratch.

He held his breath, fighting the urge to change course as the image of the space cruiser filled the screen.

Mierda. He was wrong. They *were* going to crash.

At the last minute, the cruiser veered. The power of her back-thrust washed over *El Cazador*, rolling her, and for a minute, he hung upside down from the harness. He ignored the crash and subsequent yelp as someone collided with the ceiling.

When the ship righted itself, the screen was empty. Rico released his breath and assessed the place for damage. A few red buttons blinked on the console, but nothing too drastic.

Skylar picked herself up off the floor. He should have guessed she'd be the one to disobey orders. She winced and rubbed a spot on her hip, but otherwise she appeared okay. Perhaps he would offer to kiss her bruises better… later.

Everyone else was where they should be. He paused to study Al. The boy's eyes gleamed with excitement. He caught Rico watching, and the excitement was immediately replaced by abject fear. Strange. Very strange. But Rico didn't have time to ponder the young boy right now.

"That was great," Daisy said. "Can we do it again?"

Rico grinned. He clicked open his harness and crossed to where Skylar leaned against the wall. "You okay?"

Her eyes narrowed. She opened her mouth to answer just as Tannis strode onto the bridge, radiating raw fury, her head bleeding from a small scalp wound.

Another one who couldn't follow orders.

"Do you want to tell me what the fuck is going on?" Tannis snapped.

"We had someone on our tail."

"Who?"

"That space cruiser we bumped into the other day."

"I'm not getting this. Did they attack?"

"Not quite."

Beside him, Skylar snorted. "This big, stupid, brain-dead, bloodsucking idiot thought we'd attack first."

"All-dead, actually," he inserted cheerfully.

Tannis frowned. She reached up and rubbed at the blood trickling down her forehead. Rico followed the movement with his eyes. Danger always whetted his appetite. He reined in his hunger.

"I don't understand." Tannis shook her head. "You attacked that space cruiser?" Her voice rose with each word. "The space cruiser that's bigger than us, faster than us, with ten times more firepower?"

"I wanted to know if they would finish us off. And the answer is no. Whatever they're after, they don't want us dead."

Tannis didn't look impressed with his explanation. "And what if they had wanted us dead? Then, guess what—we'd *be* dead!"

"But they didn't."

She gritted her teeth and made a visible effort to bring herself under control, then spoke into the comm unit. "Trog, what's the damage?" She listened for a moment. "Hey, don't shout at me. I'm not the one who nearly blew up your engines." She turned back to Rico. "The cooling system is fucked. I suggest you get down there and fix it."

Rico took one last look at her fixed expression and decided the cooling system sounded like a good place to be. Besides, he needed time to think.

• • •

Skylar watched him go.

What the hell had that been about? Her hands shook, and she knew it wasn't just the physical shock.

How had he known the ship was tailing them?

"Have you got anything to say?"

The question cut into her thoughts. Tannis looked pissed. And who could blame her? She had a madman flying her ship. It hadn't occurred to Skylar when she'd done the planning for this mission to factor in that the pilot was a complete suicidal idiot.

Or was he?

She couldn't get away from the nagging doubt that Rico knew more than he was letting on. But that couldn't be the case. Otherwise, why was she still alive?

"Well?" Tannis asked.

Skylar frowned. She'd already forgotten the question. "I think I need to go lie down." Not waiting for an answer, she turned and walked away.

Al caught up with her in the corridor. "Are you all right?"

She nodded.

"Do you want me to come with you?"

"No." She set off again and then stopped. "Where's the cooling system?"

"Down on the lower level, next to the engine room. Do you want me to show you?"

"Thanks, but I'll find it."

She felt Al's gaze boring into her back all the way along the corridor, until she took the ramp down to the lower levels.

She had to find out what Rico knew, whether her mission was compromised.

Shit. She was totally fucked if she had to get out now. No way could she set this up again in the time left. Her first mission, and she had messed it up. She just wasn't sure how. Maybe Rico had picked up that message she'd sent, but she'd been quick, and the frequency wasn't one they monitored. And that was days ago. Why wait to confront her?

She knew she'd arrived at the cooling room from the billows of steam wafting under the black door. She pressed her hand on the door panel. Nothing happened. It figured she wouldn't be cleared to go everywhere on the ship. For a moment, she considered turning back, but she needed to know. She tapped her hand on the door. Still nothing. Drawing her laser pistol, she hammered on the metal with the butt.

The door glided open. Rico stood in the opening. "Skylar, what a nice surprise." He glanced down at the pistol still clutched in her hand. "Planning on shooting somebody?"

She was tempted. Maybe she could shoot him, toss the body off the ship, and no one would be the wiser. She was almost certain he hadn't shared whatever it was he thought he knew.

Could she do it?

He stood there, slanting her his lopsided grin, and the muscles in her belly tightened. His clothes were soaked, clinging to the strong lines of his body, his hair damp, his skin gleaming with a fine sheen of moisture.

She holstered her pistol. "I just wanted to know what's going on."

"I'm fixing the cooling system—you want to help?"

She gritted her teeth. "I meant up there, with the space cruiser."

"Nothing you need to worry your pretty little head about."

His eyes gleamed with amusement, and she forced herself to take a deep, calming breath. He was trying to wind her up, and she wasn't going to let him succeed. She curved her lips into the semblance of a smile. "That's sweet of you, but it's my brother's life at stake here. I can't help but worry."

"Hmm, for a moment, I'd actually forgotten about your brother. How remiss of me." He stepped to the side and gestured into the room behind him. "Why don't you come inside, and I can set your mind at rest while I work."

Skylar peered past him into the steam-filled room.

"I can't stop right now," Rico said as she hesitated. "The Trog's threatening to jump ship if I don't fix this fast."

The thick, wet heat enveloped her as soon as she stepped into the room. The door slid shut behind her, and immediately sweat oozed from her pores. Breathing in the hot heavy air, she felt as though she was drowning, and she took quick, shallow breaths until she was sure she could get enough oxygen into her lungs.

The room was small, with a large cylinder in the center, steam hissing from the seals around the base. Rico stood with his back to her, tapping into a console, and the muscles shifted beneath his skin-tight clothing. Even from behind, he was quite possibly the most beautiful thing she had ever seen, with broad shoulders, lean hips, and long, muscular legs.

After working for a minute, he swore under his breath and banged his fist down hard. "There, that should do it. Give it a few minutes to reset, and we can get out of here."

He swung round to face her, leaning against the counter, his arms folded across his chest. His skin was slick with steam or sweat, his thick lashes spiky with moisture. Her gaze dropped to where the shirt clung to the hard muscles of his chest. She could see the outline of his nipples beneath the damp silk.

She swallowed and looked away before her gaze could drop lower. Instead, she focused on a large red button on the wall beside him. "What does that do?" she asked.

"Sets off the emergency cooling system."

"Isn't this an emergency?"

"Not yet."

She wiped the sweat from her forehead. "Can't you press it anyway?"

He shuddered. "I'd really rather not. Now, what did you want to know?"

She licked the moisture from her lips and saw his eyes follow the movement. She hadn't thought it could get any hotter in here, but the temperature shot up. She forced herself to concentrate. She needed answers. Though, if Rico suspected her of something, he was hiding it well.

"Do we need to call off the rescue?"

Surprise flashed across his face. "Why would you think that?"

She frowned. "That space cruiser—"

"—was nothing to do with you or the rescue," he interrupted. "Just someone who reckons I owe them. That's how I knew they wouldn't shoot. This guy doesn't want me dead. Well not yet. He wants me to pay him back—then he wants me dead."

"Wasn't it a Collective ship?"

"Yeah, but this guy has friends in high places."

"So why didn't they board us?"

He shrugged. "I guess he's letting me know he's found us, but don't worry, this baby"—he patted the ship's wall—"has some fancy maneuvers in her. We'll shake them off."

There was something not quite right here, but Skylar couldn't work out what. Maybe the heat was getting to her, or the fact that Rico suddenly seemed much closer. She took a step back and looked around her—the thick haze of steam appeared to have dispersed a little.

"Is it done yet? Can we get out of here?" she said.

"Not yet." He moved closer again and stroked her cheek. "Are you feeling okay?" Curling his hand around her throat, he cupped the back of her skull, massaging her scalp with his fingers. "Did you bang your head when you fell?"

"No. I bruised my hip, that's all." At the memory, her anger surged. "What in the name of Meridian were you doing? You could have killed us all."

"I did tell you to strap yourself in."

"Yeah, right, and that would really have helped if they'd zapped us into tiny little pieces."

He laughed softly, and his hand slid down her body, to rest against her hip, rubbing the sore spot gently. "You want me to kiss it better?"

At his words, the muscles in her belly clenched. She had a flashback to the feel of his mouth on her. Her legs clamped together, and she almost came from the memory.

She needed to get her mind off sex. She couldn't allow herself to relax around him. Closing her eyes, she ran a quick, calming mantra through her mind. When she had her unruly body under control, she brushed his hand away and stiffened her spine.

If she was sensible she'd leave right now, but this might be the last time she would see him alone and there was something she wanted to ask him, a few things, actually.

He was the oldest person she had ever heard of, yet he didn't seem like the other long-lifers she had met. "Can I ask you a question?"

"You can ask. I might not answer."

"Do you like living forever?"

He slanted her a smile. "Well so far, I've always preferred it to the alternative."

"But don't you get bored?"

"No, I've never gotten bored. There's a whole universe out there waiting to be explored." He grinned. "Besides, I've learned to keep myself entertained."

She decided not to pursue that. "So, did you choose to become what you are?"

"A vampire?"

"Yes, did you choose it because of the immortality?"

He shook his head.

"So why?"

For a minute, she thought he wouldn't answer, then he shrugged. "I was married once. She was killed, and I wanted revenge."

His voice was expressionless, and Skylar had no clue what he was thinking. "What happened?"

"The Church—the Inquisition, to be precise—took her. They accused her of being a witch—"

"A witch?"

"She was a healer. The Church didn't care that she helped people. They came for her when I was away. By the time I returned, she was dead. Tortured and burned at the stake."

"I'm sorry."

"Don't be—it was a long time ago. Afterward, I went hunting for the darkness. If you look hard enough, you'll always find it. You could say I sold my soul for revenge, but I had that many times over, so the bargain was good."

The thought of Rico married made her feel uneasy, and the next question slipped out before she could stop it. "Did you love her?"

He shrugged. "It was a marriage arranged by our families, but I came to care for her."

. . .

Her skin glowed with moisture, her hair slick against her scalp, her eyes huge and shadowed by the death of someone she had never known. A death that had happened so many centuries ago.

A wave of unexpected tenderness rose inside him. For some reason, Skylar pulled at emotions he'd thought he'd lost. Perhaps emotions he never had before.

In view of what he suspected, it wasn't wise to care for her.

But, *dios*, she had him tied in knots.

The material of her jumpsuit molded to her full breasts and slender legs. He breathed in and caught the lingering scent of her arousal on the warm air. She wanted him, and at the knowledge, his own body responded, heat coiling in his belly. He allowed his hunger to rise, pushing the doubts from his mind.

Leaning in close, he whispered in her ear. "Enough questions. You still owe me an orgasm."

Her eyes widened, and he took advantage of her shock, slipping a hand between their bodies, between her thighs, feeling her tremble against him. He saw the moment she gave up the fight, all the tension draining away.

Pressing upwards with his fingers, he rubbed her core, and she moaned low in her throat. She was already poised on the edge, and she came quickly—her whole body shuddering with pleasure, a small scream escaping her throat.

He waited for the tremors to stop, then kissed her lightly on the lips. "Two orgasms," he murmured.

She raised her head. Her eyes half-closed, her face flushed. "I always pay my debts."

She dropped to her knees in front of him. He'd been hard since the moment she walked in the room. Now he throbbed with need.

He held himself still as her light fingers traced over the length of his erection. Her fingers fumbled on the fastening of his pants, but at last she peeled open the damp material and his cock sprang free.

She sat back on her heels for a moment staring at him. Her tongue came out, licked her lips, and he groaned. He couldn't help himself. Reaching for her, he stroked his hand over one shoulder, cupping the back of her head in his palm, pulling her closer. Her warm breath teased across the sensitive tip, and it jerked toward her. Beneath her lashes, her hot gaze caught his as the blood pounded through his veins, pulsated in his cock.

Then she licked him.

He closed his eyes, rested his back against the wall as

she explored him with her velvety tongue. Her touch was tentative at first. Rico was used to whores whose practiced mouths knew exactly what to do, but he found this far more erotic. She kissed the tip, and his hips pushed against her. She ran her tongue around the rim, and he bit back another groan.

Finally, she took him in her mouth. He opened his eyes and stared down the line of his body to watch as her red, full lips encircled his cock. His fingers tightened in her hair, pressing her closer, and she sucked harder.

He forced his hand to relax, stroked her hair, her throat, anywhere he could touch as he continued to thrust leisurely into that hot, wet mouth. The pleasure built inside him. He was so close now, his breath coming in short sharp pants. She cupped his balls with her hand, squeezed, and he exploded.

Pleasure shot through his balls, up his shaft, melting his spine. His back arched and he came. For long moments, he pumped into her mouth, unable to stop. Finally, she drew back, her tongue snaking out to lick her full lower lip. "Umm."

"Umm?"

"You taste…" She licked her lips again and a tremor of residual pleasure shot through him, jerking his hips. "…delicious."

At the word, another hunger rose, and his gums ached with the need to taste her. "Come here." He tugged her to her feet, pulling her close against him. Everything was hot and wet. He kissed her mouth, her cheeks, burrowed his face in the curve of her throat, licking the moist skin, finding the point where the blood flowed close to the surface, touching his tongue to the pulse. She wasn't fighting him off now, and he knew he could have her. His hunger rose as his fangs grazed the tender flesh. It had been days since he had fed, but still he couldn't bring himself to make the final move.

If he tasted her, what would he discover?

Right now, he only suspected what she was. If he knew for sure, would he have to put a stop to this charade? Put a stop to Skylar? And even if he did prove she was a liar, it wouldn't explain what she was really up to. He doubted he could make her talk, and he wanted to know.

Actually, he wanted her to tell him of her own free will, and for that he needed more time.

When he didn't move, she wriggled against him. His hunger roared, straining against the fierce hold he had on his control. If she moved again, he knew he would lose it, take her. Then she ground her hips into him, and his control slipped away. There was only one sure way he could stop himself now. He stared at the red button on the wall beside him.

Dios, he hated cold water.

He shifted Skylar so he held her in one arm, and taking a deep breath, he slammed his other hand onto the button.

The effect was instantaneous.

Skylar screamed, and this time it wasn't from pleasure.

CHAPTER SEVENTEEN

"Security is going to be much lower going in," Tannis said. "They're not going to think anyone would risk attacking a heavily armed ship for a few supplies. So we hit before they reach Trakis One."

The whole crew had gathered to go over the final plan. Skylar rested her back against the wall, arms crossed, as she watched Rico out of the corner of her eye. A shiver ran through her. After twenty-four hours, she still felt frozen to the bone.

She was certain he'd done it on purpose, despite his protestations of innocence.

What she didn't understand was why.

She'd given in. She would have let him do anything, but instead of doing the obvious, he'd pressed that stupid button and nearly froze them both to death.

"So, Skylar goes ahead," Rico continued. "It's an all-male crew, so she dresses in that skimpy outfit and sends out a distress signal. They're going to be suspicious but with a bit of luck they should only go to a code-yellow alert. We can work with that."

"What if they go to a code red?" Skylar asked.

"They go to a code red and we're fucked." He grinned. "Well, actually, at that point it's just you that's fucked, because we'll be out of there."

"Great plan so far."

"But we don't think they will," Tannis added quickly. "Once you're on board, your job is to see that they do not go to red. Stop them anyway you like, just make sure it doesn't escalate when we come on board, and if possible switch off the yellow. You also need to cut their external shielding so we can board. If you can do that from the control panel—great. If not, Janey's got something that should help you."

Janey was sitting a little apart from the group, her perfectly manicured fingertips gliding over a hologram screen in front of her. Engrossed, she seemed unaware that everyone had turned to look at her.

"Janey?"

She glanced up with an irritated frown as Tannis spoke her name. "Yes?"

"That 'thing' you have for Skylar. Can you give her a quick rundown?"

Janey's expression brightened. "You're going to love this. I've been working on it all night."

She held up a disc, so small Skylar had to move in closer to see. About the size of her smallest fingertip, and paper-thin, it didn't look particularly impressive. "What is it?"

"A radio wave emitter, and get this—it's triggered by a

medical scanner. Which fits in great with your cover story. You tell them you think you were hurt when your ship was attacked and get them to scan you. If you time it right, it will knock out the shields and the alarms long enough for Rico and Tannis to board."

"Where does it go?"

"That's the clever part—I'll slip it under your skin," she patted her rib cage just below her left breast, "right here."

"Lovely," Skylar muttered, but she was impressed. She was starting to believe they could make this work. "Will we have the ship's codes?"

"I'm hoping so." Janey waved at the screen. "I'm working on them now."

"Good." Skylar turned back to Rico and Tannis. "So, I keep them contained. You board, we persuade the crew to cooperate, or we put them out of action. We go in to Trakis One on the transport ship, pretend we're them, drop off the supplies, pick up my little brother, and we're out of there before they realize anything is going on." She frowned. "You know, it all sounds a little too easy."

"Well, the going in is going to be the tricky part," Tannis said. "Rico has to get us past that black hole. That's what keeps them safe. Also, according to Fergal they've gotten sloppy. This whole 'impossible to break out of' crap has gone to their heads. That should work in our favor. So—any questions?" she asked. "No? Well then, I suggest those of you not on watch get some sleep. It's a big day tomorrow."

Rico strolled across to where Skylar lounged against the wall. "Sweetheart, how about you and me go somewhere quiet, have a drink?"

She didn't move, just examined him, one lip curled in what she hoped was a disdainful sneer.

"Hey, I said it was an accident. My hand slipped."

"Yeah, right."

"Come on. Don't be like that. After all, this time tomorrow, we might all be sucked into a black hole."

He flattened his palms on the wall on either side of her head; she could smell the musky male scent of him, feel the whisper of his breath against her cheek. "Do you really want to die not knowing how it could be between us?" His voice had sunk to that low, husky drawl that sent prickles racing across her skin. "I thought you always paid your debts, Skylar? You're still one up on me, remember."

Yes, she did, and at the memory of his agile fingers working on her body, a fire burst into life inside her, banishing the last of the cold.

He leaned a little closer. "What if I promise no biting—just good, old-fashioned sex?"

His words conjured an image of him on top of her, inside her, and the fire threatened to rage out of control. She swallowed, bit her lower lip, and slowly unfolded her arms from her chest. Reached up to…

"Skylar, are you coming?"

Skylar jumped. The voice came from behind Rico, and she glanced over his shoulder. Daisy stood in the entrance watching them, amusement gleaming in her emerald eyes. "You said you wanted to see the navigation room."

Skylar's tongue flicked out to moisten her dry lips. Her gaze lingered on Rico's hooded eyes for a moment, and then she nodded.

"I do." The words came out as a croak, and she cleared her throat. "I do. Yes, I definitely want to see the navigation room."

She ducked under Rico's arm, but could feel his eyes on her back as she walked out.

"Skylar?"

She turned back at the doorway. "What?"

"You won't be able to run forever."

Once they were a safe distance down the corridor, she released her breath. "Thank you."

"Hey, a deal's a deal," Daisy said. "Besides, you're paying us, and you looked like you were about to cave."

"No, I wasn't."

Daisy snorted. "Right." She gave Skylar a sideways look. "You won't hurt him, will you?"

"Hurt who?"

"Rico."

Shock stopped Skylar in her tracks. She turned to face Daisy. "How could I possibly hurt Rico?"

"Well, he's changed since you came on board."

"How so?"

"He used to be really aloof. He'd talk to the captain, but the rest of us, he'd pretty much ignore. Then the last week, he's been talking to us, he's more…human, and we know it's because of you."

"You've been discussing this?"

"Of course. He obviously likes you, but we reckon you'll be leaving after the job's over." She studied Skylar, head cocked to one side. "Or will you? You could stay. I mean, you obviously like him as well."

"No, I don't."

The response was automatic, and Daisy snorted again. "Of course you don't. You should think about it though—staying on, I mean. Anyway, we'd like you to. You saved Janey that night. You could have left us, but you didn't."

She shoved her hands in her pockets and sauntered off, leaving Skylar staring after her.

They'd like her to stay?

Why should that make her feel all warm and fuzzy?

The feeling didn't last. Running a hand through her hair, she pressed her fingertips to her scalp, trying to ease the pressure. She'd never allowed herself to consider a different existence; she'd made her choices long ago and always believed that was the way things would be.

Forever.

Now, thoughts of another life teased her mind. What would it be like to turn her back on everything that was safe, to stay on *El Cazador*, to explore the universe with Rico?

For a brief moment, she imagined it was possible. But the notion was fleeting. What about duty and honor? Besides, after tomorrow, they wouldn't want her to stay.

They'd want her dead.

• • •

Skylar hit her palm to the shuttle door pad but hesitated for a moment at the top of the ramp, tugging the silver tube dress a little higher over her breasts. She'd decided against the wig—long hair could be a liability if she got into a fight—but otherwise she was identical to the first time she had boarded *El Cazador*. When she was sure everything was firmly in place, she tottered down the ramp into the docking bay, trying not to trip over her heels.

She had a feeling of déjà vu, but this time she had a welcome committee to meet her. Tannis paced the floor of the docking bay, Janey stood close to where Rico leaned casually against the curved silver wall. A mocking smile was on his face as his eyes ran hotly down over her body.

"You look gorgeous, sweetheart. I'd let you board my ship anytime."

"Let's hope the crew of the transport ship feel the same way."

"I'm sure they will. So are you all set?"

"I just need to get Janey's device implanted, then I'm good to go."

"Okay."

"I've got it here," Janey said, lifting up what looked like an old fashioned pistol. She examined Skylar, a small frown on her face, then reaching out she tugged the tube dress down so at least half of Skylar's breasts spilled out over the top. "And you've got to lose the pistol," she said, "You're supposed to be looking like a helpless damsel in distress. And really, a laser pistol does not work as an accessory to this outfit."

"Personally, I think a laser pistol is the perfect accessory for any outfit," Skylar mumbled, but she unstrapped the weapons belt and handed it to Janey.

"Okay, where do you want me?"

"We can do the implant in the shuttle."

Rico held out his hand. "I'll do it," he said. "I want a word with Skylar before she goes."

Janey glanced from one to the other, and then nodded.

"Okay, it's easy, you need to aim the tip of the gun between two ribs, about here—" She touched Skylar, just under her left breast. "And depress the trigger." She placed the gun in his outstretched hand.

Rico took Skylar's elbow and steered her back up the ramp onto her shuttle, then pushed her down into the single chair.

"Put your arms up," he said.

Skylar lifted her arms above her head. Rico tugged the dress down over her breasts. For a second, she felt self-conscious, but he didn't take advantage of the fact; he seemed all business. Crouching down beside her, he rested his hand flat against her rib cage, then his fingers stroked her, finding the spot between two ribs. He held the gun just under her left breast and depressed the trigger. Skylar felt a slight jolt of pain, but it faded to a dull ache almost immediately. Rico put down the gun, and rubbed his fingers over the spot.

"Okay?"

"Yes."

She lowered her arm. His hand went still, then slowly slid up to cup her breast. A fleeting caress and then he pulled the dress back up. Skylar tried to ignore the heat that washed over her skin, the urge to lean in close to him.

She took a deep breath. "What did you want to talk to me about?"

He straightened, turned away briefly, shoved his hands in his pockets, then looked at her. "It's not too late to back out of this."

"Out of what?"

"The whole thing. This breakout. Forget it."

Skylar searched his face. A longing rose up inside her that she could do just that. Forget the mission. Stay here; pretend she wasn't who she was. But she knew that wasn't a possibility any more than it had been yesterday. Once Rico knew what she was, she'd no longer be welcome on *El Cazador*, and it was inevitable, if she stayed, that he would find out.

"I have to help my brother," she said. "I'm all he's got."

Rico studied her for long moment, then shook his head, an unidentifiable expression flitting across his face— disappointment maybe. But why should he be disappointed? More likely, it was suspicion. The old fear came back. Did he know? But if he knew anything, then why go on with this charade?

"Okay, we go through with this," he said and she released her breath. "But before you go…"

He leaned in close and kissed the swell of her breast just above the dress, his mouth cool and soft against her skin. Then higher, his lips pressing against her throat, his tongue licking over the rapid pulse. His big hand came around the back of her neck to hold her steady while his lips plundered hers. His tongue thrust inside, filling her, tasting her.

A loud banging made her pull back. Rico crossed the small space and opened the door. Tannis stood outside, her face stamped with annoyance.

"This is your fault. You know that don't you?"

"Probably, but what's my fault this time?"

"The cooling system has broken down again."

"Shit," Rico muttered. "What does the Trog say?"

"You broke it—you fix it. He said you shouldn't have used the emergency system—it's for emergencies."

Rico flashed Skylar a glance. "My hand slipped."

"Why do I find that hard to believe? Anyway, stop canoodling and get down there and fix it."

Rico gave Skylar one last, brief, hard kiss and stepped away. "Be careful," he said.

Tannis turned to follow him, but glanced back over her shoulder. "You're going to have to go or you'll miss the interception point. Don't worry—we'll fix it and be right behind you."

"What happens if you don't fix it?"

Tannis grinned. "You're fucked." And she strode out of the shuttle, the door sliding closed behind her. Skylar stared at it for a moment, then started the takeoff sequence.

It occurred to her as the shuttle drew away from *El Cazador* that if Rico did suspect her then he need do nothing more than leave her to her fate.

• • •

Rico gave the cooling system one last bash with his hammer and stepped back. The system worked—enough to get them moving anyway. Though at some point in the not-too-distant-future they would have to dock somewhere and do some serious repairs.

The Trog waited outside the door.

"She's good," Rico said.

He received a grunt in response. The Trog turned to vanish back inside the engine room, and Rico stopped him with a hand on his arm.

"The reporter—could he have recognized you?"

"Maybe."

"Look, I don't give a fuck who you are as long as it doesn't put my ship at risk. So will it?"

"Maybe."

Rico sighed. "When this is over—we talk."

Relief washed over the Trog's face. What the hell was he hiding? Rico hoped it wasn't anything too bad—he didn't want to have to find a new engineer. The Trog was the best he'd ever come across.

"In the meantime," he said, "talk to Janey. She can check out your cover and make sure you stay hidden."

The Trog nodded and disappeared into the engine room. A minute later, Rico felt the ship vibrate beneath his feet— they were moving. He made his way up to the docking bay and into the shuttle. It was larger than Skylar's, with two seats in front of a bank of consoles.

Tannis was strapped into the copilot's seat, her shoulders tense, her eyes gleaming yellow. Daisy sat in the pilot's seat, readying the shuttle for takeoff and looking very pleased with herself. She'd be on her own, piloting the shuttle, once he and Tannis transferred to the transport ship, and Rico reckoned she might as well settle in.

He stood behind her, his fingers drumming on the console in front of him, while he stared at the comm unit, willing it to do something. It was two hours since Skylar had left, and they needed to hear she was in place before they headed out. They were already behind schedule, and Skylar would have to spend more time on the transport than he would have ideally liked. But she was a good actress—he had no doubt she would pull it off.

Finally, the comm light lit up. "Skylar, here."

She sounded cheerful, and some of the tension eased from his muscles. He'd been worried about her. The thought brought him up short. He couldn't remember the last time he'd cared enough to worry about anyone.

"Hi, sweetheart," he answered. "You in position?"

"Yup, and it's on schedule. I should intercept in less than two hours. How about you?"

"We're good to go. We'll be right behind you."

"I'll be waiting."

Rico closed the connection and turned to the others. "Well, looks like we're on."

Tannis grinned. "Everyone ready?"

"I'm ready," Daisy said, and Rico could hear the barely suppressed excitement in her voice.

"Right, let's go."

At that moment, Janey appeared in the open hatchway. She peered inside. "Captain?"

Tannis swiveled her seat. "What is it?"

"I thought this might be important. You know the cruiser that's been following us?"

"How could I forget?"

"Remember the first time it appeared, the day Skylar came on board? Well, just before it showed up, there was a comm sent from the ship."

Tannis frowned. "A comm? How did you pick it up? Or more to the point, why did you even look?"

"Rico suggested I check back for anything unusual. I nearly missed it. It's not like anything I've ever heard before—more like brain waves than electrical—and I still can't pinpoint exactly where it came from."

Tannis sat for a minute, tapping her booted toe on the ground. "How did you know?" she asked Rico.

"I didn't. I just thought the whole thing was odd."

"Hmm, well, the obvious suspect is Skylar, but it can't have been—she was with Rico."

Rico smiled at the memory. "Yes, she was, wasn't she?"

"So, does that mean we have a traitor on the ship? One of the crew?" Tannis ran a hand though her hair. "I don't believe it. Do we abort the mission?"

"No. As you say, it couldn't have been Skylar."

"But we might be compromised."

"It's probably unrelated. We'll look into it when we get back. We need to leave now if we're going to do this."

Tannis stood for a moment deep in thought. She looked at Rico suspiciously.

He kept his expression blank. "Think of all that money."

She sighed. "Okay, let's do this."

Rico turned to Janey. "Have you managed to isolate the frequency?"

"Not yet, but I will soon."

"Good. Comm it through to me when you have it. Now, I suggest we leave."

• • •

Skylar was in range. She stared at the comm unit for a minute and wondered whether she should check in again. But no—what was the point? If they did plan to let her board the transport ship and then abandon her, they would hardly be likely to tell her.

Taking a deep calming breath, she pressed the button that

sent out the shuttle's distress signal. The response came back almost immediately, which was unsurprising. Most ships and crews followed a code of ethics, and they wouldn't ignore a call for help.

"This is transporter 334, give us your identity and coordinates."

"Please," Skylar said. "I've been injured, I need medical help." She also needed visual. She pressed a few keys and leaned in close to the monitor, squeezing her arms together to show her cleavage to the best advantage.

"Switch off your engines, we're bringing you in."

The three crew members were lined up, waiting for her as she tottered down the ramp in her high heels—only too eager to help a damsel in distress. They were an unimpressive looking lot, and curiously alike; medium height and build, dressed identically in dark grey uniforms, and all three were gawping at her cleavage. Skylar's hand slid down to her waist instinctively, only to remember that her laser pistol was missing.

She tried to picture how Janey moved, slowing her steps and giving her hips an exaggerated sway. She must have been at least partially successful because the three sets of eyes never left her. Then she remembered she was supposed to be injured, so she clutched her side and added a limp. But not too bad. What she needed was to get to the bridge. She couldn't look so hurt that they took her straight to the sick-bay.

The tallest of the three stepped forward. "I'm Captain Thomas, this is Joe and Evan, Miss…"

"Skylar, Skylar Rossario. Please, don't let me stop you from your business. I just need to sit for a moment."

"I'll help you, ma'am," Captain Thomas said.

"Call me Skylar." She added what she hoped was a seductive smile. It seemed to work. The captain clamped his hand around her arm just above the elbow and hustled her along.

She sighed in relief as they came to the bridge and he insisted on helping her to a seat, refusing to relinquish his hold when they got there. Every few seconds, he squeezed her arm, while the other two stood on either side, leering down the front of her dress.

It was becoming increasingly obvious that while they were more than willing to help her, they expected her to be suitably grateful for their services.

Lovely.

But not even in the line of duty would she let any of these assholes touch her.

She considered taking them out. She could probably do it, even without her weapon, and it would feel so good. But she really couldn't take the risk, not when they were armed and she wasn't.

Putting her hand to her forehead, she let out a little moan of simulated pain as she studied the layout of the bridge through her fingers. She'd gotten used to the sleek, graceful lines of *El Cazador*. By comparison, this ship was utilitarian, bordering on downright ugly. She spotted the control panel she needed directly opposite where she sat, but she had no chance of getting to it with the crew sticking so close.

She dropped her hand. "I'm really not feeling too well. Could I possibly have some air?"

She hoped they'd take the hint and move away—no such

luck.

"You look fine to me." The captain gave her arm another squeeze. "Doesn't she look good to you, Joe?"

Joe licked his lips. "Good enough to eat."

Now she really did feel ill.

El Cazador would be in range by now, just waiting for Skylar to knock out the shields. She wasn't too worried yet. If she couldn't get to the control panel, she still had Janey's gadget as backup. All she needed to do was convince them to scan her. She clutched her stomach. "Please, I think something is seriously wrong."

No one moved. Heartless bunch—she could be dying here.

Gritting her teeth, she raised her head, widened her eyes, and batted her lashes at the man beside her. "Please, Joe, I hurt. Right here." She ran a hand over her left breast and pressed her ribcage. Three sets of eyes followed the movement. She licked her lips. "Check me out, and I promise I'll be grateful."

Joe grinned. "I'll go get the scanner."

At last.

He was back in seconds. He ran the scanner over her breasts, frowning as he read the readings. He shook the machine, and Skylar bit back her frustration.

"I said, here." Grabbing his hand, she guided the scanner to the right place.

Nothing happened.

Had Janey's brilliant gadget failed?

Skylar gritted her teeth and pressed the scanner a little closer. The shrill sound of the ship's alarm rang out of the bridge.

"What the fuck…?"

Skylar made to rise from the chair, but the grip around her upper arm tightened, and she was shoved back into the seat.

"What's happening?" She tried to keep her tone innocent. Right now was the most dangerous time, but with a bit of luck, they wouldn't suspect her.

"Perhaps you could tell us."

The captain rammed his laser pistol into the side of her neck, and she clamped her lips together. There was no point in saying anything now. All she could do was wait. Joe still stood beside her chair, the scanner hanging from his hand. The third man was stationed at the control panel, and after a minute, the shrill scream of the alarm ceased.

He turned. "There's no damage. It must be a malfunction."

"A very convenient malfunction." The captain jabbed the pistol harder into her throat, and Skylar winced.

"Talk."

When she remained silent, he drew back the pistol and smashed it across her cheekbone. The blow slammed her head against the seat, and warm blood trickled down her face.

Holy fucking Meridian that hurt.

He hit her again, and for a moment, her vision blurred.

Where the hell was Rico?

She blinked, clearing her sight, and when she opened her eyes, there he was, standing in the doorway, legs braced, laser pistol held loosely at his side, a small smile playing across his gorgeous face. The rest of the room faded, and Skylar couldn't prevent the grin from spreading across her own face.

"You all right?" Rico asked.

"Brilliant."

The pistol jabbed in her throat again, bringing her back to reality.

"Anyone moves," the captain said, "and the bitch is dead."

"Oh, please." Skylar rolled her eyes at the cliché, but held herself perfectly still.

Rico turned his gaze to the captain, the lazy smile sliding from his eyes, leaving them cold as black ice. "I don't suppose you would consider surrendering?" When no one replied, he shrugged. "I thought not." He cast Skylar a wry grin. "Sorry, sweetheart."

For a moment, the words made no sense. Then he raised the laser pistol smoothly, aimed it straight at her heart.

In that final second, thoughts raced through her mind.

Did he know? Was it all a setup? Had he always known?

Her vision narrowed on the pistol. The laser flashed, and the blast slammed into her, breaking the grip on her arm and crashing her to the floor. Everything went black.

She must have been out only for a few seconds. When she blinked her eyes open, nobody had moved. Except her. She was lying on the cold, metal floor—and it looked like it hadn't been cleaned since the ship was built. She ran a quick internal diagnostic and realized she was basically unharmed. Nothing but stunned.

Rico hadn't tried to kill her.

Still, it hurt like hell.

A laser fired over her head, and a body crashed to the floor beside her. The face was half gone, burnt away, and the smell of roasting flesh filled her nostrils. It was the captain, and she crawled to him on her elbows and tugged the pistol from his clenched fingers.

She lifted her head and peered around. Tannis stood just inside the door, Rico beside her. As she watched, a laser blast spun the pistol from his hand. He snarled and hurled himself across the floor, a blur of speed, slamming into the second man, gripping his skull between his large hands. Skylar winced at the sound of bones snapping. Rico released his hold, and the body dropped to the floor.

Of the crew, only Joe remained standing. He appeared bewildered, the scanner still dangling from one hand. When Rico turned toward him, he dropped the machine and fumbled for his pistol. Rico stalked closer, nostrils flaring as though he scented prey.

Skylar wanted to look away, but her gazed remained fixed on the tableau in front of her. She had seen a lot of killing in her life. But nothing like this.

For the first time, it struck home that Rico was not human. He'd told her he had been at one time. Now, he was something else. And that something was pure predator.

A pair of boots appeared in her field of vision. She managed to tear her gaze from Rico and look up. Tannis stood over her, her face impassive, one hand extended. Skylar took it and pulled herself to her feet. They both turned back to watch. With the urgency gone, Rico appeared almost languid as he reached out, wrapped his fingers around Joe's throat, and pulled him close.

She realized the first two crew members had been fortunate—they had died swiftly. Joe was not so lucky. Rico held him in a powerful embrace, close against his chest, his fist clenched in the man's hair. He pulled back the head, baring the line of his victim's throat. For a moment, Rico held himself still, then he stared straight at Skylar. She shivered but couldn't look away—his eyes glowed with crimson fire as he lowered his head, and his fangs pierced the man's vein.

"Does he do this often?" Skylar asked in a low voice.

"Not often," Tannis replied. "Thank God. He's actually pretty well-behaved for a bloodsucking monster. He told me recently that regular sex kept the monster at bay. I thought it was just an excuse, but"—she looked from Skylar back to Rico—"I guess he hasn't been getting any."

"Right, blame me," Skylar muttered. She rubbed at her chest where the laser blast had hit her. "The bastard shot me."

Tannis grinned. "All part of the plan. And I did offer to do the shooting but I don't think he trusted me to switch my laser to stun. Come on, we have work to do. Eyeballs and blood samples to collect. Then we can clear up this mess and get on with the job."

Skylar blinked and forced her gaze away. Kicking off her high heels, she tugged up the neckline of her silver tube dress, and took the knife Tannis handed her. "Okay, which one's first?"

She kept an eye on Rico as they worked. He'd finished feeding, casually dropping the body to the floor, but he kept his distance, pacing the room. His hair had come loose from its ponytail during the fighting and hung across his shoulders. He ran a hand through it, then his eyes caught hers and he smiled, flashing his fangs. He appeared totally wired. She'd known what he was, but that was still different from seeing it with her own eyes. A shiver ran through her. She swallowed, shook herself, and got to work.

CHAPTER EIGHTEEN

Rico couldn't drag his eyes from the black hole that filled the screen. It was beautiful, a vision of whirling iridescent gases surrounding a gaping maw.

For so long, he'd battled the pull of his own personal darkness. Now, something in the stygian blackness called to him, and he had to fight the urge to dive headfirst into that well of eternal night. Discover whatever awaited him on the other side.

"Rico!" Tannis spoke sharply from behind him.

"What?" he said, without turning from the screen.

"We're getting awfully close to that black hole."

He shrugged. "We haven't hit the Event Horizon, yet."

"Isn't that the point of no return? The point where that thing sucks us in and totally obliterates us? Don't you think it might be a good idea if we *never* hit the Event Horizon?" Her voice was even, but he could detect a hint of panic underneath.

Rico sighed and forced his gaze away from the darkness.

Not today—he wasn't ready quite yet.

And they *were* getting close. He switched the ship to manual. This was going to be tricky, and he was old-fashioned enough to trust himself above a machine. The navigation system of the transport ship was sluggish and heavy after *El Cazador,* and he could feel the gravitational pull of the black hole, dragging the ship closer.

"There it is," Tannis said.

He saw it then. Trakis One, dark ochre encircled by spiraling radiation rings of palest yellow to blood crimson. A single moon revolved lazily around the planet. He knew from their research that the orbit and size of Trakis One kept it from the pull of the black hole. But anything approaching had no chance. Except for the brief period when that moon passed between them. Denser than the planet, despite being smaller, it would provide sufficient cover for a ship to reach the planet's surface—he hoped.

Beside him, Tannis was counting down. "You ready?"

He nodded.

"Right. Three, two, one, go!"

Rico slammed on the forward thrusters. Not a lot happened. They slowed a little, but were still heading into the darkness.

"We're still getting closer."

He ground his teeth. "I know."

"Holy crap. We're going in. Do something, Rico."

"I am doing something." He focused on the screen. It did indeed seem as though they'd be swallowed, but at the last moment, the moon slipped fully between them. Freed of the pull, the ship shot forward, around the orbiting moon, and they were on a direct course for Trakis One.

"*Dios mio*," Rico muttered.

They were heading straight for what appeared to be a ball of fiery gases. After only a couple of minutes, he felt the heat burning through the strengthened hull. *El Cazador* would have been ashes by now. Rico wiped the sweat from his forehead before turning to look at Skylar.

"Have we got those codes from Janey yet?" he asked. "We're not going anywhere without them."

Skylar frantically tapped into her console. After a second, she flashed him a grin. "Got them. Or at least she thinks so."

"Thinks?"

"We'll soon find out."

She came to stand beside him, rested a hand on his shoulder, and showed him the screen. She fizzed with barely suppressed excitement, and he reached up and squeezed her hand. She started in surprise but then smiled.

"Here goes nothing," Rico said and switched on the comm unit. "This is Transporter 334, requesting permission to dock."

"Enter your access codes."

He tapped in the codes and held his breath.

"You are cleared for docking. Switch off your engines, and we'll bring you in."

He flipped off the comm, switched off the engine, and swiveled his chair to face Skylar and Tannis.

"Wow, we did it," Skylar said. "We're actually in."

"Did you ever doubt it?" He grinned. "After all, we are the best."

Skylar still wore that sexy little dress, and the vast amounts of bare skin on show gleamed with sweat in the heat. Rico gave in to the urge and dragged her down into his lap. He breathed in the scent of hot, excited woman, and then he kissed her. Her mouth opened beneath his, and he pushed his tongue inside, losing himself in the taste of her.

Behind them, Tannis coughed loudly.

Rico pulled back. "Soon," he murmured in Skylar's ear.

"Could you please leave off the somewhat nauseating celebrations until we're out of here," Tannis said. "We have less than an hour. If we're not away by then, we're stuck here for another fifteen days, which probably translates to forever. So let's be quick."

Rico kissed Skylar one last time and released his hold. She scrambled to her feet, and brushed down the dress, but a small smile still lifted her full lips. They all turned to stare at the screen as the ship was pulled relentlessly toward Trakis One. Up close, the planet didn't appear any more hospitable; nothing on the surface showed any sign of life.

A hatch opened beneath the shuttle. Rico's hands tightened on the arms of his chair as the tractor beam caught them and slowly sucked them inside. They landed, and the hatch closed above them.

"Right," Rico said, "let's get the supplies unloaded, find Jonny, and we'll be back in no time."

"We'd better be," Tannis muttered.

Rico ignored her. He and Tannis were both dressed in the uniforms of the transport crew. Luckily, they'd been able to find spares in the cabins. They were clean or at least cleaner than what the corpses had been wearing. His was uncomfortably tight around the crotch, Tannis's was too loose, but they'd pass. Skylar was still in her silver dress, as she wouldn't be getting off the ship. She looked good enough to eat and he couldn't resist a quick kiss on the lips. She tasted as good as she looked. "Don't do anything I wouldn't do," he said, stepping back.

"Well, that doesn't narrow things down much." Tannis replied. "Come on, we have company."

"They're here to collect the supplies," Skylar said. "At least I hope that's why they're here. I'll open up the cargo hold."

"And we'll be off."

"Good luck."

Rico gave her one last look as they left the bridge. He still had no clue how this was going to play out, but his gut was tight with anticipation.

They passed a group of men in grey all-in-one outfits that he presumed must be convicts here to unload the ship. He ignored them and led the way across the docking bay as though he knew where he was going. If they were questioned, then chances were they would have to fight. It wasn't the end of the world—he was guessing he and Tannis were more than a match for the guards here, however many there were. But he'd rather it not come to that. He was full-up, and he hated waste. The only thing he wanted to taste right now was Skylar. Soon. He tugged at his too tight pants.

"Get your mind off your dick and concentrate," Tannis said from beside him.

They came to a halt in front of a small door at the far side of the docking bay. They were out of sight of the ship, but Tannis glanced around before she pulled a small bag from inside her jacket and took something out.

A flash of distaste crossed her face. "Ugh."

It was a severed hand, the skin already tinged with grey.

Tannis pressed it against the door panel. For a moment, it seemed like it wasn't going to work, then the door opened with a hiss.

Rico followed Tannis into a grey corridor, the walls and ceiling curved like a tunnel. As the door shut behind them, a shudder ran through him.

"I hate prisons," he said. Just the smell—too many people, too close together—that hung in the air was enough to make him want to whirl around and get out of there. Fast.

"You ever been in prison?" Tannis asked.

"Oh, yeah." Over fifteen hundred years, and he could still remember what it was like to be chained, his freedom taken from him. "And it's never going to happen again."

He'd been locked up in other places since then—Tannis had once rescued him from one—but he had only one experience of a real prison, and it was imprinted indelibly on his mind. The stench of hopelessness.

Far off in the distance, he could hear the muted sound of thousands of incarcerated souls. He shook off the feeling. Whatever happened here, no one was ever locking him up again.

Tannis led the way down the corridor until they reached a junction. She flipped on the palm screen and studied the map Fergal had given them. "This way."

The sound of voices grew louder, but hopefully, if all went to plan, they wouldn't even have to enter the main prison.

Would Skylar betray them in some way? He didn't think there was much danger at this point, because he could see no purpose in luring them here just to imprison them. No, if she were going to double-cross them, then it would be after they got the prisoner away from here. That would be the time to watch her. Even so, a trickle of sweat ran down between his shoulder blades.

Tannis stopped and held up a hand. The corridor had widened, and up ahead a single door, with a clear panel at the front, blocked their way. Through it he could see what he hoped was the main control room for the prison. It seemed full of men, but when he counted, there were only five.

"Maximum stun," Skylar whispered.

Rico nodded and drew his pistol. They sidled up to the door, and Tannis once again pressed the severed hand to the panel. This time, nothing happened. It wasn't entirely unexpected—Fergal had told them that the transport ship's crew didn't have access to the control room. Even so, Tannis swore softly.

Then she shot out the panel.

Rico kicked open the door as the raucous scream of the alarms sounded overhead. He quickly assimilated the scene and took out the two men standing to the right of him. Tannis shot the one on her left and Rico blasted the fourth sitting at the console just as he was rising. He fell back into the chair, which toppled over with a crash. Only one man remained standing. From the description Fergal had given them, this had to be 'mean as a snake' Peters. He looked mean, with a narrow face, dark slits for eyes, and sickly pale skin. His hand went to the pistol at his side.

"Don't," Rico said in a low voice.

He pointed his weapon at Peters. "And could you turn off that goddamn noise? It's giving me a headache." Peters didn't move. "Now. And send out the message that it was a false alarm."

Peters reached out with a trembling hand and pressed something on the console. The noise vanished.

"Right," Tannis said, "we can do this two ways. This way." She held up the severed hand. It took Peters a second or two to realize what she was holding, and then the color leached from his face. Tannis smiled. "Or you can cooperate. Your choice."

Peters opened his mouth and no sound came out. Tannis drew the serrated blade from the belt at her waist. Peters cleared his throat and tried again. "I'll cooperate."

. . .

Skylar sat on the bridge of the transport ship, drumming her fingers on the console in front of her. The end was so close now, but she hated the waiting.

She tried to concentrate on her next move. Once they had the prisoner off-planet, her best bet was to get him into her shuttle and straight to the Corps space cruiser, which she presumed was still somewhere close by. The original plan was to take the prisoner to *El Cazador* and rendezvous with her people there. But if she did that, then there was a good chance the whole crew would be heading for the mines. On the other hand, if she didn't go back to *El Cazador*, her crew might have enough of a head start to get away.

She had a suspicion that sidestepping Rico and his reward wouldn't be that easy, but she'd find a way. She had a brief, sharp pang of—she didn't know what—disappointment, regret maybe. But she couldn't allow herself to think like that. She had limited choices here. There was no future for her on

El Cazador.

Rising to her feet, she paced the floor until she tripped over her shoes. She stared down at herself—she still wore the stupid dress and ridiculous high heels. Why hadn't she brought a change of clothing? She considered a quick trip to her shuttle, but she didn't want to leave the bridge in case something happened.

Flinging herself back in the seat, she flipped between the external cameras, trying to locate Rico. Nothing moved in the docking bay. The area was huge, cavernous, and empty except for a small space cruiser that stood, partially hidden, in the far corner.

Her gaze moved past it, then back again.

There was supposed to be no way off Trakis One apart from the transport ship Skylar now sat in. She clearly remembered Tannis saying no ships were stationed on the planet—another of the security measures.

The ship was clearly modified for the radiation on Trakis One, but otherwise bore no name, no markings. A trickle of unease ran down her spine. Kicking off her shoes, she rose to her feet and searched the bridge. She spotted the laser pistols taken from the dead crew and strapped one over her silver dress. She started to walk away, then turned and strapped on a second, so a pistol hung at either side.

Outside the ship, the air felt cool against her sweat-damp skin, the floor icy beneath her bare feet. She made her way around the outside of the docking bay, coming up behind the unmarked cruiser. It was locked up tight, and Skylar was pretty sure no one was on board. She stood for a minute, eyeing the ship, deciding what to do next. Should she warn Rico? But warn him of what?

She had to think this through. It made no sense. The ship must have been stationed here since the last lunar cycle. Fifteen days. Five days before she'd ever boarded *El Cazador*.

It couldn't be tied to their hijack of the transport ship.

Of course, it might be totally unrelated. But she didn't believe that. Which meant that someone who knew of her mission had sent the ship to Trakis One. Had the information been leaked? The colonel wouldn't be happy.

She turned on her internal comm unit, but nothing came through, only a buzz of static. Obviously, no one wanted to talk to her.

A door opened opposite where she stood. Skylar took cover behind the cruiser as four men stepped through, the familiar black uniform of the Corps instantly recognizable.

"Shit," she whispered.

She watched as they crossed the floor. One of them entered the transport ship through the open hatch. He came out a minute later, shaking his head, and they all disappeared behind the ship. Drawing her laser pistol, Skylar took a step forward.

"Stand down, Lieutenant."

She stopped in her tracks as the colonel's words came through her internal comm link.

"Sir?"

"Stand down. You've achieved your mission."

She frowned. *"No, sir. My mission was to get the prisoner off Trakis One."*

"No, Lieutenant, your mission was to prove that the security here is inadequate."

It took a minute for the words to make sense. When they did, disbelief flooded her. *"You're saying this is nothing more than a training exercise?"*

"Correct. Now, stand down."

Anger coiled in her gut when she thought of what she had been through to set this up. She was aware the colonel hated the officer in charge of security here, but she was finding it hard to believe this whole thing came down to nothing more than political infighting. Her boss trying to prove a point.

And what about the crew of the transport ship? They'd been assholes, but they hadn't deserved to die for a fucking training exercise. Was that really worth anyone dying for? *"You should have told me."*

"This was need to know." The colonel spoke sharply. *"Is there a problem, Lieutenant?"*

She ground her teeth. *"No, sir."*

"Good."

"Sir?"

"Yes?"

"What happens to the crew I hired?"

"If they surrender, they'll be shipped to the Meridian mines with the prisoner. If not…"

Skylar could almost hear his mental shrug. If not, then she had no doubt they would be eliminated. She slid the pistol back in her holster, forced her tight muscles to relax.

"I understand, sir."

She turned and stared at the door where Rico and Tannis would emerge. And walk straight into an ambush.

CHAPTER NINETEEN

"Hey, wouldn't it be funny if we took the wrong one back," Rico said, eyeing the line of cryo-tubes.

"Fucking hilarious," Tannis replied. "But no worries, they're labeled and lined up alphabetically." She turned to Peters and nudged him with her pistol. "I'm impressed—very organized."

Peters didn't answer, and Tannis moved down the line, reading the little plaques on the bottom of the tubes. She tapped on one of the tubes. "Here he is."

Rico wiped the front with his sleeve and peered inside. "Yup, that's him."

"How do you know?"

"I asked Skylar for a picture—thought we might need it."

"You're *so* clever." She didn't sound pleased with the idea. "Okay, let's get him out of here. We need our friend to unlock him from the line. Peters?"

Rico tapped his foot on the floor while he waited for

the scanner to do its stuff with Peters. He wanted out of this place—they had what they'd come for, now it was time to head home. The thought made him smile—how long since he had had somewhere he actually considered home? He couldn't remember.

"You know," Tannis said as she pulled the cryo tube free from the line, "I reckon security has gotten pretty sloppy in this place. I mean, we shouldn't have been able to do this so easily." She turned to Peters. "You reckon you'll get a slapped wrist over this? Maybe we can do something to prevent that. Now, make yourself useful—push."

They made it back to the door leading into the docking bay without seeing anyone. Tannis nodded to Peters, and he pressed his palm to the panel and the door opened. All appeared quiet outside. The unloading looked like it was finished. Now, all they needed was a nice clean getaway.

"What do we do with him?" Tannis asked, waving her pistol in the direction of Peters.

Rico didn't hesitate. He remembered what Fergal had said about this man—a sadistic bastard. "Kill him."

Tannis shrugged, raised the pistol to the back of his head, and squeezed the trigger. Peters fell to the ground.

"Now, let's get out of here."

Rico pushed the cryo-tube through the door. "Piece of cake," he said to Tannis.

He kept his pace steady, but the spot between his shoulder blades itched with the need to get out of there. He couldn't understand why he felt so uneasy.

Everything had gone according to plan. They were only a few feet from the transport ship when a voice called out behind them.

"Stop where you are."

From the pitch of the man's voice, Rico could tell they were in trouble. He stopped and slowly pivoted, easing his hand onto his laser pistol.

Tannis turned beside him and swore softly.

Rico counted six guards, but at least their weapons were still holstered. They probably weren't expecting a fight when the numbers were on their side. A tall man with sergeant's stripes stepped to the front of the group.

"Take your hands away from your weapons and place them behind your heads."

Like that was going to happen.

Rico glanced sideways at Tannis and saw the almost imperceptible nod of her head. His muscles tightened in readiness.

They drew their lasers in unison. Six blasts took the six guards down before they had a chance to unholster their weapons. Rico stood for a minute in the ensuing silence, laser aimed until he was sure no one was going to move again. Ever.

Tannis released her breath and shoved her pistol into its holster. "Right," she said. "Can we go now?"

"Not so fast," Rico murmured. "They know we're here." He crossed the room and opened the control panel, blasted the insides. "Just disabling the tractor beam."

"What about opening the hatch."

"It has proximity sensors, it should open."

"Should?" She shook her head. "Come on. We have five minutes to get off this piece-of-crap planet."

Rico started pushing the cryo tube toward the transport

ship. He'd only gone a few feet when Tannis stopped him with a hand on his arm. "What now?" he muttered.

"Look, Rico."

Four men appeared from behind the ship. Rico's breath caught in his throat as he recognized the uniforms.

"Shit, Rico," Tannis said from beside him. "They're Collective."

"They're not only Collective—they're Corps."

"Look at their eyes." Her tone was full of awe.

All four sets of eyes glowed violet, inhuman, and a shiver of unease ran down his spine. Unlike the guards, their weapons were already drawn. He wondered, briefly, what had happened to Skylar, and a wave of regret washed over him. Damn, he'd wanted to get to know her. Too late now.

"Well, it was nice knowing you," he said to Tannis.

"We going to fight?"

"You *want* to end up in the mines?"

She shook her head. "We fight."

"Are you ready?"

"No."

Rico grinned. He took a deep breath and…

"Rico, get down!"

Skylar's voice. But from behind them. Rico grabbed Tannis, hurled her to the floor, and covered her with his body. The heat of the laser shots passed close over them, and he kept his head down. After a few seconds, the shooting stopped, and he peered up.

The four men were down. Skylar stood, still in that sexy silver dress, her feet bare, her legs braced, a laser pistol in each hand.

She raised an eyebrow. "You going to lie there all day?"

He'd never seen anything quite so beautiful in his whole life.

"They're down for now, but they're not dead, and there'll be others," Skylar continued, when he didn't move. "Besides, we only have three minutes to get off this planet."

Rico got to his feet and pulled Tannis up. "Thanks," she said. "Now let's get the fuck out of here."

...

Rico pushed the cryo tube the last few feet and then up the ramp and into the transport ship. For a second, Skylar hovered, unsure what to do. It occurred to her fleetingly that she should stay, but decided that was a bad idea. Instead, she raced after Rico. Tannis followed close behind, smashing her hand into the panel so the door closed behind them.

When she reached the bridge at a run, Rico was already in the pilot's chair and the engines were rumbling. They rose from the ground, and she waited for him to hit the boosters and get them the hell out of there.

"Rico, now would be good," Tannis said.

"*Dios*—problem—looks like those proximity sensors are fucked after all." He stared down at the console. "Where the hell are the bloody blasters?"

"There," Skylar said, pointing to a red panel set in the console. Rico thumped his hand down and the ships guns shot out. The blast missed the exit hatch and blew a hole in the wall instead. Rico swore, adjusted the range, and shot again. This time the blast took the hatch dead center.

They couldn't see through the flames and smoke, but they

headed for the middle. Skylar closed her eyes, waiting to hear the scrape of metal, but then they were through. She opened one eye and peeked out. They were heading away from the planet fast.

Up ahead, on the monitor, Skylar could see the moon and behind that the black star, just peeping out, but getting more visible with each second. A huge, gaping hole in the fabric of the universe. What was on the other side?

As she watched, the ship slowed.

Tannis had been pacing the bridge, now she came to stand in front of Rico, hands fisted at her hips. "Rico, we have less than a minute to get past that thing before we won't be going anywhere except maybe headfirst into that black hole."

"I know."

She gritted her teeth. "So? Could we shift here?"

"We could, but maybe not just yet." He flicked on a second monitor, which showed the view behind and a ship growing bigger as it raced toward them. Skylar recognized it as the cruiser that had been parked in the docking bay on Trakis One. She was closing fast.

Up ahead of them was the hole, behind them the ship, and Skylar realized what Rico meant to do—if they timed it right, went through at the last moment, then the cruiser would have to give up or…

"If they have a brain between them, they'll realize what I'm doing and they'll fuck off back to the planet. Where they will have to wait fifteen days before they can come after us. If they don't have a brain…"

They'd keep going and be sucked into the black hole. Skylar shuddered, but couldn't help but hope that somewhere on the ship following was someone with a brain.

"They're coming into range," Tannis said.

The blast took them straight on. The lights flickered, but the shielding held. It wouldn't for long.

"They're shooting to kill," Tannis said. "They are not playing games here—the next one will get through."

"I'm guessing they're pissed," Rico said. "Time to go." He slammed his palm down on the boosters, and they shot forward. They were skimming past the moon and Skylar could feel the gravitational tug. Had he left it too late? But then they were out of the gravity range and the ship was running free and at top speed.

Skylar stared at the monitor; the cruiser was still coming. She bit her lip but couldn't force her gaze away. Briefly, it seemed as though their pursuers might make it, then the cruiser suddenly lurched to the side. Almost as though in slow motion, she was dragged inexorable toward the darkness. For a second, her lights shone bright against the stygian blackness, and then the cruiser was gone.

· · ·

Once they were clear of the planet, Rico switched the navigation system to automatic. Skylar leaned against the wall next to the cryo-unit. She'd put her shoes back on, and the heels made her legs appear endless. *Dios*, she was sexy in that dress, and the weapon belts strapped to her waist just made her sexier. Her eyes caught his, and she looked away quickly.

She was going to try to avoid paying her debt. He wasn't about to let that happen. She might have saved his life back there on Trakis One, but a deal was a deal. Besides, it wasn't as though she wouldn't enjoy it.

Tannis strolled across the deck. She stared in through the glass window of the cryo-unit. "That's *little* Jonny?" she asked, and Rico could hear the disbelief in her voice.

He peered in and grinned. The man was enormous. Rico turned to Skylar. "He doesn't look much like you."

"He's actually only a half-brother. Same father, different mother. I call him little because I was ten when he was born so he was…" She shrugged. "…little. It just became habit. How long until he wakes up?"

Tannis examined the control panel. She pressed a few buttons. "There, it's started, but a good few hours, I would think."

"Perhaps we could load him into my shuttle. Do you want me to transfer the balance of the fee now?"

"Actually," Rico said, "that can wait until we get back to the ship. And little Jonny stays here for the moment."

Skylar dragged her gaze from the cryo-unit to Rico. "I'd like him with me."

No way was he letting Skylar out of his sight. Certainly, he wasn't going to let her take their new friend and disappear as he suspected she might. He wanted his reward. He wanted answers even more. He'd considered waiting until they were all safely back on board *El Cazador,* but he had a feeling that things could go badly wrong very quickly. This might be his only chance to get her alone, show her a little of what they could have together, convince her that she had options.

"Darling," he said, "I'll be with you. We have some unfinished business, you and me."

Her eyes widened. "We do?"

"Oh yeah. And having your brother present might just cramp my style."

"But…."

He didn't give her a chance to say anything further. He moved in close, took her arm, and hustled her toward the door. He turned to Tannis. "We'll see you back at the ship. We'll be a couple of hours. At least."

On board the shuttle, he slammed the hatch and sat down in the pilot's seat. Within minutes, they had undocked and were heading into space. Away from *El Cazador*.

Rico set the autopilot and swiveled his chair to look at Skylar.

• • •

Why not?

The words echoed in her mind as she stared at Rico. He sat in the only chair, his long legs stretched out in front of him, arms clasped behind his head, his eyes half-closed as he waited for her to come to a decision.

She knew he wouldn't force her, and she wasn't sure that made it any better. At least if he forced her, when the world came crashing around her ears she could tell herself she'd had no choice. But that was the coward's way, and she'd never been a coward.

He was beautiful, with the lean, masculine grace of a predator, and she wanted him more than she had ever wanted anything in her life. And she'd had a long life.

But it was more than mere lust. She'd been alone since Daniel had died. She could have taken lovers, but she'd chosen not to, and now the need to connect physically with another being rose inside her. Something about Rico called to her as no one else had done over the years. She wanted to hold him, to make love, but she also wanted to lie with him afterwards, feel him close to her.

Why not? Just the once.

There were lots of reasons why not. The main one being, she needed to get the prisoner and deliver him back to the Collective. If she did that, she might just avoid demotion, though she doubted it. The colonel had to be really pissed off at her right about now. They would probably toss her out of the Corps. At the least, she had put her career back a good many years.

But right now, her brain couldn't seem to concentrate on that. All she could think of was how good it had felt to give in to him. She remembered the taste of him and licked her lips. He'd been so big and hard and…. She shifted from one foot to the other.

She knew that if he could tell all about her from the taste of her blood, then afterward she'd have no option but to kill him. Her gaze shifted to the cabinet where she'd hidden the long blade—just in case. A wooden stake would have been better, but there had been nowhere to get one of those. And according to her research, beheading should be enough. She flinched at the thought, but realized she'd prepared for this, that all along she had known she would give in. The thought made her stomach churn.

"Come on, sweetheart," Rico murmured. "You're giving me a headache with all this thinking." He rose to his feet, never taking his eyes from her. "Both you and I know this is going to happen."

He took a step toward her, and she held up a hand. He stopped.

"Just one thing," she said.

His eyes narrowed. "As long as it's a quick 'one thing.'"

"The whole bloodsucking thing is spooking me out." She bit her lip. "I'm not trying to back out, but will you make love to me first?"

Rico considered her for a moment. Finally, he nodded once. The tension oozed out of her, and she pushed the last of her doubts to the back of her mind. At least she would have this.

His hand went to his waist, and he flicked the fastener of his weapons belt. Then to his thigh. He flicked the second, and the belt clashed to the floor. He took another step toward her. She swallowed.

"I love that dress, but take it off," he ordered softly.

A fire roared into life in the pit of her stomach. She unfastened her own weapons and dropped them to the floor at her feet. Hooking her fingers in the top of the silver tube dress, she peeled the clinging material down and stepped out of it, to stand before him in nothing but a silver thong and the silver platform shoes. She made to kick them off.

He shook his head. "Leave them on."

His eyes burned over her skin, lingering on her breasts until her nipples tightened to hard little points that ached for his touch. Then lower, so a fire coiled in her belly, and moist heat welled up between her clenched thighs.

She watched as Rico studied the cabin of the shuttle. There weren't a lot of options; the shuttle was small. His gaze finally settled on the pilot's chair. He slid his palm into hers, led her across, and pushed her down gently. Her legs gave way, and she collapsed back, staring up as he perused her, his head tilted to one side, dark eyes gleaming with hunger and need. And the realization that he needed her as much as she did him soothed away any doubts that still lingered.

Reaching down, his fingers slid between her thighs. He lifted first one leg, then the other and placed them over the arms of the chair.

She sprawled, quiescent, her body throbbing with arousal, her breath coming in short, sharp pants, waiting for his next move. He trailed his hand over her breast, across the flat plane of her belly, then hooked a finger in the silver thong and ripped it away.

"*Dios*, but you're pretty."

He sank to his knees between her thighs and breathed in deeply. His cool breath brushed the sensitive skin of her inner thighs, and every muscle she possessed clenched tight.

"Payback time," he murmured and slowly lowered his head.

At the first touch of his tongue, Skylar's eyes drifted closed. She held her breath as he licked from the cleft in her buttocks, over her already drenched opening, pushing his tongue inside, up toward the inflamed nub between her thighs, stopping just short, so she moaned in delicious need. He repeated the move, always leaving her wanting more until she reached up and curled her hand around his skull and dragged his head toward her, pushing herself up against his mouth.

He laughed softly, took her swollen clit in his mouth, and suckled. Her hand dropped from him. Her head fell back, and she moaned. He bit down and pleasure poured through her, arching her back as she immediately came. She struggled against him, out of control, and his hands grasped her thighs. His fingers dug into her flesh, holding her open while his tongue continued to work. Pleasure pulsed through her. Finally, he kissed her one last time and raised his head. She forced her eyes open.

"I was planning on taking my time," Rico said, his expression faintly rueful.

She opened her mouth, but no words came out, the pleasure still buzzing through her. He ran the pad of his thumb over her sensitized clit, and she nearly leapt from the chair.

She lay back and watched as he undressed for her. He pulled his shirt over his head, tossed it on the ground. His skin was pale, smooth over the swell of muscles. A narrow line of hair disappeared into his waistband, and she held her breath as he opened the fastener and dragged his pants down. He was already fully aroused, his shaft thick, the head swollen and blushed dark with blood as it arched up against his lean belly. She licked her lips, and his cock twitched. Taking it in his fist, he squeezed. His head went back, and he groaned. "Tell me what you want," he said.

"I want you," she whispered.

. . .

She looked so beautiful sitting there. Beautiful and bemused as though the pleasure had taken her by surprise. Swiping his tongue over his lower lip, he tasted the salty sweetness of her. His gums ached with the need to savor her blood.

She had come much too fast. He'd wanted to prolong her pleasure, force every other man she had ever known from her mind until there was only him.

Now, she was sitting almost primly, her thighs clasped together, and she kept shooting wary glances at his cock; it did nothing for his control, but she seemed unaware of the effect she was having on him.

"I get the impression it's been a long time for you," he said.

Surprise flashed across her face. He could see her mind working, deciding whether to deny it. Instead, she shrugged. "You don't want to know how long."

Actually, he did want to know, but he didn't push it—that wasn't a conversation to have just now. He reckoned it would be a definite mood killer. And right now, he wanted to sink himself into her hot, silky depths. "Tell me if I hurt you."

She looked at his cock and nodded, and the muscles in his belly cramped. Rico picked her up, and she wrapped her legs around his waist. Turning, he sat down in the chair, positioning her knees on either side of his hips. For long moments, he held her close, breathing in the wild, musky scent of her sex. He stroked a hand down over her breasts. She was lean, no spare fat, but her skin was soft and her breasts were a heavy weight in his palm. Bending over her, he took one swollen nipple into his mouth while one hand went between her thighs and parted her sex with skillful fingers. The head of his cock nudged at her opening. He raised his head to look at her, and her eyes were wild.

"Ready?" he asked.

Without answering, she put her hands to his shoulders, held his gaze as she pushed herself down, sheathing him inside her. She was so tight, and he held himself still, savoring the feeling.

When he could wait no longer, his hands moved to her hips and lower to cup the firm globes of her ass, and he moved her on him. The drag of her muscles was exquisite, and he shoved into her harder this time. He could already feel the orgasm building in his balls, sending ripples of pleasure through his spine. He grasped her tighter, pushed her down, grinding her sensitive core against him until she whimpered. He knew she was close, and he slid one hand between their bodies, massaged her clit with the tip of his finger. She exploded against him. He released his control, holding her hips and thrusting into her, feeling the ripples of her pleasure tugging at his cock.

He wrapped his arms around her, pulled her against his chest as the waves of pure bliss pulsated from his shaft, through his whole body until it burst in an explosion of pleasure.

His head fell back against the chair and he lay, eyes closed, sated. For the moment.

Finally, he opened his eyes to find her watching him, her own eyes wary. He was overwhelmed by the urge to comfort her, tell her everything was going to be fine. He couldn't find the words, and instead he wrapped his hand around her neck and pulled her towards him. He kissed her long and deep, felt the tension ease from her as the hunger rose inside him, and his gums ached with the need to feed. He couldn't remember a hunger like this, as though he would die without the taste of her.

He backed off and stared into her eyes. "You know what I want?"

She nodded. "Rico, I just wanted to…" she trailed off and shrugged, then raised her chin, baring the smooth line of her throat.

He smiled at her fixed expression. "Don't look so worried, *querida*. This isn't going to hurt."

"Querida—what does that mean?"

"It's Spanish for 'darling.' Now relax—you'll enjoy it, I promise."

He stroked the pad of his thumb down the line of her throat then leaned in close, breathing her in. He could smell the sweet scent of her blood as it thundered through her veins, so close to the surface. He tilted her head slightly and sank his fangs deep. She gasped against him as the warm blood filled his mouth, and the power filled his body. He swallowed, and a jolt of shock ran through him. He'd never tasted anything quite like Skylar's blood, and for a moment, he went still. He forced the knowledge to the back of his mind—it was nothing he hadn't already guessed, and it would wait for later.

She wriggled against him. He lifted her with ease; never releasing his hold on her throat as he lowered her to the floor and came down on top of her. Inside the tight sheath of her body, his cock stiffened, and she gasped again.

This time, they made slow, erotic love, the thrust of his hips keeping time with the pulse of her blood. He was careful not to take much, just enough. Finally, he released her, swiping his tongue over the small wound, before rising up over her to stare down into her desire drenched eyes.

"That was amazing," she murmured.

Tension eased in his mind, and he realized he'd been worried she would not enjoy his blood-taking—another first. What was it about her that made him so unsure? He pushed the thought aside and flexed his hips, filling her, wanting to feel her shudder with desire beneath him.

Her blood buzzed inside him, saturating him with power. He continued to thrust slowly into her, holding tight onto his control, until finally, they came together in a rush of pleasure.

. . .

Skylar lost consciousness after the third orgasm. When she opened her eyes, it was to find Rico lying next to her on his back. She was pretty sure he was awake, but she didn't have the energy to lift herself up and look.

She waited for him to say something, to denounce her, ask her what was going on, but he didn't move.

She should get up, go get that blade or something, be prepared, but her body refused to obey. She felt boneless, weak. Complete for the first time in her life. The thought brought her up short and she sat up abruptly.

"You're thinking again," Rico murmured.

Her throat hurt, she reached up, ran her fingers over the puncture wounds and hissed under her breath. They had stopped bleeding, but still stung.

"Come here, *querida*." He tugged her, so she fell on top of him. Nuzzling her neck, he kissed her, running his tongue over the small wounds. The stinging stopped, and she pulled away and rose to her feet. She kicked off the silver shoes, then dragged a clean jumpsuit out of the small closet and pulled it on. Boots followed. Finally, she fastened her weapons belt around her waist. And all the time she waited for Rico to denounce her. Instead, he stayed silent.

Her gaze shifted to where he still lay on the floor. He'd rolled onto his side, his head resting on one hand as he watched her. Skylar could read nothing from his expression. Flinging herself down into the pilot's chair, she reset the coordinates to head back to *El Cazador*. She stared at the screen for a long while, but her gaze was drawn back to Rico. He still hadn't moved. She allowed her eyes to wander over the length of him. She'd never met anyone so comfortable in his own skin. Finally, she reached his face. He raised an eyebrow.

"What?" she asked.

He sighed and pushed himself up. "You think too much."

"Yeah, I know. Can't seem to stop."

Rising to his feet, he grabbed his pants and shirt from the floor and pulled them on. He leaned on the console beside her chair. "What do you plan to do now? Take little Jonny and go back to the rebels?"

Why wasn't he confronting her? After tasting her blood, he had to know she'd lied about everything.

Her gaze narrowed on him. "I told you, I can't go back. I stole their money."

"Hmm, so you did. So, what will you do?"

She shrugged. "I don't know."

"You could stick around for a while."

She glanced at him in surprise. Why would he say that? She considered the idea of staying on, then berated herself for even allowing the thought to cross her mind. It was never going to happen. She was an idiot to even think about it. Besides, if she didn't get out of there before Jonny woke from his cryo, she doubted Rico would be offering her a place on his ship. More likely, she'd be straight out the emergency exit without a spacesuit.

"I can't. We're fugitives. We'll bring the Collective down

on you."

"Darling, we're all fugitives after that little escapade."

"They might not have identified you."

He tossed her a look of disbelief. "You reckon?"

"No," she replied honestly.

"Well the offer's there, if you want to stay. At least until you decide on your next move."

Pain shifted deep inside her. Why had he made the offer? It just made everything so much harder. "I can't."

Anger flared in his face. "You know, we are what we are. There's no way around that truth. But that doesn't mean we have to behave in a way prescribed for us by others. There's always a choice."

"Not always."

He shifted irritably. "Of course there is. It might sometimes seem a choice between bad and worse, but it's still a choice."

"Bad and worse," she mused, and shrugged. "We're approaching *El Cazador*. Get ready for docking."

CHAPTER TWENTY

Skylar landed the shuttle, and wordlessly, they made their way to the bridge. As they arrived at the door, Rico put his hand on her arm. He had a feeling the whole world was about to go to shit. He was expecting it, but even so, he wished he could put off the moment for a while. What he really wanted to do was turn around, drag Skylar back into that tiny shuttle, and disappear into deep space for the next hundred years. Maybe longer.

But he wasn't going to do that.

All his life, he had taken what he wanted. Skylar was different; he needed her to come to him freely. Right now, he was sure she was planning to bolt, and he wouldn't stop her. But he wasn't leaving everything to chance, either. He'd left her a little something in the shuttle, for when she ran again. Something he hoped would tip the balance in his favor.

"What?" she asked.

"Just this." He took her in his arms and backed her against

the wall. Sliding his hands into her short hair, he curled his fingers around her head to hold her still while he bent down and kissed her. She didn't resist, her tongue thrusting fiercely into his mouth, her hands gripping his shoulders as though she would never let him go. He pressed into her, feeling the whole length of her against him. His cock nudged her belly, and she squirmed against him.

Behind him, the door slid open. Tannis coughed. "We have a little problem here, Rico."

Skylar went still in his arms. Her tongue slid from his mouth. Reluctantly, Rico raised his head.

"What's that?"

"Well, it seems that little Jonny has just woken up, and while he's very grateful to be rescued, it appears he doesn't actually have a sister."

Rico raised one eyebrow. "How surprising." Skylar met his gaze, her own steady. "Anything you want to add?" he asked.

The tip of her tongue came out to lick her lower lip, still swollen from his kisses. "He must be confused. I've heard cryo can do that, and Jonny never was too bright."

He watched as she strolled across the bridge and sank into a chair. God, she was cool. Even now, he was impressed. "Aren't you eager to go have a tearful reunion with baby brother?" he asked. For a moment, he wished she'd break, confess, and throw herself on his mercy. And he would be merciful. But the thought was fleeting—if she'd been the sort of woman who broke, he probably wouldn't have cared one way or the other. There was still a chance if he gave her a choice, she would choose him.

She pursed her lips. "I think I'll wait till he's a little less fuzzy. It will break my heart if he doesn't recognize me after all the trouble I've gone to."

Rico smiled in admiration. "Hmm, and we wouldn't want to break your heart, would we?"

Tannis stood, hands on her hips, her gaze flicking between the two of them. "Is someone going to tell me what's going on?"

Skylar remained silent, and Rico shrugged. "She's Collective."

Tannis stared at Skylar. "She can't be. Her eyes are the wrong color."

"Have I mentioned the word gullible before?" Rico shook his head. "Skylar?"

Skylar reached up and removed the contact lenses, dropping them on the floor. Her eyes glowed with the violet of Meridian. She turned to Rico, a look of resignation on her face. "When did you know? Was it the blood?"

"Actually, no. I suspected almost from the start, but Janey confirmed it. You were the only one who could have called up that space cruiser, and as you were with me, you must have had some internal comm link. The only people with that are the Collective. It gave you away. Why did you do it?"

"I had no choice. You were about to munch on me, and you'd just told me you could tell how old I was from my blood."

"You could have said no." He studied her face. "So, how old are you exactly?"

She shrugged. "Two-hundred and thirty-two."

"A baby." He shook his head. "When the ship attacked, at first I thought you'd had a lucky break, then I got to thinking."

"I make my own lucky breaks," she said.

. . .

Skylar was furious with herself. How could she have not prepared for this? She looked up at where Rico lounged, one shoulder against the wall. She couldn't believe that all the time he'd been making such sweet love with her, he'd known what she was. She should have chopped off his head after all. One thing was sure; he was a damn better actor than she was.

Time to get off his ship.

There was a good chance that they would attempt to kill her before her backup got there, but right now, she couldn't think of an alternative. She closed her eyes and opened her internal comm link.

And hit a wall.

She tried again. Nothing. They had cut her off, and the first stirrings of panic awoke inside her. She opened her eyes to find Rico watching her, an amused smile on his face.

"Janey reconstructed the frequency," he said. "She's put up a wall. I'm afraid there's no calling for help." He grinned. "Oh, and *you* told them to rendezvous about two hours from here. So don't be expecting them anytime soon."

A sense of fatality settled over her. This was it. It was over. They even had an assassin on board who knew exactly how to do away with the Collective on a permanent basis.

"If you knew all this, why am I still alive?" she asked.

"Good question," Tannis said.

"I had planned to kill you," Rico said. "I don't like being double-crossed. But you went back for Janey that night, and you saved our lives back on Trakis One. Those Collective would have killed us and by now you'd be back with your own kind."

She scowled. "It was a reflex action."

"Of course it was. Whatever, we owe you, and, like you, I pay my debts."

"What does that mean?"

"You can go. Get in your shuttle and leave."

She looked from him to Tannis. The captain's face was set, but she didn't speak. Skylar rose slowly to her feet.

"Just one thing," Rico said.

She turned to him.

"What was this all for? Why go to the bother of freeing a man condemned by the Collective?"

She shrugged. "I don't know. I was told it was a training exercise."

For the first time she saw a real reaction. "A what?" His tone was outraged.

She didn't blame him; she was outraged herself, but she kept her tone bland. "You said it yourself. They were getting sloppy. The Collective houses a lot of political prisoners on Trakis One. We needed to be sure it was secure. Plus my boss hates the guy in charge of security."

"And just who exactly is 'we'?"

"The Corps."

"Jesus," Tannis muttered.

"So why don't you introduce yourself," Rico said.

"Lieutenant Skylar Ross."

Rico studied her for a moment, and she wondered if he would make the connection. She saw the moment enlightenment struck. "Would that make you related to Aiden Ross?"

She nodded. "He was my uncle."

"So Jonny assassinated your uncle."

"It's not personal." She shrugged. "I never liked Uncle Aiden anyway. He was a pompous ass."

"So what was the plan now? Call in your space cruiser, arrest us all, and ship us off to the Meridian mines with Jonny?"

"Something like that."

Tannis took a step toward her. "I'm letting you go because, as Rico said, you saved our asses back there. But if I ever see you again—I'll kill you."

Skylar narrowed her eyes. "You might try. I doubt you'd succeed."

Briefly, she wondered whether it was worth suggesting she take the assassin off their hands, but one look at Tannis's ice-cold expression and she decided not to push her luck. Instead, she whirled around, strode off the bridge, and headed for the docking bay, aware of Rico keeping step behind her. She slammed her palm onto the lock and the door to her shuttle slid open. She stepped inside and turned to face him.

He grinned. "Thanks for the sex, and the blood. That Meridian sure tastes good."

"I enjoyed it."

"I noticed."

She reached up to shut the door, and he leaned forward, kissed her lightly on the mouth. "Remember, *querida*," he murmured against her ear, "there's always a choice."

Her gaze flashed to his face. "Really? You heard what Tannis said. Somehow, I don't think staying is an option now you all know what I am."

He ran a finger down her cheek. "I've always known what

you are, *querida*. The question is, does it matter?" He gave her one last, fleeting kiss, and then he was gone.

Skylar moved automatically, strapping herself in, setting the engines. She expected any moment for them to change their minds and come after her. And all the while, in the back of her mind, something niggled.

She'd been flying for ten minutes when she crashed her hand on the emergency stop button. The shuttle spun to an immediate halt. She sat for a moment, staring out into the vastness of space.

Rico had always known what she was.

He already knew she was Collective when he'd asked her to stay. Her pulse roared in ears with the realization.

There's always a choice.

But what were her choices?

No one had ever parted company with the Collective before. That didn't mean it couldn't be done. Skylar thought of going back, of taking the fallout from her impetuous decision, and of the tedious years that stretched ahead. Did boredom have to be the price of immortality?

She thought of Rico and had an instant flashback to the feel of him on her, in her, filling her completely. That low, husky voice whispering *querida* in her ear. A wave of heat rolled through her body. She didn't understand her feelings for the vampire fully, but she did know that things would never be boring on his ship.

And there was another thing to consider. Her husband, Daniel, had died. Despite being offered the Meridian treatment, he had chosen a normal life and a normal death. But unlike Daniel, Rico would never grow old, and he would never die. Well, not of natural causes.

Skylar wasn't sure what they had, or what they could have together, but whatever it was, she knew they'd have plenty of time to explore it.

All the time in the universe.

She leaned forward to switch on the engines and something glittered in the corner of her eye. For a moment, she was sure her heart stopped beating. A ring lay on the console; a purple jewel on a slender band of white metal. She picked it up and held it to the light, turning it so fires danced in the heart of the stone.

For a brief moment, she thought the ring might be a farewell gift, but the idea didn't linger. This was an offer of a new life. A symbol of eternal love, Rico had said.

Skylar wasn't sure anything could last forever.

But did that really matter?

The important thing was, right now, she wanted it to. For the first time in years, the thought of eternity filled her with anticipation rather than dread.

She slipped the ring on her finger and grinned as she remembered Tannis's farewell comment. Hopefully, it had at least been in part rhetorical.

And if she survived Tannis, there was 'Jonny.' She had an idea Jonny wasn't going to turn out to be a big fan of the Collective either.

At the thought of Jonny, something stirred deep in her mind. Something that had been bothering her since Trakis One. Closing her eyes, she visualized the scene, and a light clicked on in her brain.

Shit.

She'd been so stupid. She had to get back, warn them.

Switching on the engine, she swung the shuttle around, and headed back to *El Cazador*.

. . .

The door slid open.

Rico stood exactly where she had left him, as though he'd been waiting for her. They stared at each other, neither moving.

After a minute, Skylar raised her left hand with the ring sparkling on her finger. "Eternity, huh? Sounds like a long time."

"You scared?"

She considered the question. "Yes."

"Me, too."

"But I kind of like it."

He slanted her a smile. "Me, too. But don't worry; we'll take it one day at a time."

Eternity, one day at a time. It sounded good to her. She closed the space between them, wrapped her arms around his neck, and kissed him. His mouth opened over hers, his tongue filling her, starting the slow burn in her belly, and the docking bay vanished, the Collective and Jonny driven from her mind.

Behind them, someone cleared her throat, and Skylar went still. She peeked over Rico's shoulder. Tannis stood in the open doorway.

"Shit," Skylar murmured, "here comes trouble."

She wriggled out of Rico's arms, though he kept a tight grip on one hand. Leaning in close, he whispered in her ear. "You want me to protect you?"

She raised an eyebrow. "Sweet of you to offer, but do I look like I need protecting?"

He stepped back, his gaze wandering slowly over her body. Her insides melted.

"Hell, no."

For a moment, she forgot Tannis and swayed toward him. The soft scrape of a laser pistol being drawn stopped her. Skylar sighed. "Just one thing," she said. "If she really looks like she's going to shoot me, you might ask her not to. Nicely, of course."

"I can do nice."

"Good." Skylar turned and watched as Tannis strolled across the docking bay toward them, the pistol held loosely at her side. She came to a halt a foot from Skylar.

"What are you doing back here?" she growled. "I thought I'd made my position clear—I see you, and I kill you."

"And as I said, you can try."

Skylar searched her face, but had no clue what Tannis was thinking or whether she would shoot. She must know the blast wouldn't kill Skylar. The Meridian treatment made her almost impervious to normal weapons, and she could repair any amount of damage.

But Skylar didn't want it to come to a fight. She wanted to stay on *El Cazador,* and to do that she had to reach some sort of understanding with the captain. Also, the Collective would waste no time coming after Jonny; they could be out there right now, ready to pounce. She needed to find a way defuse Tannis and quickly.

Curving her lips into the semblance of a sweet smile, she waggled her ring finger in Tannis's face. "I had to come back—

you see, Rico made me an offer I couldn't refuse."

The yellow eyes widened, the pupils narrowing to slits. "No freaking way."

Raising her hand, Skylar held the ring close to her own face, and batted her lashes. "Look—it even matches my eyes."

Tannis glanced from the ring, to Skylar, to Rico, back to the ring. "Excuse me while I lose my lunch."

Skylar bit back a laugh at the response. She nodded at the laser pistol. "So, are you going to use that thing?"

"Actually, after that bit of news, I might just use it to shoot myself."

But she jammed the pistol back in the holster and turned away, running a hand through her short hair, and muttering under her breath. Skylar reckoned Tannis deserved a minute to come to terms with the news, but she was impatient to talk about Jonny and work out what they could do. Maybe she could contact the colonel and offer to send his prisoner back, but she suspected they had moved beyond that being a viable option.

For the first time, she noticed the rest of the crew had edged into the room and were watching avidly. Daisy caught her eye and grinned.

Skylar inched closer to Rico and nodded toward Tannis. "Is she going to be okay?"

"Probably."

"Do you think she could be okay sooner rather than later? There's some information you all need to know."

He obviously saw something in her face. "Tannis! Get over it and get over here. We might have a problem."

Tannis stopped pacing. "A bigger problem than my pilot

losing his mind?"

"Much bigger," Skylar said. "Where's the prisoner? Has he talked yet?"

"Your baby *brother?* No, he's sleeping off the cryo. Why?"

"I think the Collective are going to come after him."

"Well, obviously. They'll want him back."

"No. I think they want him dead."

Rico looked at her sharply. "Why? If it was nothing but a training exercise, why kill him?"

"I don't know. I just know something's not right."

"Explain," Tannis snapped.

"I couldn't work it out until just now, but then it struck me. The soldiers I shot on Trakis One—the Corps—they weren't carrying laser pistols. They were carrying blasters."

"So?" Tannis didn't attempt to hide her impatience.

"So, they were an assassination squad. All along, they meant to kill him."

"That makes no sense. They've had him in prison for weeks. If they wanted him dead, why not kill him there?"

"If he'd died in prison, there would be all sorts of questions. I think they wanted it to look like a failed escape attempt. For some reason they didn't want him to come round from the cryo. I'm guessing he has information they don't want to come out."

"And what would that be?"

She shrugged. "How should I know? I'm a soldier. I'm on a need-to-know basis."

"Hmm. So they would have just blasted us all to pieces?"

Skylar nodded.

"And they're going to come after us."

"With everything they've got."

"Great, just great. And I bet there's no chance of me getting the rest of my money either." She gave Skylar a black look. "You do know this is your fault?" She turned her cold gaze on Rico. "And yours."

"Why the hell is it *my* fault?"

Tannis snorted. "She probably only picked this ship because she'd heard what a pushover you were. Forget that 'I heard you're the best' crap. I bet it was more a case of she'd heard all she needed was to flash a big pair of tits in your face and your brain would fly out the airlock."

Someone sniggered. Tannis glared at the crew, and the sound was cut off abruptly. Shoving her hands in her pockets, she turned and stalked away.

"Well, that went well," Rico murmured.

"It did, didn't it?" Skylar waited until Tannis reached the door. "Captain?"

Tannis paused, but didn't turn around. "What?"

"You still planning to kill me?"

"I'm thinking about it."

EPILOGUE

Tannis slapped a bottle down on the table.

"What's that?" Skylar asked.

"Iron supplement," Tannis said. "I think you're going to need it."

"Oh." She only narrowly resisted lifting her hand to her throat, where she knew the marks of Rico's fangs still showed. "Thank you."

It was later that evening, and they'd all gathered at the table in the galley for the final meal of the day. *El Cazador* was heading away from the Trakis system as fast as she could go. Tomorrow, they had a planning meeting, but tonight, by unspoken agreement, they'd been keeping the conversation light. Rico sat next to her, his hand resting on her thigh.

"Tannis looks after her crew," he said.

Skylar stared up into Tannis's cold, yellow eyes. "So, am I crew?"

Tannis nodded curtly, and something tight unraveled in

Skylar.

"We just haven't decided what position yet," Rico murmured, stroking his hand along her thigh. "We can discuss it later—try a few out."

"Yes, we have. She's our security officer," Tannis said, kicking out a chair and sinking down opposite her. "So does this mean you've left the Collective?" she asked.

Skylar shook her head. It always amazed her how little outsiders understood about the Collective. "I can't leave the Collective," she said. "I *am* the Collective. We all are. I could no more leave than you could chop off your arm and expect it to have a life without you."

Tannis frowned, and Skylar struggled to explain. "The Meridian joins us together until we're part of a single being. If we open ourselves, we can think as one, expand our minds."

"A gestalt," Rico said. "The whole is greater than the sum of its parts."

"Yes, that's it."

"So, they'll be able to find you?" Tannis asked.

"I really don't know. No one's ever tried to leave before, but I'm sure we'll find out."

She didn't mention that although she had clamped down her internal links, she could already feel them nudging at her, trying to get in.

They were all silent for a minute, then Al spoke up from the end of the table. "The Church believes the Collective is evil."

Skylar frowned. "Why do you say that? It's certainly not an official stance."

Al shrugged one skinny shoulder. "They say it takes a

hundred men a hundred years to mine enough Meridian for one treatment."

"Well, I think that might be a slight exaggeration."

Al ignored the interruption. "But they also believe Meridian ties your soul to your body. That's why you can't die, and why you'll never go to heaven."

He rose from the table, picked up a plate, and started piling it with food.

"Who's that for?" Tannis asked.

"Jon."

"He's not a prisoner—he can come and join us."

Al shifted uncomfortably and glanced at Skylar. "He says he won't sit in the same room as a piece of Collective…" He bit his lip on the last word.

"Hmm," Tannis said. "Well, we'll let it go for tonight, but if he stays on this ship, he eats with my crew."

"I'll tell him," Al said.

They watched as he took the plate and left the galley. Soon after, the rest of the crew drifted away, leaving Skylar alone with Rico. Once they were gone, he pulled her onto his lap. "Security officer," he whispered into her ear. "Does that mean you get to tie me up, maybe even handcuff me, if I misbehave?"

She giggled, but pulled back slightly.

"Do you think it's safe?" she asked.

"What? Tying me up?"

"No. Al with that criminal?"

"Why shouldn't it be?"

"Well, Al's …" she trailed off, unsure if she should giveaway Al's secret.

"A girl?" Rico said.

She stared at him in surprise. "You knew?"

"Only just guessed—the kid got me interested. It was easy to see once you looked."

"Don't you want to know why?"

He shrugged. "There're a whole load of reasons people want to hide—I reckon Al's reasons are her own."

"Yes, but—"

He dragged her closer and kissed her. For a moment, she relaxed against him. But something was tugging at her mind. Something to do with the Church. She pictured Al, that shock of dark red hair, the huge grey eyes, and suddenly it came to her.

She sat up straight, eyes wide. "Holy Meridian!"

Rico sighed. "What?"

"I just realized who Al is."

"Really? Well, Al can wait until tomorrow." He kissed her throat, his tongue stroking along the length of the vein, and Al vanished from her mind.

Picking up her left hand, he twisted the ring on her finger. "Did you really pick this ship because you heard I was the best?"

"Oh, yeah."

"And what do you think now?"

She looked down into his hard, handsome face and thought about forever. "Why don't you ask me again in a few hundred years, and I'll let you know."

ACKNOWLEDGMENTS

To the fabulous ladies at Passionate Critters for reading my stories and letting me know what they really think. And to my editor at Entangled, Liz Pelletier, for her help, her suggestions, and most of all, for her wonderful enthusiasm.

Keep reading for a sample of Katee Robert's sexy and wildly entertaining science fiction romance

QUEEN OF SWORDS

"Intricate world-building, a wounded hero, and a fabulous love story. Queen of Swords *is Sci-fi romance at its best!"*
- Nina Croft, author of the Blood Hunter series

"Robert's Sanctify series kicks off in high gear. Readers will root for the alpha hero, whose determination is easily matched by spunky, gritty Ophelia."
- RT Book Reviews

When the cards tell Ophelia Leoni she's supposed to marry the Prince of Hansarda, the gunrunner grits her teeth and boards the starship that comes for her. It doesn't matter if the ship's commander is the gorgeous stranger she just spent a wild, drunken night with. As a Diviner, she's painfully aware the cards don't lie. Ever.

Boone O'Keirna knows Ophelia is trouble the second he sees the way she moves. Not about to let the little hellcat marry his sadistic half-brother, Boone pretends to be the Prince's emissary and kidnaps Ophelia. Too bad they can't be in the same room without him wanting to throw her out an airlock–or into bed.

Even as they fight each other—and their explosive attraction—Ophelia and Boone sense something is wrong. Too much is going their way. Soon, they realize while the cards may never lie, the truth is sometimes hidden between them…and the future king of Hansarda is not one to take defeat lying down.

CHAPTER ONE

Ophelia couldn't find her underwear.

They had to have been around there somewhere. She'd been wearing them last night, after all, but she was hard pressed to find that small piece of silk amongst the other clothing scattered about the room.

She stood up, hands on her hips, and scowled. Against her better judgment, her gaze slid to the man taking up more than his fair share of the bed. He was delicious. Absolutely delicious. Even relaxed in sleep, his muscles stood out beneath tanned skin marred by scars. The marks crisscrossed up his back and over his shoulders, perfect, shiny lines made by some kind of blade, or maybe giant claws. They were enough to make her reconsider her morning-after policy and crawl back into bed with him.

Her link beeped again, setting her teeth on edge. The damn thing was what woke her in the first place, and now she couldn't even find it. Ophelia moved around the room, picking up her clothes. Yeah, she should definitely crawl back into bed with the hot man. She'd do damn near anything to escape the memories of Sanctify's white hull looming before her ship, her crew's frightened faces…

Nope. Not thinking about it.

And still no underwear.

Oh well. She shimmied into her pants and pulled on her shiny silver tank top. In the hazy light of morning, she felt rumpled and twitchy. Her link beeped again, giving her a better idea of where it was—under the bed. Growling uncomplimentary things, she sank to her stomach and peered into the shadows. Sure enough, the link's small screen was lit up against the back wall. Ophelia grabbed it and headed into the bathroom, locking the door for good measure, and brought up her messages.

Her stomach clenched when her mother's voice came online. "Good morning, daughter. I trust you slept well last night."

It was like she knew what Ophelia had been doing. Considering she was a second-level Diviner—known as a *Tyche* by their species—it was likely she did. Ophelia shoved the hair out of her eyes, refusing to feel guilty. Or at least making a good effort at it. She'd lost her whole damn crew, for the Lady's sake. A failure like that deserved a little drinking.

Her mother continued on, looking remarkably put together despite the fact the call had been placed before Keiluna's twin suns breached the horizon. But then, Mama always looked put together. It was downright unnatural. "In any case, your father and I need to speak with you immediately. We will see you for breakfast."

Corpse's fingers traced up Ophelia's spine and down her arms, raising goose bumps in their wake. Damn. Her mother might support Azure Enterprises, might agree with their mission, but she also never involved herself with the dirty details, let alone something so small as a run.

Something was up, something to do with the Lady's business. That's the only reason Mama would be the one making this call.

Double damn.

She cast a quick look around the bathroom and frowned at the flash of red in the hot tub. Crossing the black-tiled floor, she peered in. Sure enough, her underwear floated along the surface. Ophelia grimaced as she hooked them with a single finger and raised the dripping cloth. The dripping *ripped* cloth. All evidence pointed to her having the time of her life last night.

Too bad she didn't remember it.

She frowned, thinking hard, but last night was one big blank. Which had been the plan, of course. It had started at her favorite pub, The Hammer, and she vaguely remembered deciding to go dancing after midnight, but then everything faded into a pleasant grayness. She was going to have to make sure she tipped Lacy next time she was in—those drinks had been strong enough to make even *her* wince and Ophelia was all about more bang for her credits. Still…pretty soon she would have to tone it down on the whole blacking-out thing. Too much could go wrong, from her killing someone to getting kidnapped.

Dropping the underwear on the floor—something to remember her by—she walked out of the bathroom. After pulling on her boots, she took one last look around the room. Whatever else happened, she must have had a universe-shattering time. The bed covers were tangled on the floor, and the entire bed skewed sideways where the springs had broken in. And there were the telltale remains of spray-on condoms scattered about. Thank the Lady, because the last thing she needed right now was a baby. She couldn't even take care of her own crew.

The man rolled over and she tensed, her gaze flying to his face. When he didn't open his eyes, she breathed a little sigh of relief. He really *was* delicious. Those cheekbones were sharp enough to cut and that jaw certainly wasn't weak. Still…he wasn't pretty by any means. Such a waste when paired with a body like that.

She found her bag near the door and a quick check told her nothing was missing, so she walked out the door without looking back. It was bad luck, after all.

The prominence of red and black in the decor was enough to indicate where she was. Death's Door. It wasn't the safest area during the best of times and, since the riots, it was damn near fatal for someone like her. What in the hells had possessed her to come to this part of town last night? Especially with the patrols Sanctify had scouting the streets, ready to scoop up anyone who showed signs of being less than human. Gods knew they'd jump at the chance to nab one of their dreaded Diviner enemies. What happened to those unfortunate souls didn't bear thinking about, especially knowing her crewmembers had suffered the same fate.

To save her.

Surely it wasn't too early to start drinking?

She shook off the memories of those final moments on the *Dutchman*, before Akito and Kana drugged her and tossed her into an escape pod. She'd need to keep her head straight if she planned to make it out of here. Death's Door wasn't a place for nonhumans, no matter the flavor. Ophelia couldn't begin to imagine how she got through the door in the first place. Sure, she looked human, but only until people saw her eyes. Even with the implants and upgrades available to anyone with enough cash, no one besides Diviners had eyes this shade of blue-violet.

Right now the only thing that mattered was getting back to her parents' house. Mama's call had her on edge, her mind full of questions, her instincts screaming warnings. Bypassing the elevators—too easy to get penned in—she took the stairs down, thankful no one else was up and around at this ungodly hour. As soon as she was outside, the band around her chest loosened a bit.

Above her, the sky stretched wide, a color somewhere between yellow and orange that would change several months from now when the winter storms hit. Ophelia slipped on a pair of red-tinted glasses, glaring at the flickering posters depicting the ancient High Priest of Ba'al. Attached to the walls of nearly every building on the street, they were larger than life, each taller than her nearly two meters, and their damn tech was so good the bastard actually moved. He waved an age-spotted hand and smiled, the words "Purity Will Protect You" flashing below his face. It made her sick knowing there were those who actually believed shit like that.

Unable to stand the sight any longer, she turned her attention to the thin crowd filtering through the streets. The only people out were dressed in muted colors and moved quickly about their business, hoods pulled up to conceal their features. As Ophelia watched, a small group of dirty teenagers skirted the edges of the buildings, their shifty eyes suggesting they were looking for their next score.

They were all human.

Shifting her bag higher on her shoulder, she started walking, keeping her eyes to the ground and her pace up. As long as no one looked too closely, she could pass for human. But the trick was not to draw attention to herself. Even as the thought crossed her mind, she heard militant steps that could only mean one thing. A Sanctify patrol, and one closing fast.

As if her morning could get any worse.

Ophelia kept her stride even, acting as if she had every right to be there, hoping to the Lady they wouldn't look too closely at her. Those bastards jumped at any excuse for a public bonfire, and nabbing a Diviner would be a huge coup. They passed her at a fast clip, obviously having somewhere to be. The closest one, a tiny man with tattoos depicting Ba'al, cast a searching look her way but didn't pause.

She waited until they rounded the corner before breathing out a prayer of thanks to the Lady. That had been close. Too close. Keiluna used to be the perfect place for Azure Enterprise's base, lots of people coming and going, a population diverse enough for anyone to blend in. But then Sanctify had turned its bloody eye their way and taken over.

Oh, officially it was still owned by the Delegate of Quadrant Four, but those monsters had slipped in, whispering poison until the perfect opportunity arose. This time it came in the form of an "attack" on a human child by one of the

Bolkerians. If anyone had stopped for half a second to think, they would have realized the alien meant the little one no harm, that the boy just got underfoot and the Bolkerian didn't move fast enough to avoid him. It was a terrible, terrible accident that he'd been impaled, but it had been enough to spark a fire of hate directed at anyone different.

The riots had gone on for days, a bonfire set up in damn near every intersection, until the alien population was decimated.

And now Sanctify held the reins, ruling a people suddenly fearful of anything different.

Though her thoughts were consumed with darkness, the streets around her had begun to take on a more cared-after look, the busted windows replaced by metal bars and eventually by higher-end materials—the homes of people with enough credits to replace what was lost in the fires and violence. The faded paint, streaked with soot, changed as well, evolving into cheery blues, greens, and yellows. There were even carefully tended flowers blooming, the pretty purple ones so common on this planet, bunches of heart-shaped petals so full, they trailed over the window ledges to hang above the street. Their subtle scent teased her, as if this dash of beautiful could cover up the ugliness lurking within.

After a quick look around to make sure no one was paying attention, Ophelia jogged up the three stairs leading to a yellow house with a muted blue door. She'd been trying to convince her parents to move somewhere more secure since even before the riots, but Mama liked to be accessible to her clients and Papa claimed the best place to hide was in plain sight, that no one would expect the leader of Azure

Enterprises to be hiding on a planet controlled by their enemy. Ophelia thought it was bullshit, but once Papa got an idea in his head, there was no moving him. Mama was supposed to be the calm and rational one, but she wasn't much better.

So Ophelia was forced to content herself with ensuring they had multiple escape routes and hideaways in case things went south.

The muzzle of a gun met her as soon as she entered the door.

She froze, a small smile tugging her lips. "Papa, put that antique away. It's only me."

Her father lowered his gun and Ophelia rolled her eyes. The damn thing was so old it probably didn't even work. Then again, this was her father she was talking about. He wouldn't haul around a useless weapon.

"Your mother is in the kitchen."

An icy chill of foreboding snaked its way through her. "What's going on, Papa?"

He shot her a look and stalked down the stairs. The fact he was cranky but not battening down the hatches should have been comforting. Instead, her anxiety skyrocketed. This was definitely about the Lady's business, and she knew all too well how nasty things could get when someone didn't heed the Lady's warnings. It shouldn't be so terrifying, since readings were an integral part of her world, but Ophelia couldn't shake the feeling her life was poised on the precipice, readying to fall.

Lady, but she hoped not.

• • •

Boone woke the moment the Diviner got out of bed. He listened to her mutter and curse as she moved around the room before finally retreating into the bathroom.

Last night had been a mistake. He was only supposed to scope her out, see what was so special about some woman from Keiluna that made Kristian send spies to watch her.

She'd looked so untouchable sitting there with an entire bottle of the clear alcohol they brewed on-planet, wearing a tiny top revealing more than it covered and black pants looking painted on. But it wasn't her body that held his attention—there were plenty of beautiful women flaunting themselves in the bar—it was the way she moved when she went for her second bottle. The loose way she walked, as if she were ready to spring into violence at any moment. It was a radical opposite from the pretties Kristian had carted back to Hansarda to populate his harem.

Really, she was more Boone's type than his half brother's. Her obvious battle training paired with the sweeping black hair and delicate features were quite the package.

Even with those damned violet eyes.

But the part that drew him in the most was the vulnerability on her face when she thought no one was looking. Her shoulders slumped, and her fingers framed the bottle in front of her as if it were the most precious thing in the universe.

He'd had to talk to her, to see if her personality held up the physical promise. Surely she was as empty-headed as the other women Kristian cultivated, a pretty face who could barely hold a conversation.

Boone really should have known better.

He was in trouble as soon as he heard her throaty sex-vid-star-would-kill-for voice. It didn't help that she'd been telling some poseur to shove off before she jammed his balls down his throat. The combination of strength and weakness was an intoxicating one he had no hope of resisting.

The bathroom door swished open, jerking him back to the present. He listened to her breath hiss out as she sat across from the bed.

Boone contemplated trying for another round. He could still taste her on his lips, and it was driving him crazy. They'd been together more times last night than he could count and still he craved the feel of her skin against him. But last night was a mistake, and not one he could afford to repeat. Maybe if he kept thinking that, he'd start to believe it. Besides, she'd hate him soon enough. All of Kristian's floozies did. Just because she seemed different from the countless others didn't indicate a different outcome.

As soon as she left the room, he rolled back over and stretched. He was tired and sore and felt fantastically used. The woman really was something.

His wrist unit beeped, and Boone sighed. Couldn't Jenny give him a few minutes to enjoy the afterglow? He opened the call, leaving the screen blank. His little sister didn't need to see where he was and start asking questions. "What?"

"Now, now, is that any way to speak to your favorite sister?"

"You're my *only* sister."

Jenny laughed. "Technicalities." Even without the screen on, he knew her gray eyes, so similar to his own, were dancing with mischief. Which meant trouble for anyone in her sights.

Boone flopped back on the bed and propped his head on

his free arm, the movement pulling at old wounds. He rolled his neck, fighting against the tide of memories threatening to drown him. Kristian coaxing him down to the dungeon to hide from the old man. The chains digging into his wrists. The knife, gods, that damned knife…

"You're not even paying attention to me!"

He could have kissed his sister for pulling him free of the past, even as Boone hoped to the gods he wasn't going to have to clean up another of her messes. "What do you want, Jenny?"

"What's she like?" She was only snooping. Thank the gods for small favors.

Boone glared at his wrist unit, but it wouldn't have intimidated her into silence, even if she could see him. Jenny wasn't afraid of anything. "You are not calling to ask about Kristian's new whore." To call her that felt like a betrayal, but he slapped down the feeling. She may have been amazing last night, but if she became a member of the prince's harem, she was an enemy, plain and simple.

"Bo-oo-ne." Jenny stretched his name into three syllables. "Stop playing with my emotions and tell me what she's like. Is she vapid? Lazy? A royal bitch like the last one? Come on, I'm dying here."

"No."

Jenny was silent for what felt like an eternity. A new record. "No? That's interesting."

"Yeah." He pictured those violet eyes gone hazy with passion. "She's not at all like we expected."

"Can we use her?"

That was the question. Judging from last night alone, the

Diviner wasn't a woman someone used lightly. Hells, she'd probably fillet anyone who tried. "I don't know."

"You sound weird. What happened?"

Of course Jenny would pick up on his distraction. "Nothing. We'll talk later." He reached over and ended the call. Almost immediately, the unit rang again. Boone clicked it on. "Damn it, Jenny—"

"Hello, little brother."

He froze, his gaze glued to the screen showing the man who had been his enemy for nearly ten years, ever since he'd chained Boone in the dungeon and tried to cut the skin from his back.

Dread curled in his gut. "Kristian."

For more of Boone and Ophelia's wild adventure, pick up

Queen of Swords

online or in a bookstore near you!